I See You've Called in Dead

Also by John Kenney

Talk to Me
Truth in Advertising

Love Poems for the Office
Love Poems for Anxious People
Love Poems for People with Children
Love Poems for Married People

I See You've Called in Dead

A Novel

John Kenney

Zibby Publishing
New York

I See You've Called in Dead: A Novel

Copyright © 2025 by John Kenney

All rights reserved. No part of this book may be used, reproduced, distributed, or transmitted in any form or by any means without the prior written permission of the publisher, except as permitted by U.S. copyright law. Published in the United States by Zibby Publishing, New York.

ZIBBY, Zibby Publishing, colophon, and associated logos are trademarks and/or registered trademarks of Zibby Media LLC.

This book is a work of fiction. Names, characters, places, historical events, and incidents are the product of the author's imagination or are used fictitiously. Any resemblance to actual persons, living or dead, events, or locales is entirely coincidental.

Library of Congress Control Number: 2024943194
Hardcover ISBN: 979-8-9899230-1-4
eBook ISBN: 979-8-9899230-3-8

Book design by Westchester Publishing Services
Jacket design by Emily Mahon

www.zibbymedia.com

Printed in the United States of America

10   9   8   7   6   5   4   3   2

For my brother Tom

Someone has to die in order that the rest of us should value life more.

—Virginia Woolf

Sometimes I wish my first word was "quote," so that on my death bed, my last words could be "end quote."

—Steven Wright

INTRODUCTION

The good news, of course, is that someone died today. That came out wrong.

My name is Bud Stanley. I am an obituary writer. Here is what I know after writing 724 obituaries.

I know that you are more likely to be killed by a cow than by a shark.

I know that you can be declared dead in some states in the United States but considered alive in others.

I know that in the year 897, Pope Stephen VI had the corpse of a previous pope exhumed, perched on a throne, and questioned about his crimes.

I know that the term *mortician* was invented as part of a PR campaign by the funeral industry, which felt it was more customer-friendly than *undertaker*. The term was chosen after a call for ideas in *Embalmer's Monthly* (a magazine I will admit that I have leafed through).

I know that in China, roughly 27,573 people die each day. In India, it's around 26,520. In the United States, 7,700, give or take. In Switzerland, it's about 179. In Micronesia, it's just 2. In Liechtenstein, 1. Why not move there?

Mostly what I know is this. I know that you—all of us—should have the answer to one question: What would you write if you had to write your obituary? Today, right now.

What comes to mind? What memories, days, moments? What people and experiences?

I realize, at first glance, that the idea of writing one's own obituary while still alive may sound morbid. It's not, though. I promise you. It's a needed reminder of who you are, of what truly matters. Because it's your life and there's still time to write it. Before I have to.

BLIND DATE

My death and eventual afterlife began on a cold, rainy Sunday evening in April that now feels like another lifetime. It was eight months ago.

It began harmlessly enough, with the mistake of agreeing to go on a blind date. Well, that was certainly one of the mistakes. There were several that evening.

But I'm getting ahead of myself. Let me back up to the beginning of this year.

It was going to be an amazing year.

This is what I had told myself, had promised myself. It had been about two years since my ex-wife left (another man, which I kind of thought was off the table with the whole being married thing). She was able to secure an uncontested divorce in about eight months (yay for her) and I needed to make a clean start.

And so the year had started, as years often do, with wide-eyed resolutions, illusions of a new life, as if the turn of a calendar page, the drop of a ball, could somehow jump-start a life in quicksand, change long-ingrained patterns. *That's negative thinking, Bud!* So said the books with the bold covers, colorful and confident, that promised radical transformation:

Be the You That Not Even You Will Recognize.
Happiness Is Daring You to Grab It. Grab It!

Everyone Kind of Thinks You Suck.

The self-help books did what self-help books often do: go largely unread. But they did act as a catalyst to begin making a list of things I would change, places I would go, hints of the person I would become.

I was going to learn Japanese, for an eventual visit to Japan, to the shrines of Kyoto. I would exercise, join a gym, perhaps lift weights and stretch things. I would drink less, just on weekends, and then only a glass or two. I would start my day early, clearheaded, by sipping hot water with lemon, a drink that holds the benefits of alkalinity (which apparently is a thing). I would avoid coffee, tea, caffeine in general. I would ingest goji berries for their superfood properties. I would meditate. I would listen to the soothing voice of a man from Minneapolis who espoused Buddhist mantras and wisdom and who also sold T-shirts on his mindfulness website with clever sayings on them such as *Being present is a present* or *Let that shit go.*

I would meet someone. I would go online, put up a photo that looked vaguely like me but better and write something charming and funny. A wonderful woman would find me intriguing and we would date and have absurd amounts of sex. I would stop regretting things, like not having invested in Google years ago when a colleague told me to, that colleague now worth somewhere in the neighborhood of $50 million. ("Tech is a fad," were, I believe, my exact words.) I would start reading again, something I used to do instead of what I now did, which was watch things. I would read philosophy and poetry and internal-monologue-altering, new-way-of-thinking, all-enlightening books by calm-faced TED speakers who had discovered the secret to happiness. Or at least the secret to a very compelling presentation. I would change, on a cellular level. Neuroplasticity. The brain's neural pathways are malleable. It's possible to rewire ourselves. I had read this in a dentist's waiting room in a back issue of *Us Weekly*. I would rewire, be a better me. More patient, more hopeful, more empathetic. I would be the change I wanted to see in the world. Because I would change. I would not be me.

It lasted a day.

It lasted as long as it takes to listen to Japanese for Beginners and think, *Hmm, maybe not.* It lasted as long as the one-day free-trial membership at the gym where I pulled a muscle while yanking incorrectly on a machine. It lasted as long as it took to log in to my TD Ameritrade account with $21,000 in it invested in GE (the company of the future!). It lasted as long as it took me to scan the lovely faces and intimidating résumés of women so far out of my league on the dating sites. It lasted as long as it takes to try and fight the voice in my head that says, *Other people can change. Not you.*

The blind date.

This was at a bar in Brooklyn, not far from where I live. My office mate set me up. Tuan. His name is Tuan. You'll meet him.

I arrived early, having stopped at a bodega to pick up flowers. Flowers are a nice touch. Who doesn't like flowers? It was a quiet Sunday evening at one of those small hipster bars without TVs. Zinc-top bar, a working fireplace, a jazz trio that seemed to take a lot of breaks. I sat at the far end of the bar and ordered a beer.

It was early April and the clocks had moved forward, more light in the evenings but still cold, winter holding on. The band played and I checked my watch. She was twenty minutes late. I looked at the flowers on the bar and was struck by a sense of embarrassment. Why had I bought flowers for a blind date?

The bartender—a handsome man with superb facial hair and a topknot—pointed to my empty beer glass. I nodded.

The trio—a drummer using brushes, a stand-up bassist, and a guitarist—played standards: "Ain't Misbehavin'," "The Girl from Ipanema," "In a Sentimental Mood." After a while the band took a break and I finished my beer. She was forty-five minutes late and I considered leaving.

The door opened and a woman walked in. She was wearing a trench coat and her auburn hair was windblown, cut in a bob. Her face was dotted with drops of rain.

Oh look, my wife just walked in. We're having a quick drink and then it's off to a dinner party. No, a play. Wait. A concert. No. A flight to Rome. I'm the new bureau chief there. Actually for all of Europe. I know, amazing. Phoebe works for Doctors Without Borders. Her name is Phoebe. Why, yes, after Holden's sister. She speaks Italian. Italian and French and Farsi. And Urdu. She went to Princeton. How did we meet? That's a funny story. She was being robbed and I killed the robbers. No. Wait. We were on a flight together and she fell asleep on my shoulder. Drooled on me. Actually threw up because of some bad fish. Nope. Wait. We met online, in an adult chatroom for people interested in dressing up as Teletubbies . . . no, no. Friends, mutual friends . . . She said she knew I was the one. We had sex in the cab on the way home. No. We talked and walked the streets of

Manhattan, watching the sun come up on the Brooklyn Bridge, where we were later murdered by crack addicts. Nope. Stayed up all night and had coffee and pancakes at a diner. I proposed two months later in Paris. I've never been happier. In fact, we have a little one on the way.

Men are stupid. Or maybe it's just me. How foolish to tell myself a life story about a person in four seconds, based on her hair, how she moved it back from her face, behind her ear, only to have it fall again, the black skirt and black tights and large, darting eyes, lips shining from the rain. What a waste of time to feel that almost desperate pang of—what is it?—desire, I guess. Not merely sexual. Not some teenage lust. But a far more unfair, unreachable illusion. Still. No harm in dreaming.

"Bud?" she said, having somehow closed the distance between the door and the bar.

"Yes. Phoebe. Hi."

"It's Diane."

"I meant Diane."

She looked confused. "You're Tuan's friend Bud, yes?"

"Yes, I am. I can show you my license." I started to take out my wallet.

"Oh . . . no, that's okay."

I stopped, forced a laugh, and put the wallet back.

Why was I acting this way? Surely part of it was my lack of practice, the paucity of dates over the last few years. Dates where within minutes we both knew there was nothing there but continued for a drink out of politeness. Nothing much to say after the cursory chitchat, what do you do, what was your last vacation, have you ever considered suicide. Fine, I made up the last one. Dating in one's forties is a radically different experience than dating in the carefree days of one's twenties. More pain now. More history. More exes and sometimes children. More lonely, more longing, more guarded. There was the morning TV show producer who arrived mildly tipsy and proceeded to get fall-down drunk. There was the big-law-firm attorney who looked like Grace Kelly but who seemed to get angrier as the night went on. And there was the social worker who spoke quietly and who made me laugh and whom I fell hard for. Three amazing dates and then I never heard from her again.

Now I rarely made an effort. I'm not sure why. Instead, I waited, a kind of magical thinking, for life to mend itself, for someone to find me. Superb plan, I know.

Diane said, "You said, 'We have a little one on the way'?"

"I did?"

"When I walked over. What did you mean?"

"Oh, God. Who knows." I laughed again. Well, forced a laugh.

"I am so sorry I'm late. I just . . . It's a long story but . . ."

"No worries at all. Please, sit."

"I can't, actually."

"Did you hurt yourself?"

"What?"

"Is that why you can't sit? I have sciatica sometimes. I have to stand all day working. And once a particularly savage case of hemorrhoids." I couldn't stop talking. I hated myself.

"God, no. No, it's not that I can't sit. I mean I can't *stay*."

"Oh. Why?"

"This is super awkward but . . . I . . . got a call . . . right before I was leaving the house. My old boyfriend."

"That must have been nice. To hear from him, I mean."

"Yeah. Um . . . we broke up last year . . . anyway . . . and . . . this isn't important and it's just that . . . he wants to . . . I do too, not just him . . . but we both realized we want to get back together."

"Wow. That is . . . such great news . . . for both of you."

"Thank you. It is. It's just . . . like when you find that one person . . ."

"Totally."

She looked at the flowers on the bar.

"Are those for me?"

"What's that?"

"The flowers."

I looked at them as if seeing them for the first time.

"These?"

"Yeah. Who are they for?"

"The . . . well . . . they're for . . . the bartender."

She appeared confused. As was I.

"He's . . . going through some . . . you know . . . so I thought . . ."

"That's very sweet," Diane said.

I nodded in the bartender's direction, a signal he mistook for my need for another drink.

"Another?" he asked.

"Ah, no," I said. "I'm good. I just wanted . . . to give you these . . . flowers."

He stared at me, then looked at the flowers, then back to me. I hoped that somewhere deep in our shared male psyches he could sense my pain.

"Okay. Well . . . thank you. I . . . will . . . put these in water, I guess." He picked the flowers up, turned to Diane, and said, "Can I get you anything?"

I jumped in. "Happy to buy you a quick drink since you're here. We can celebrate your being back together with your old boyfriend."

"Oh. Yeah. Thank you. But . . . he's kind of waiting for me . . ."

"Well, one drink and we'll get you on your way." I winked at her like we were old friends. I was floundering badly, watching myself, a kind of out-of-body experience where I was repulsed by this person. Me.

"No, I mean he's waiting for me. He's outside."

"He's outside now?"

"Yeah." She looked over to the door. "Actually, it looks like he's made his way inside. There he is."

She smiled and waved at him. I did the same. So did the bartender.

"Cool," I said. "I don't think I've ever been on a blind date where someone brought their boyfriend."

"Well, former boyfriend."

"I'd say invite him over for a drink, but you probably have plans."

"We do."

We both smiled and nodded and looked back over at her ex-boyfriend.

"He's very handsome," I said, regretting it immediately.

"Isn't he? I will tell him you said so."

More nodding.

"Okay. Well. I should go," she said, wincing. "I'm sorry."

She turned and I watched her walk over to her ex-boyfriend and watched them walk out the door. I waved and for some reason shouted, "Don't be late! You know how your mother and I worry!"

I sat back down, trying to make sense of what just happened. The bartender placed a fresh drink in front of me, rapping the bar twice with his knuckles.

"On the house," he said. "Largely because I've never seen anything quite like that," he added, shaking his head, turning, and walking to the other end of the bar.

BURY THE LEDE

I live on the top floor of a 150-year-old three-story brick town house in Brooklyn owned by my friend Tim. Creaky wide-planked floors, a view onto a large, lone ash tree out back, and an ivy-covered wall where talkative birds gather. I've furnished it in the spartan fashion of a man whose ex-wife has taken most of their belongings, retaining the couch I had before our marriage, two overstuffed chairs, and a small dining table that I use when I work from home. I found it on the street when I first moved in. Sturdy, plain oak. It had scratches and a few stains that fine sandpaper got out. I am fond of the table. It suits me. On occasion I buy flowers and place them in an old glass milk bottle on the table. When I do this I feel like an adult. Three days later, when they're drooping and lethargic, I throw them out.

It was after nine and I had an unpleasant buzz and a deep chill. I took a long shower, the kind where you drift, the warmth so enveloping, so primal, the smell of the shampoo, clean chemical scents.

I should have gone to bed. I remember thinking that. But I found myself in that near-end-of-evening hour—too late to make other plans yet maybe too early to turn in—where I was caught between opposing camps. One side made a reasoned, persuasive argument for a good book, some tea, soothing music: simple, wholesome actions that would contribute to a restorative night's sleep, one that would birth a fresh, life-affirming worldview come Monday, a renewed vigor to my of late less-than-enthusiastic attitude toward work.

The other side made a half-baked, mildly buzzed argument to screw it; pour yourself a whiskey, put on some music, maybe open a bag of Cheetos. Sleep when you're dead. The argument was brief, foolish, and embarrassing. The jury went for the latter in a unanimous decision.

I took down a bottle of sixteen-year-old Lagavulin from a shelf in the kitchen. My boss, Howard, gave it to me at our company Christmas party a few years ago.

On occasion—a damp, cold evening, the house too quiet—I pour myself a glass, give it a gentle swirl, inhale the heady, fiery aroma, and imagine my ancestors in Ireland a long time ago, in a cottage, by a peat fire, rough hands, so tired, so much labor, wondering, perhaps, if there was something else out there, a better life, if they had the courage to find it, knowing they would, that they had to, that they owed it to themselves and their family, afraid, excited, eternally hopeful, dreaming of possibility for their children, their children's children, for me, this person sitting here now. Surely that was worth a toast.

I sat on the couch with my computer and got lost, aimlessly clicking through cnn.com and tmz.com, nytimes.com, YouTube, Instagram, Facebook, the algorithms knowing my tastes, pulling me in deeper, mindlessly following every new link. A Nick Drake video, a Stephen Fry talk, a *Fry & Laurie* skit, *The Two Ronnies'* "Fork Handles" skit, great catches in baseball, vintage wristwatches, yoga women of Malibu, Bill

Maher, news anchor bloopers, a garbage truck that bursts into flames, Norman Mailer drunk on *The Dick Cavett Show*, squirrels dancing.

The videos—half watch, click, half watch, skip ad, click—alternatingly intrigued and annoyed me, engaged me, sucked life from me. It was after eleven. *Go to sleep, Bud.* But Bud wasn't listening. Bud had pushed past tired into numbness, the brain buzz of too little sleep, the mistake of topping off his drink. What's the worst that could happen?

The email surprised me, froze me for a few seconds. The name. *Jen Finch-Atwell.* I knew it but I didn't. My ex-wife, known to me as Jennifer Bennett. Here I will try to describe what transpired in the perhaps three or four seconds before I opened the email.

I thought, for just a moment, just a surprisingly powerful spark-of-hope-inducing yet just as quickly wince-inducing moment, that she was writing to get back together. As that little neuron fire was happening, I caught sight of the subject line, which read "my mother." At which point I assumed, again for just a moment, that she was referring to my mother.

But all it took was two words to bring me back to reality.
Hello Bud . . .

The formality of it. The distance. We never spoke like that, texted like that.

> I wanted to let you know that my mother died last week. There is a wake tomorrow evening and I mention it because I know how fond you were of her and she of you.

I understand completely if you can't make it. I hope this finds you well.

Jennifer

P.S. I heard you're living near Tim Charvat. Please tell him hello for me.

At the bottom of the email, she'd attached a link to her mother's obituary. I clicked on the link and read, taking in bits of information. I knew she had taught high school art but had not known she'd had a debutante ball in New York on her coming out. I knew her father had been from a very wealthy oil family but had lost a large portion of his money in speculative real estate investments abroad. I knew she was survived by her daughters but did not know that she was survived by a granddaughter. Jen had a daughter name Chloe.

I read once that there are something like one hundred billion galaxies in the universe. And that once, at the start, the moment before time, 13.8 billion years ago, the universe was a million, billion, billion times smaller than a single atom. And that temperatures of a million, billion, billion, billion degrees caused the explosion that formed the ever-expanding universe. I can't get my mind around that. I can't imagine that smallness, that vastness. I can't make sense of how the universe began. What came before it? What remains when we go? Where do we go?

Somehow the Drum tobacco had come out and I rolled a cigarette. It was a casual habit I gave up a decade ago. And by "gave up," I mean I smoke once in a great while, usually when I've had too much to drink. And I don't usually drink too much.

I sat by the window, opened a few inches, listening to the rain. And just that clearly, in the muddled, whiskey-soaked place where terrible ideas pose as good ones, I knew what I had to do. It made perfect sense. I would write my obituary.

(I should add that it wasn't entirely out of the blue. On occasion, I write my own obituary. I know what you're thinking. *How is this guy single?*)

I put music on shuffle. I began to type.

Bud Stanley, the first man to perform open-heart surgery on himself, died today in a hot-air balloon accident. He was 44. His wife, Miss France, has confirmed the death.

Interesting. Keep going.

Bud Stanley, one of the original Pips for Gladys Knight, has died. At the hands of the other Pips.

Yes. This was very good.

Stanley was born in Nepal, the Dalai Lama's younger twin brother. Their father was a police officer and their mother a homemaker from Boston.

The Standells now, "Dirty Water (Boston You're My Home)." Might explain the Boston reference.

Although he didn't speak his first words until the age of four ("Where are my pants?") he had a command of seven languages, in which he wrote, taught, and lectured. He was a competitive ballroom dancer.

"Everybody Wants to Rule the World" by Tears for Fears.

Mr. Stanley would go on to form the band Tears for Fears, though refused to take credit for the songs he wrote. Stanley was married anywhere from four to nine times. His ex-wives, all friends, praised his unique lovemaking technique, one they said could last upward of twenty-eight seconds.

Type. Fast. Go.

Stanley began his career in soft-core pornography as a script doctor, but was fired for insisting on more plot and less nudity.

Excellent.

Your identity is more interesting than your biography. That was another one from one of the self-help books or the podcasts or talks that Tim sent me. Aren't we all more than our résumé? Aren't we more than the college we attended and the places we've worked? Aren't we a million things that are so subtle and nuanced that most people never see them or experience them? Aren't we also that moment—that nothing moment—on a cool spring day when, stopped by a lilac bush in bloom, by the breeze moving the leaves and full violet flowers, the hint of the perfume smell in the wind and the sound of birdsong, when we close our eyes and feel deeply, profoundly grateful, before it slips away, gone, and we're back to the noise of our own head? Aren't we that too?

It got late.

The mistake, looking back, was logging in to the company's password-protected website, access to which was granted only after one attended a training seminar, after which you signed many legal documents. It is a site I log in to routinely. At work. For the death of someone who has, in fact, died.

Did it make sense to log in on a Sunday night, after several whiskeys? I would vote no. At the time, however, it seemed—and I want to choose my words carefully here—funny-ish.

Another mistake was going into the obituary section, where Tuan and I routinely laid out our work. Once, this work was done by typesetters and printers. But they were long gone now in the cost-cutting digital age.

Yet another mistake (so many, really, though the hearing committee substituted the word *felony* for *mistake*) was deciding to upload a photo of myself after college when I briefly sported a mustache, looking much less like, say, a young Tom Selleck and more like Borat. Looking at it, that's when I snorted. Innocent enough, yes? I snorted and was enjoying myself on this rainy, cold Sunday night where I was imagining my own death, a sentence that, upon review, I fear does not convey the frivolity of the moment.

That's when I reached for my glass. Picture it if you will. I'm snorting, at my photo, at the idea of the obit itself. What fun! Of course I don't want to die. Oh sure, who doesn't think about it from time to time. Fine, maybe fewer people than I'd thought. The point is I'm about to delete it, the photo, the copy in the layout—which looks pretty good, I had to admit. I'm going to delete it and go to bed and get up and try harder. Except I reached for the glass. I wish I hadn't done that. Maybe it was the late hour, my fatigue, the softness of the whiskey, the delayed and grandpa-on-the-remote-controls-of-an-Xbox flailing quality of my reaching to catch my glass after knocking it over, causing the entire side of my hand to accidentally hit the keyboard. The fatty outside of my hand, the one I used to bite in grade school when stressed. I believe I also emitted a noise. "Whoa!" Something awkward. Several buttons were depressed. One of them being the return button. The one that posted my obituary, live, on the website of the world's largest wire service news organization, to be picked up by news organizations around the world. No delete possibility. I made a mental note to speak with IT about that flaw in the system.

EMPLOYEE REVIEW

This is all bad journalism on my part, starting a story so randomly, without context. *Who what when where why.*

A bit about me.

I spent an unimpressive four years in college, neither lazy nor diligent (potential gravestone epitaph?), wasting weekends, not smart enough yet to understand Hamlet or Prufrock, drinking too much beer, trying in vain to meet women. I possessed the universal college worldview that everyone else had it figured out, felt passionately about their major, and had a keen sense of the kind of life they wanted, and that I, alone, was clueless.

After several short-lived declarations of a major course of study—sociology, business, pre-med (two weeks), philosophy (one day)—I settled on journalism. The idea of cracking a big story, typing fast as the camera panned over my shoulder (I assumed they would make a movie), international travel, carrying one of those thin reporter's notebooks making notes I would later be unable to decipher due to exceptionally bad penmanship thereby rewriting the quotes, was thrilling. Plus, and forgive the pathetic ego here, I would see my name, my byline, in print. It's hard to describe what that's like.

Graduation begat a year of odd jobs: golf caddy, house painting, busboy, landscaping. Some at the same time. Friends were doing internships at law firms, at investment banks. They were applying to graduate schools. The only point on the horizon that seemed appealing to me (besides earning money to begin paying off my student loans) was travel. What happened out there in the world? In Europe? In the Far East? So, after squirreling away a bit of money for almost a year, I packed a bag and left.

My naïve hope was that dragging myself halfway across the world would somehow change me. I thought I would find clarity in what my life should be, perhaps a change in personality and outlook, a newfound confidence, a worldly-wise demeanor, an answer to what to do.

What happened instead was that I ran out of money after three months of train travel around Europe and found myself no closer to understanding much about myself. This other self, this other me, seemed to be out there, waiting, if only I could find him. In the meantime, I worked. More odd jobs for a few years—plasterer's assistant, moving company, midnight to eight at a warehouse unloading trucks—and, along the way, I lost a goodly portion of my twenties.

I applied for reporter's jobs in Hartford, Boston, Portland, Maine, Columbus, Ohio, and Concord, New Hampshire. I got one, in Concord. It was an entry-level job covering police, town hall, and local sports. To my great surprise, I loved it. I loved learning how a newspaper was put together. There was an energy to it. The days weren't the same. The news was ever-changing. Power outages and car accidents and minor scandals involving affairs by local officials. I knew things before others did, knew that something had happened. It was a strange and thrilling feeling. Plus, I was out of the small, ink-smelling office most of the day, talking with people. I found I was good at listening, that a simple question—*Excuse me, ma'am, what did you think of the city council's vote on afternoon trash removal over morning trash removal*—could elicit bizarre, fascinating answers. ("'I hope they rot in hell,' an angry Concord resident said today in reaction to the city council's controversial vote to . . .").

The job became my social life. Drinks with colleagues after work. During long, frigid New Hampshire winter evenings, I played pickup hockey with guys from the paper and went out for beers after, occasionally engaging in casual, deeply unsatisfying hookups.

I wanted more. I wanted a change. My clippings were good enough to get me a job in Providence, a big step up (certainly in terms of weather). I did some feature writing—a long piece about coastal erosion for which I interviewed fishermen about the challenges and dangers of their work (joined them on the boat during what they said was a mild storm and vomited excessively)—and had a brief and ill-fated affair with a professor of philosophy at Brown who enjoyed full-on conversations during sex—about her day, about grocery shopping, about a call with a friend—which I found challenging.

Late one summer, as a favor, I filled in for our obit writer while he was on vacation. I was surprised by how much I enjoyed it. Perhaps that's the wrong word. It wasn't enjoyment so much as fascination, as intensity. There was—is—a meaning to the writing of an obituary that transcends the filing of a daily news story. Whole lives. I found it strangely life-affirming, oddly thrilling, this thing where you tried, if only briefly, to capture the essence of someone's life.

Fortunately—well, it's a matter of perspective, of course—the obit writer I was filling in for died while on vacation (hang gliding, Arizona). The editor asked if I wanted the job.

I'd like to think I was good at it for a long time. I will freely admit that of late I do it poorly.

From my last employee review, six months ago:

"You haven't had the best year, workwise. This isn't news to you, right?"

Howard Ziffle sat with his back to the window of his large and pleasantly cluttered office. Behind him, the avenues of the West Side far below, the Hudson River, New Jersey, the country, the world we reported on.

Newspapers from around the globe littered his desk. One could only assume there was a desk under the piles of newspapers, files, books, and empty Werther's candy wrappers, Howard's go-to instead of cigarettes, which he quit decades ago.

Dozens of books appeared to hold up one wall. Framed photos dotted the others. Howard and his father and grandfather. Howard and his daughter. Howard and former New York mayors and three former U.S. presidents. Behind him, on a small desk, the one neat place in the office, a silver-framed photo of Howard, his wife, and their daughter on a beach in Cape Cod many years ago, Howard's grin gorgeous.

Howard has been my boss for nine years. Here is a not-atypical sentence from Howard regarding my work: "One advantage for the dead is that they never have to read your writing."

"I'm off my game a bit," I said, wincing, fully aware of how little these words captured reality.

"Really? That's how you'd put it? You write obituaries. It's not a moving target. They're dead. You get the facts, type it up. It's not that hard. And yet . . ."

He looked back at the file and read aloud in a breezy voice, as if he were reading out a list of tourist attractions he and I might visit along a driving tour of the coast of Maine.

"Jean Carlson, aged eighty-nine. She was wounded in Korea. Imagine the surprise of Jean's wife and family when they learned you got Jean's gender wrong. As you did with Alex Shapiro and Kit Spader. Men, all."

I started to open my mouth to respond, but Howard held up a hand, forcing a thin smile.

"No, no," he said with an unnatural lightness. "I'm just getting started."

He returned to the page.

"Wrong age of the deceased," he continued. "Nine times." Here he looked up, smiling. "Nine times in the last year."

He licked a finger, turned a page.

"Oh. Here's a good one. Wrong spouse and children's names. Fourteen times. That would explain your use of Ramon O'Brien and Sloane Lopez."

He sighed and plowed ahead.

"Wrong affiliations. Twenty-one times. Wrong birthplace. Twelve times. Here's a favorite: Wrong cause of death. Four times. You claimed an eighty-one-year-old grandmother of five who died peacefully in her sleep had, instead, died by suicide by leaping off a bridge."

Here he looked at me. "Imagine the little grandchildren. *Why did Nana kill herself?*"

"That was a typo," I lied. "Well . . . I mixed up two deaths and . . ."

"Don't speak."

He reached for a pack of Werther's on his desk without looking, only to hit them and knock them to the floor. He either didn't notice or didn't care. He was too busy rubbing his face with both hands, as if trying to dislodge bees.

Howard once said that the trick to being a good obituary writer was keeping people alive. The moment they stopped being alive to you, that's the death of an obituary writer.

There are, essentially, two types of obituaries: those of the rich/famous/successful and those of everyone else. The former are written well in advance of the death of the rich/famous/successful. Think of a Hollywood star, Fortune 500 CEO, NBA power forward, rock star, and, weirdly, their life story has already been written. Strange to think, but Britney Spears's obit is ready to go. Just need the time, place, and cause of death.

We have a team in Washington that writes these obits. But on rare occasions, Tuan and I are allowed to write the minor celebrity ones. The inventor of the Flowbee, for example. The heir to a mustard fortune. A Finnish scientist who made major strides in poison ivy research. I don't want to brag, but I wrote the obituary for the chemical engineer who invented Dippity-do, the wildly popular hair gel of the 1960s, '70s, and '80s that was said to be a favorite of KISS's second drummer, Eric Carr. (I reached out to the band's publicist but never heard back.) I wrote the obituary for the man who created the longest word in the English language, *pneumonoultramicroscopicsilicovolcanoconiosis*. It means silicosis. The man who invented it was a former president of the New York Puzzlers Club. I made the mistake of asking a spokesperson for the club what their mission was. He said it was to find creative ways to express the language in as many letters as possible. I responded by saying, "So you complicate English, not make it simpler." He hung up.

There is a Society of Professional Obituary Writers. I am a member. I have a card. I have no idea what it entitles me to. Perhaps a free obituary. Their motto is *We write about the dead for a living.*

Most journalists, at some point in their apprenticeship, spend a bit of time in obits, but then they move on. They move up. They find their beat, their passion: features, sports, politics. Maybe a move to Washington, maybe a sought-after overseas posting. No one stays in obits. In fact, there is a saying in the newspaper business. *What are they going to do, put me in obits?* It's not a great saying, but you get the point.

The irony is that the art of obituary writing is dying. As newspapers die, with a few exceptions, so do the local obits. Seemingly small lives writ large—the ones that cause you to pause over your morning coffee, stopping midsentence in the kitchen, the smell of toast in the air, a finger wrapped around the handle of the cup, a vague memory, perhaps, of the last time you saw the grocer/dentist/mechanic—that pull you back to yourself, to the fleeting nature of life, to the shiver-inducing fact that that will be you one day, that it can and will all be taken away, that it can and will end. You bring the coffee cup close to your face, you need something, someone, to hold on to, to ground you, to bring you back to the small moments of life and not the vast, cold universe where death awaits. Best to table that thought. Time to butter the toast now, to make a list, to begin another day with the assumption, the hope, please God, that there will be so many more, that they won't just end. So your mind, on overload, thinks of the day to come, the errands to run, the meetings, so much to do. Too early for existential dread. But then your wife, your husband, your partner enters the kitchen, heading for the coffee, and doesn't understand the hug, the intensity of it this early, doesn't understand that you've been reading an obituary and drifted, if just for a moment, to wondering about your own.

I SEE YOU'VE CALLED IN DEAD

The following day started poorly. And much had transpired while I had slept.

For starters, the world was under the impression that I was dead. My anemic LinkedIn page—so few connections there—had condolences from fellow obituary writers, from people at the company. There were several likes of my posted obituary on LinkedIn (though far fewer than I'd hoped for). I liked it as well, under my own name.

I had a voicemail message from my brother, in China, his voice a curious balance of annoyed and mildly frightened. "Bud. What the hell. This isn't true, right? Call me as soon as you get this." In the background, a child's voice said, "But how can he call you if he's dead?"

From Howard. "What have you done? Oh, God."

From my friend and landlord, Tim, who was visiting his sister in Los Angeles.

"Assuming news of your death is premature? If not, hope it's okay to keep the security deposit."

I arrived late to work, around midmorning, feeling a first-day-at-a-new-school terror. My magnetic keycard didn't work at the lobby turnstiles. Lev, the day-shift security guard—a large and polite man originally from Belarus who smelled powerfully of cigarette smoke and a pungent aftershave—came out from his desk and tried it but had no better luck. Perplexed, he took it and went back to his computer, where he tapped away. Whatever he saw confused him, if his expression was any indication. He looked up at me, then down at the screen, then back up at me.

"Emmm . . . I am so sorry, Mr. Bud," he said. "But . . . it appears you are . . . maybe expired?"

"It's possible, Lev."

He seemed more confused. "Please," he said, picking up the phone and dialing. I couldn't make out what he was saying, but someone must have agreed to let me in.

I reached for my magnetic card, but Lev, with an embarrassed look now, said, "I am sorry but . . . I have to keep this."

A bad omen, surely.

"You look well for a dead man."

It was Tuan, my office mate. He held an oversized mug with both hands mere inches from his mouth, blowing gently on steaming tea. He stared at me as if watching a subject in an experimental drug trial.

"Do you know how I know you're dead?" Tuan asked, uninterested in an answer. "I read your obituary on our website. I briefly hoped it was true. But alas."

The looks on people's faces as I had gotten off the elevator at reception, as I walked through the newsroom. I'd stopped for a coffee in the kitchen area on our floor and our office manager, Phyllis, a woman of at least seventy, looked at me, screamed, and dropped a bagel with cream cheese on her shoe.

"I've waited for this day for many years," Tuan said, smiling. He lifted a triangle of egg salad sandwich on white toast to his mouth. Tuan ate lunch at 11 a.m. whether he was hungry or not. Tuan ate egg salad every day. I hate the smell and he knows it. Tuan is the brother I never wanted.

On a good day he is perhaps five foot five, although he is fond of boots with heels as well as cravats, French cuffs, and vests. Where once he grew his jet-black hair long, he now sports closely shaved sides and back and a kind of cupcake frosting on top. Despite his age he has a lineless face, feminine and pretty. When he smiles he involuntarily puts his hand over his mouth, embarrassed of his crooked and discolored teeth.

I sat at my desk and sipped from my cup of now tepid black coffee.

"Funny, I don't remember writing that obituary," Tuan said. "And yet it has my byline."

I winced involuntarily, remembering the last thing I did before accidentally hitting send late last night. I typed "By Tuan Nhat, United World Press Staff."

"Yeah. Sorry about that," I said.

I looked out the window. One of the perks of our office is our remarkable view, facing southwest to Hell's Kitchen and the Hudson. Tuan and I are housed on the twenty-sixth floor, in a far-off corner, away from the main newsroom, which occupies the great bulk of the floor. With few exceptions—my boss, Howard, for example—there are no traditional offices. Open spaces dominate the company's many floors.

Where once newsrooms were places bustling with energy and noise, typewriters clapping, lead keys snapping actual ink on paper, the bell of the line return, the air thick with cigarette smoke, now it feels more like a place where microchips are made. Clean, quiet, thickly carpeted floors, noise-reducing ceiling tiles, midrise partitions for a modicum of privacy. Phones don't ring; they hum, cricket-like. Almost no one speaks, as they are plugged in, headphones on, looking like air traffic controllers.

Tuan and I feel that our physical distance from the newsroom is a slight, a sign that we are lesser. Our nearest neighbor is Austin Aronson, the health reporter. Austin is diabetic and currently on leave after emergency open-heart surgery due to staggeringly high cholesterol that he ignored. Still, he was nominated for a Pulitzer a decade (and fifty pounds) ago.

Tuan chewed and pretended to smile, nodding slowly.

"I take it the blind date didn't go well?" he said.

"She showed up with her old boyfriend."

"How awkward. My friend Kevin assured me she was ready to move on. Fixing you up would be much easier if you were gay."

"I blame you."

"For you not being gay?"

"For my life now. For suggesting the blind date. For then causing me to go home, drink too much, write and publish my obituary, and now sit here in this Kafkaesque waking nightmare."

"You're welcome."

Tuan was enjoying this too much to stop.

"Look," he said, gesturing with his hand, a wannabe Vanna White. "Flowers."

I raised my head to see a large bouquet of flowers in a glass vase on his desk.

"Because you're dead and all. There's a note," Tuan added. "Do you want me to read it?"

"I'll give you twenty dollars to stop talking."

He read. "So sorry about Bud. He seemed nice. Your friends in Finance."

I moaned and sipped the coffee.

"You promised you'd let me write it when you died," he said.

"Sorry to disappoint."

"No, I liked it. I liked the headline."

"Remind me," I said.

"Bud Stanley, forty-four, former Mr. Universe, failed porn star, and mediocre obituary writer, is dead."

Tuan took an emery board from his desk drawer and began carefully tending to his nails. "One out of three isn't bad."

I have worked for United World Press for nine years. For five of those years I have shared a workspace with Tuan. He refuses to tell me his age, but I would guess he's in his early fifties.

I tend to arrive at the office a bit late, closer to nine thirty, sometimes ten. Once there, I procrastinate, waste time searching the internet, wander to the cafeteria to buy a coffee I don't really want but drink anyway. Tuan, on the other hand, is a model of early-morning efficiency, jumping into his assignments. By the time I am ready to get to work (in the afternoon), Tuan is done for the day. His real work can then begin. Annoying me.

"Straws," he will say, apropos of nothing, leafing through newspapers from around the world that the company delivers to the office each morning.

"What?" I'll foolishly respond.

"Plastic straws. Sea turtles choke on them. California is banning them. You use them. I see it. I see you drinking from them, essentially complicit in the death of millions of sea turtles. Babies."

"What are you talking about?"

"This is how the Nazis came to power. People like you."

"What?"

"Dead sea turtles. Global warming. China. Don't you see? Don't you get it?"

He'll sit in silence for a time. Then, "I wish you'd let me cut your hair. It's an abomination."

"Tuan, please."

"Do you believe in God?"

"I'm trying to work."

"You're an obituary writer. You're a man in midlife. It's *the* question. Any thoughtful person has an answer. God. Go."

"Yes. But his real name is Todd, he loves yoga, and he lives in Darien."

"God would never live in Darien. Too bland, too white. He'd live on the Upper West Side, just off the park."

Of late we talk of race, gender, sexuality. All the fun topics.

"Do you worry about your whiteness?" Tuan will ask, typing, not looking at me.

"You mean because I'm pale?"

"Because you are a straight white man."

"Oh. Well, I can't really control that."

"Do you feel you're inherently racist?" he'll ask.

"I don't think I am."

"That answer tells me you are."

"How?"

"Because if you *weren't* a racist, you would admit that you are."

"Okay, I'm a racist."

"The problem with that answer is that I believe you *are* a racist."

"You told me that if I said I was racist, I wouldn't be."

"True. But then you admitted it. Your whiteness, your privilege, your history of colonial domination." Here Tuan straightened his arms out in front of him, palms open, making small circles in the general direction of my face. "This is a problem."

"Is there anything I could do to prove I'm not a racist?"

"Not be white."

"Would a skin bronzer help?"

"The fact that you would joke about it shows me that you are a racist. I'm tempted to report you to HR. I'm getting a Diet Dr Pepper. Do you want one?"

Tuan has been unlucky in love (his words). Mostly because he likes to date much younger, often quite cruel men. His last serious relationship was with a Dutch man named Jerome who carved pumpkins for a living. They didn't last.

Tuan was, I believe, around five years old when his family fled Vietnam, after the fall of Saigon. The family settled in San Diego. His father got a job as a school janitor and worked at a car wash on weekends. Tuan said his father refused to accept the idea that he had a gay son and doted on Tuan's two younger sisters instead. Tuan mentioned casually, sarcastically, at an emotional remove, that he was bullied mercilessly in school, this slight, sensitive boy with the strange accent. My sense is that he forgot that he told me, one drunken evening, about the time he got an erection in the showers after a soccer practice, others pointing and laughing and how he wanted to kill himself.

After putting himself through college at San Diego State, working in the university laundry, he left for New York, where, he said, he found home. It was the mid-'90s, and he found an apartment share in the East Village near Alphabet City and discovered the freedom of living openly as a gay man. He tended bar at night and searched for a career by day, landing an unpaid internship at *The Village Voice*, at a time when the *Voice* mattered. He found his calling.

I remember Tuan's first words to me: "The good news is that someone died today."

I also remember I stared, not sure what to say. He shook his head. "You don't understand yet."

Tuan continued looking over my obituary, as if for typos, for hidden clues.

He said, "I was unaware that your father invented the hovercraft."

"It says that?"

"Third graph. It also says that you had a successful YouTube channel where you interviewed garden gnomes."

"Please stop."

"HR called. I should have mentioned that. And Howard's office. HR is expecting you."

"Any chance it's a promotion?"

"They're going to fire you for this, you know. Although, come to think of it, your performance postmortem might be an improvement."

"You're enjoying this," I managed.

"Best morning I've had in a long time," Tuan said.

THE BOSS WILL SEE YOU NOW

An urgent-sounding email said I was to go to Human Resources at four that afternoon and meet with a woman whose name may or may not have been Amy or possibly Megan and who may or may not have been an actual human being, if her soulless demeanor was any indication.

I announced myself to the receptionist on twenty-nine and was told to wait.

I had to use the men's room. While washing my hands, I looked in the mirror and saw, behind me, a stall door open and the wide-eyed face of Dylan Weiss from Accounts Payable. "Fucking hell," he said.

"Hi, Dylan," I said.

"I thought . . ."

"Yeah. I got better."

Megan came out to get me, a formal head nod, a surgeon about to give me bad news. I followed her to her office and we sat. Her desk, her office, her hair, her outfit were all unnaturally pristine. She adjusted an eco-friendly water bottle with the company's logo on it, moving it about an inch. She took hold of a company pen that sat atop a manila folder with my last name on it. She opened the folder, using the pen to trace the sentence that she appeared to be reading, then looked up at me.

"As of this minute you are suspended, with pay, pending an investigation and a hearing, which will take place within ten days." She then, for some reason, forced a smile.

"At this time I will need your building pass and company ID." She was an assassin, unblinking.

I took my company ID from my wallet and handed it over. "Lev from security took my building pass this morning."

"Lev?" she asked, squinting. Maybe it was the human name and not the employee number that was throwing her. She made a note and then ticked a box on the file.

Megan turned and typed at her computer and said to her screen, "Your computer has been removed from your desk and your company email is now disabled."

"Wait," I started, but didn't know what to follow up with. The reality of it was stunning. She stared, as if daring me to say more.

"Okay then," she said. "So there are a series of questions I'd like to ask you about your employment with us."

Again she consulted the file in front of her. I wondered briefly if she brought the omniscient file with her everywhere. Her guide. How to speak with children, gas station attendants, her partner during lovemaking. *I'd like your penis to become erect and then . . .*

"What did you like best about your job?"

"I was fond of the money."

Also noted.

"Do you feel like your achievements were recognized throughout your employment?"

"I'm not sure I'd call them achievements," I said. "I did my job. Fairly well. For a long time. Then less well. Have you ever written an obituary?"

More blinking. This was off script. She asked the questions.

"I . . . no." Blinking. Then, "What suggestions do you have for the company?"

"Maybe a group trip to Disney World?"

"Logistically, that would be almost impossible."

She pushed a packet across her desk, in the space between the silver framed photos of, I could only assume, her alien pod offspring and AI-generated 3D hologram husband.

"In the event of your termination, I've taken the liberty of providing a packet, including information about COBRA, the benefits center, and a crisis helpline."

"Crisis?"

"It's simply their name. There's no crisis. When and if there is, there's a number to call. If no one answers, leave a message."

I took the package. I was waiting for it to end, for all of it not to be real.

"One last question," she said. "Do you feel your manager gave you what you needed to succeed?"

"Howard? Well, for my birthday one year he gave me a thing called a genius paperclip holder. It's Einstein's head and he's sticking his tongue out and Einstein's head is magnetized so you can keep paper clips on it. So, how do you not succeed with that?"

She looked up. Something seemed to change. "Is that supposed to be funny, Mr. Stanley?"

"It was supposed to be. I guess it wasn't."

"Do you understand the severity of what's happening? There is a very good chance that you will be fired."

I could almost hear her think, *Make a joke of that, funny man.*

She stared, then turned to type, while I ran through a cocktail of shame, embarrassment, and regret.

She looked down at her file. "Your boss," she continued.

"Howard is the best boss I've ever had."

Perhaps it was the way I said it, because she looked up, noting the change in my voice. She nodded and made a note.

"Do you have any questions for me?" she asked her computer.

I wanted to summon the gods of gastrointestinal toxicity and vomit on her desk. But of course all this wasn't her fault. It was mine.

Tommy pointed at my half-empty beer glass, eyebrows raised.

"No, thank you," I said.

"He'll have another," Howard said to Tommy.

Howard's office had called and told me to meet him across the street at Gallagher's. The place had been there for just shy of one hundred years. It had been the site of countless after-work drinks, company parties, and interoffice hookups. It was Howard's favorite haunt.

Tommy placed a fresh beer in a frosted glass on a coaster in front of me and topped off Howard's scotch on the rocks. Like all the bartenders and servers at Gallagher's, Tommy wore a starched white shirt and a black bow tie. His black hair Brylcreemed back, full military mustache, a character from a Gatsby party, a man best photographed in sepia. Tommy rarely spoke. Instead he made small facial gestures, hand motions, a tilt of the head. His dark eyes darted, looking for tells, close-to-empty drinks, a newly vacant stool to guide a regular in the standing-room-only crowd to a coveted seat at the bar.

"Your stupidity takes my breath away," Howard said as he stared at his glass.

Did I mention that Howard's great-grandfather started United World Press? He did. Despite the vast family money, Howard appeared most days like a man who had slept in his clothes. The collar of Howard's old J. Press button-down shirt was frayed and there was a small hole on the elbow of his sweater. Antenna-like hairs leapt from his wildly overgrown eyebrows. His hair was an ungroomed mess. These things took a distant second, though, to his ocean-storm, blue-green eyes, sparkling and alive.

"What were you thinking?" he added.

"Well, I was a little drunk."

"A superb answer for the defense."

"I messed up."

"You think? You know what the crime of it was?"

"That I'm not actually dead?"

"That it wasn't a very good obit."

I happened to be the first person Howard told that his wife had died. This was about five years ago. It was late, the office largely empty. I had been making a point of checking in with him before I left. His wife, Emily—the rock upon which his world rested—had been in and out of the hospital with stomach cancer. Most nights Howard left early and was at the hospital, but he'd had a meeting about a terrorist attack in Kabul.

I stopped by his office to find him standing by his desk, coat on, one hand on the phone.

"You good, Howard?"

He looked up at me. "The, ah, the hospital just called. She died. She just died."

"Jesus, Howard," I managed to mutter. "I'm so sorry."

He was looking at the phone, as if he were expecting it to ring. He looked up and said, "I have to get to the hospital."

I drove his old Saab to Mount Sinai, on the Upper East Side. It was a very cold evening and we had to walk several blocks. The only thing he had said in the car was "I was supposed to pick up her dry cleaning. Today. I forgot to."

I wrote her obituary. Emily Keating, fifty-seven. Born in Portland, Maine, in old-money Cape Elizabeth. She was a skier as a child, good enough to captain the team at Dartmouth, where she first met Howard. She hadn't cared for him in college, she'd told a friend. Too much of a frat boy, too full of himself. A few years after she had moved to New York to become a schoolteacher, she ran into Howard at a party. He proposed six weeks later. After raising their children, she worked to turn the unused Brooklyn Piers into public playgrounds, tapping wealthy friends. A life, in other words, rich and full, dinner parties and beach vacations, nights up with sick children, days shopping for dinner. I shared my final draft with Tuan, who made it better, added nuance and grace.

Something happened after his wife's death, me being there, that drive to the hospital. I saw behind a door normally closed to others, these things in our personal lives that coworkers never know about. How well do we know a colleague? The ebb and flow of workdays, weeks, years. We might notice a new suit, a haircut, a bit of weight put on. We talk of work, a bit about life, we have drinks at office parties. But something changed in a way I couldn't quite explain. We had inched closer. How can you not, standing in the doorway of a hospital room as this man I had known for so long—this man I barely knew at all—wailed and sobbed over the body of his dead wife?

I wondered how I could ever put that in an obituary.

In the weeks that followed, during the time he took off, I would, on occasion, show up at the house unannounced. I'd show up, and if he was home, if he was in the mood, we would go for a walk. We might walk the Promenade in Brooklyn Heights, where he lived. We might continue down along the piers, his old coat open against the wind and spitting rain, a kind of painful cleanse. We'd walk until he stopped, looked around, as if unsure of how we had gotten there, and turn around. Sometimes he wouldn't say a word, just walk back into the house. Sometimes we'd go for a beer and not say much. Maybe words don't matter much. Maybe it's all in the unsaid.

"There's going to be an investigation by HR," Howard said now. "This is largely so they have proof in the event you ever sue them for wrongful termination. And then there'll be a hearing to determine the outcome."

I stared at him with the look of a man who doesn't quite understand the doctor's diagnosis.

"Meetings. Lawyers. It's exactly how I was hoping to start my week, so thank you." He shook his head, perhaps hoping to dislodge a thought. He sipped his drink.

"Oh. Almost forgot," he added. "They want to sue you."

"Who?"

"The lawyers," he said, trying to maintain a casual tone. He looked up at me, ruddy and wide-eyed. "The lawyers are involved. You broke, like, nine codes of employee conduct. You used the publishing codes for non-work business. It's . . . a felony or something."

"So you're saying I could get the electric chair?"

It took a lot to push Howard. But I had. I had gone too far. I thought maybe our past might help us get through this meeting and I could go home and start fresh tomorrow.

"Bud . . ." he said, shaking his head, unable to find the words to finish the sentence, annoyed at his own anger, at me, at the situation I had put him in.

"I'm sorry," I said.

I looked at him. "Howard. I'm sorry."

He shook his head, sipped from his drink. "Who the fuck writes their own obituary as entertainment for the evening? Have you heard of *SportsCenter*? Tinder? Pornography?"

He looked at me, trying to decode something. "Are you, like, suicidal or something?"

"No."

He held the stare.

"Howard, no. I swear. I'd just read my ex-wife's mother's obit and I . . . It doesn't sound as convincing in the light of day."

He closed his eyes and sighed deeply.

"I'm not sure you get it," he said. "You're, like, fifty—"

"I'm forty-four."

"Shut up. You're middle-aged, complacent, and your job prospects in the new world of digital media are, I would say, largely nonexistent. You know what that means? It means your days in obituary writing are over. It means your days in journalism are over. Me as your reference? *Oh yeah, he was great, except for the time he published a massive lie about his own death.*"

He stood and walked to the men's room.

When Howard returned, I saw that water dripped from his face. Not a lot, but enough that it was odd to see on a man in a restaurant. I assumed he had thrown cold water on his face. He did this throughout the day at work, his frustration at news and his journalists and editors, at life in general, causing him to need cooling.

He sat back down and we both stared at our drinks.

I stood. "I should go. I'm sorry about all this."

"Sit down," he said.

I didn't.

He turned and looked at me. "Bud."

I sat.

He picked up his drink, looked into it, swirled the caramel-colored liquid around.

"You know there's, like, wars going on. Elections, wars, the polar ice cap is melting. The steaming turd that is Putin. I mean there's news. And I'm here with you."

Tommy slid a plate of steak toast in front of us, silent as a ninja, and disappeared. We hadn't asked for it, but they did this with regulars. Small, perfectly grilled bites of dry-aged, medium-rare steak sitting upon lightly buttered toast. Howard slid the plate toward me.

"Eat."

I took one. Howard did the same.

"Fortunately, there are other people almost as stupid as you at this company. We've got a reporter in Kabul who has apparently been selling hashish to locals. So that's good. And the foreign desk editor has been caught on a security camera having sex with his assistant. In the kitchen."

"Phil?"

"Yup."

"Doesn't he lead a Bible study group?"

"Yup."

"I might start going."

I reached for another piece of steak toast.

"How's your daughter?" I asked.

"Fuck you. Stop reminding me that you're my friend." He sipped his scotch. "She's wonderful. Thank you for asking."

His face softened and he tried to hide a smile. "She does research on mushrooms at the University of New Mexico. She's in a relationship with a French woman named Lizette. They mountain bike. They cook meals together. They post videos of their life on Instagram. We talk on the phone. You should have children. Best thing. The only thing. You realize how much better they are than you. That's the hope you see."

We sipped our drinks. We ate the food. The pleasant clatter of half-heard conversations, of a sudden burst of laughter, the lingering scents of perfume, of cologne. The invisible, palpable energy of a New York night.

"The world changed," Howard said to his glass. "Broke in a way. I see things, read things, watch things, and I think . . . *I don't understand that*. The inanity, the vulgarity, the cruelty." He turned to look at me. "Is it just me, getting older?"

"I think something has changed."

"Something fundamental, perhaps. And so we retreat. Sure, we do our jobs, provide for our families. But then we seek cover. I subscribe to a channel on YouTube called Relaxing Mowing. It's speeded-up footage of people mowing their lawns, trimming their hedges. The world made clean and perfect. They put classical music over it. If someone described that to me five years ago, I would say that person was insane. Now, I love it. I watch these in bed at night. I watch videos of Fred Astaire and Cyd Charisse dancing. The elegance and grace. Where has that gone? Now we have twerking."

He reached for a steak toast.

"Do you know what's been most interesting for me to watch?" Howard asked.

"Tell me."

"My own irrelevance. I am an irrelevant man."

"I don't see you that way, Howard."

"I am. As are you, I might add."

"Oh."

He took a bite of steak. "A team of doctors have told me to avoid this type of food," he said through a mouthful of masticated meat and toast.

"Not a bad way to go, though," I said.

He gulped from one of the glasses of ice water Tommy had put in front of each of us.

"We've served our tour," Howard said. "We're done. Oh sure, we had a few bright, shining moments. The Renaissance, the Enlightenment, D-Day, the moon landing, antibiotics, Pringles. But the bad outweighs the good."

We clinked glasses.

It was evenings like this, dozens of them, listening to Howard tell a story, a natural storyteller, a mimic, self-deprecating, Irish funny, that I felt lucky to be his friend. Evenings I didn't want to end, that stayed with me when we parted. Women talked close, staring at each other, touched, hugged, said what they felt, said *I love you* out loud. We sat staring straight ahead, never touching, speaking more in the pauses, and yet still, if you listened closely, said *I love you*.

"My father fired me," he said. "Did you know that?"

He turned to look at me. I shook my head.

"Almost no one does. My father was the greatest man I've ever met. I know that sounds like clichéd horseshit but he was. He was intelligent and deeply kind. An old-school capitalist who believed in sharing the wealth. Stock for employees, unions, benefits. We had the first day care in journalism. That was my dad."

"Why did he fire you?"

"Because I was a little shit. Because I thought I knew something. I begged him for a second chance. He said, 'I'll give you two weeks. Show me what you can do. Show me you understand.' I did the overnight police beat. The worst."

"And what happened?"

"Nothing. Nothing out of the ordinary. Murders, robberies, stabbings, break-ins. The stuff that happens every night in every city in the world that we give a few column inches to."

I must have had an expression on my face that suggested confusion.

"The *thing* wasn't the two weeks, the night shift, the police beat. What he gave me was . . . he made me see differently.

He made me see that it all mattered. And I worry... I don't think anything matters to you anymore, Bud. And that kind of breaks my heart."

I felt the lump in my throat that made it difficult to swallow, felt the heat from the blood in my ears. The shock of the words, of the realization that they were true and had been true for some time. I ran my tongue hard against the back of my lower teeth, cleared my throat.

Howard said, "Maybe I care more because this thing has to do with my family. But I don't think so. I think I care because this matters to me."

And here he spread his arms out, palms up, as if offering me something.

"I happen to be dumb enough to believe that what we do matters. That journalism matters. There is a truth. That's what we do. It's not to tell people what to *think*. To look down on them if they don't share our worldview and eat kale. We're not *The Times* or Fox News. We just do what happened out there. Because in those news items from Tripoli and Seoul and Seattle and... wherever... are the stories of people's lives. And their deaths. And they matter. The facts matter. Because otherwise... otherwise their lives didn't matter."

Howard turned to signal for the check. He picked up his glass, drained what remained of his drink, then stood and worked his way into his old topcoat.

Tommy brought the check and Howard put down his American Express card. Tommy ran it, Howard shook Tommy's hand, and Tommy was gone.

Howard walked out and I followed.

We walked through the wood revolving door and out onto Fifty-Second Street. The temperature had dropped and I adjusted my coat to the wind and cold. Howard's coat was open and he seemed oblivious to the weather. I followed his gaze and saw that he was looking at a vintage car parked in front of the restaurant. He had a small garage in Brooklyn where he kept a 1968 Buick Skylark. His ideal Saturday afternoon was spent in there with his socket wrenches, a radio playing, and a few cans of beer.

"You know who cares when you die?" he asked to the bustling street. "Almost no one. Your spouse. Your kids. Your best friend. The rest? After about two weeks . . . hell . . . a few *days* . . . and you know what they're talking about? The new truffle-and-mushroom frozen pizza at Trader Joe's. Which is fucking delicious, by the way. Which is why there's you. To make it matter."

He said this while looking at the car.

"Guess the year?" he said.

"Seventy-five?"

"You're so dumb I can't process it. It's a sixty-three Stingray split-window. One of the best Corvette models ever. I mean . . . look at that."

Across the street, a man got out of a waiting black Town Car in front of our office. Howard's regular driver, Frank, a former New York City police officer. A head nod from Frank to let Howard know he was there. Howard waved back.

"Okay then," Howard said.

"Thanks for the beer. And . . . you know . . . the talk."

He looked at me, as if searching for something, then looked away.

"There are these nuns," Howard said. "We ran this story a while back. They practice something called memento mori. Latin for *remember that you die*. They sit and pray, meditating on this notion, that in every action we should remember, have to remember, that we die. When they were asked if it was depressing, they said no, quite the opposite. They said it makes life so . . . almost impossibly beautiful."

He stared at me.

"I'm sorry," I said. "I literally thought you were telling a nun joke."

His eyes went wide, like he wanted to laugh, and he placed his meaty hands on my shoulders and rocked me back and forth. "You are an obituary writer who does not understand the first thing about life. Wake up."

And here he surprised me when he leaned in and hugged me, bear-clapped my back, turned quickly, and was gone.

NO SLEEP TILL BROOKLYN

It was only six thirty or so when I left the bar. I stood at the corner of Broadway and Fifty-Second. Dusk was falling, a soft, deep-blue half-light. Traffic crawled crosstown, downtown, the sidewalks crowded, the energy of a rush-hour Monday.

People walked with New York purpose, at speed, confident strides, on the phone, crossing against the light. There were places to be and things to do. Dinner. A play. A Metro-North train to catch at Grand Central, heading home, to Westchester, to New Jersey, to family. Little League to coach, children's homework to tend to. A group of young women poured out of my office building, four or five of them, talking at once, laughing, bundling their coats tight against the wind, on their way to drinks, to an evening out, the limitless possibility of Manhattan and youth.

I dialed Tim, my landlord, friend, and emotional guardian. He had been in Los Angeles visiting his sister.

"The rumors of your death are exaggerated, I see," he said by way of answering.

I could hear him smiling. "Unfortunately so."

"I leave for a week and you fall apart. Where are you?"

"Just left work. Well, a bar. With Howard."

"What happened?"

"Big promotion."

A cab honked. Somewhere a fire truck siren wailed.

"What happened?"

Maybe it was hearing his voice, this one I relied on so much.

"I'm suspended with pay. But I think there's a chance I may also be fired."

Silence on the other end of the phone.

"Say something hopeful," I said.

"Don't worry. It could be worse. You could have drunkenly published your own obituary and gotten suspended without pay. Wait."

"You're a good friend," I said.

"Pop round when you get home." And he was gone.

I thought I would walk a bit, breathe in the cold air, make my way through Times Square, maybe go down into the subway at Forty-Second Street. But I kept walking, down Seventh Avenue to crowded Herald Square, meandering over to Fifth Avenue, past the Beaux Arts buildings south of Twenty-Third. The rain had long ago stopped and the skies had cleared. It felt and smelled as if it might snow. I had forgotten a hat.

I kept moving south, through Washington Square Park, where a man played a piano on wheels to no one, and, farther into the park, the skunky smell of cannabis. Along MacDougal, past the warmly lit chess shops, bearded men with questionable hygiene seated at tables, leaning on their elbows, studying the boards. I meandered over to Thompson, down past Arturo's pizza and the smell from the ovens making me slow my stride, close my eyes. Left on Prince, near Raoul's and its neon sign, out onto West Broadway, past the large glass windows of Broome Street Bar, a couple sitting at a small table by the window unaware of anyone else, heads close, smiling. Darker now, made all the more so by the tall buildings of lower Manhattan, the empty side streets, the closed coffee shops and bodegas that catered to the courthouses and bankers.

And then to the Brooklyn Bridge, along the footpath that gradually rises above the roadway, a thin crowd on a cold, windy night, traffic on either side. The higher up the bridge I walked, the more I could see. Standing above the river looking west to the fading light, oil painting brushstrokes, colors that defied name, orange-reds, yellow-oranges, changing each second it seemed, the cold wind stinging your eyes as you looked out at Governors Island, to the Statue of Liberty and Ellis Island, the Staten Island Ferry, seagulls flying below you, under the bridge, causing you to turn and stare in wonder at the giant ragged teeth of the buildings all the way up the island, Chrysler and Empire and ten thousand more. To feel even a small part of this place. To have come here and thought, *Perhaps I can make a go*. To come to the realization that you didn't, that your chances were running out, that time—something that once seemed to move so slowly—had sped up when you weren't looking. That it was late in the game and you were losing big.

Our little street, Covent Place, is tucked between two much busier streets. Tree-lined and quiet, you would have no reason to drive down it unless you lived there.

I moved here after the divorce. I wanted distance from our old apartment on the Upper West Side. Different shops, different walks, different borough. It was a way station, a port in the storm, some other cliché that I can't quite think of. It was a strange time and I needed a place to live. It would be temporary, before I got myself together and moved to California, Japan, London, somewhere I could start again, fresh, a new life. That was two years ago.

The street has its own seasonal rhythm. The spring thaw brought coal-like blackened snow that warm weather and street sweepers took away. The ginkgo and London plane and elm trees came into bloom. Window boxes were tended to. Older women in housecoats swept stoops and sidewalks. By summer there were more and more parking spaces, the bankers and their families having gone east to their second homes in the Hamptons, the Springs, Quogue. Fall brought the wood trucks from upstate and Pennsylvania and the smell of fireplaces in use on cold evenings, the yellow glow of lamplight, a kind of Victorian picture. Neighbors brought out sawhorses at Halloween to block off the street from car traffic. Children flooded the street as we all came out with mixing bowls full of candy. The first snow brought an almost impossible beauty, a blanket of quiet, created a kind of painting from another time.

The neighborhood bumps up against Carroll Gardens, where older Italian gentlemen still gathered on street corners, still set up a folding chair in the nice weather, in front of the old bakeries, say, or the deli across from Budget Food supermarket, smoking a cigar, dressed in shorts, white sweat socks pulled up high under dress shoes, listening to Tony Bennett on a transistor radio, saying "Hello, dahling" to the neighborhood women as they passed. It was still a neighborhood where old men out for an afternoon walk stopped at a construction site to watch, small boys again, the wonder of a backhoe. Still a place with a social club tucked in among the brownstones with signs that said *Members Only but Vets Welcome.*

There is a feeling in a city where you are connected whether you like it or not. I am not talking about the nature of city life, of the closeness of people on the sidewalk, in small shops, on the subway. This is the connection of physical intimacy, of buildings so close you can almost reach out to someone else's apartment, walls thin enough to hear sounds. I'm talking about the aroma from someone's kitchen as they prepare dinner, the clink of plates and forks and knives. The tired cry of a baby being put to bed. The sudden roar, from another apartment, as you lay in bed, windows open on a warm summer night, that tells you the Yankees won, a late-inning homer. It isn't a city so much as a collection of small neighborhoods where whole worlds take place.

Like much of Brooklyn, the neighborhood has changed, which is, of course, the nature of New York. Where once Brooklyn was the place people left, moving to the city, to Manhattan, to the mythical promise of life there, now large swaths of Brooklyn are places to aspire to, the epicenter to cool, to trendy. There were fewer cheap rentals, little in the way of reasonable home prices. The older families from forty years ago are now real estate multimillionaires with no intention of selling. Where would they go? They didn't understand the expensive coffee shops, the high-end grocery stores. Why would some pay $25 for a tiny bit of saffron? Why were there quotes on the high-end grocery stores from Gandhi and the

Buddha and James Baldwin—*The most dangerous creation of any society is that man who has nothing to lose*—next to a sign that read *Avocados $10.99 a pound*?

It was too easy to decry it, to say it was ruined. But was it better now because of it? That depended on whom you asked. Fewer cops and firefighters and teachers. More freelance graphic artists, private equity dudes, screenwriters. Fewer guys named Lou and Monte and Vic. More guys named Brent and Chip and Hunter. There were more overpriced restaurants, fewer bodegas. On our block, an adorable coffee shop called Fig's charged $15 for a coffee and a muffin because, a hand-lettered sign said, the coffee was apparently grown by a woman named Ana in Peru as part of a woman's collective and the muffin was vegan and made with organic lemons, chia seeds, and the tears of angels. Or something like that. And yet each morning they lined up, young, gym-fit men and women who seemingly had all day to sit and nibble, sip their cold brews with almond milk, the women carrying yoga mats. The men, universally bearded, sporting tattoos, carrying on production budget conversations with Los Angeles, too loud, loud enough for passersby to hear.

I wondered what they thought on those perfect spring mornings, when the world lay before them, health and riches, thinking it would all stay the same, be the same, unable, at this point, to see the world that awaited them at sixty, seventy, eighty: the medications, the hip replacements, the basal melanoma, the inability to control urination, the death of their once-fit husband from prostate cancer, the long, bedridden days at the end, glassy-eyed, weak, perhaps thinking back on those carefree days eating comically expensive muffins. Of course, they could also age beautifully or get hit by a bus next week. Either way, I wasn't going to be the one writing about it.

"Bud. There you are. I'm so glad you're not dead."

Diminutive Julia Felder was wheeling her recycling bin to the curb when she saw me, clearly unimpressed with my death. She stood on tiptoes as I leaned down and she kissed me on each cheek.

Julia had lived on the street for forty years, raised three children on her own, after her husband died. She had taught music at the public elementary school nearby and still gave lessons in the parlor of her home. In the late spring, she held a recital for her students, the old piano by the open windows, folding chairs placed on the sidewalk in front of the small brick town house and spilling onto the quiet street.

"How are you, Julia?"

"Your obituary. I'm confused."

"As am I."

She waited, looking at me with the mildly scolding face of a disappointed mother.

"I thought it might be funny," I said, wincing.

"Hysterical," Julia said without a hint of mirth. "You should consider stand-up."

"I also had a bit too much to drink, Julia."

She hit my chest, a harmless tap of affection.

"To answer your question, though," she said, "I'm splendid. Heading to Santa Monica next week to see my daughter and her children. She wants me to move there."

"Could be nice. No winter. Sunny every day."

"How awful. Nice to visit. But I like weather. I like being inside on a rainy day, making a cup of tea, listening to the radio. I like the cold, the snow. What's more magical than snow? When I taught at PS 29, the children would run to the window, stare at it, as if it was magic. I've lived here most of my adult life. How does one leave Brooklyn?"

She stared at me and winced suddenly. "Unsolicited advice?" she asked.

"Always welcome from you."

"You need a wife."

"I've tried that."

She placed her small hand on my chest, a thing she did with people, the way she spoke with them. "Could always try again," she added, with a wry little smile.

I walked inside the foyer of my building and knocked on Tim's apartment door. I entered without waiting for a response.

He'd bought the building, an 1870s three-story brick town house, twenty years earlier. He lived on the first two floors and rented out the third.

"Hello?" I said.

"Kitchen," he shouted.

I walked through his apartment, the living room with the overstuffed couch, the polished oak floors, paintings on the walls. Fresh flowers in vases around the room.

In the kitchen, Tim sat at a wood table, eating from a bowl of pasta while Esther, his housekeeper, washed a few dishes. They both turned to look at me. It was Esther who spoke first.

"Oh look. He rises on the second day, not the third. Even in death you are a disappointment."

Esther. Tim's housekeeper, food shopper, bill payer, protector. (Tim uses a wheelchair. I should mention that. Paralyzed from the waist down many years ago.) Her age was difficult to peg but I'd guess around sixty-five. Tim and Esther had been together since before the accident. They'd met when she worked the night shift at Sotheby's cleaning offices. Tim would make coffee. They talked. She lived in Carroll Gardens, though her journey there, from her native Hungary, remains hazy to me. I know she emigrated to Israel, where she was in the army, then university for a time, before following an Israeli man to New York, where they had a son. The Israeli left for parts unknown. Esther supported herself with cleaning and odd jobs. She could fix anything. A muscular build and the small, thick hands of an artisan. Her son, perhaps thirty-five now, is a dentist in New Jersey.

"Thank you, Esther," I said. "It's lovely to see you as well."

"Please, sit. Death must be exhausting."

I sat. Esther brought a glass and poured some wine. She then slapped the back of my head.

"Ow."

"Stupid." She brought a bowl of pasta and grated cheese over it.

"Thank you," I said, trying to make eye contact with her.

Esther kissed Tim's forehead. "You are both boring and I'm leaving." And with that she exited the kitchen.

"I love you," Tim shouted after her, smiling.

"Yes, I know," she shouted back.

Tim grinned.

"How was Los Angeles?" I asked him. "How's Lou?"

"She's great. Thriving. She talks with Tom Cruise. She tells him what movies to do. He trusts her."

"Wise man."

He was tanned, clearly had spent some time in the California sun, though he always had the natural coloring of someone who looked as if they'd spent the day sailing. A full head of dark brown hair graying at the temples that he combed over to the side with his hand, the haircut of a small boy from an old photo. Light-blue eyes and a mouthful of very white teeth that met at odd angles. When he smiled, which was often, he had a habit of closing his eyes. He was the kind of handsome that caused people to stare.

"I met two famous people," he said, "only one of whom I recognized."

"Do tell."

"One was a young man in a boy band. I forget his name. Turned heads in the restaurant we were in. The other was Jennifer Aniston."

"No way."

"Way. She came up to our table. Couldn't be nicer. My gosh, what a looker."

"A looker? How old are you, eighty-five?"

"We drove up to Lou's place in Santa Barbara. It's like the south of France. Stunning. I could live there. I'm getting too old for New York winters."

"Would you really move?" It was out before I could hold it back.

"I don't know. There's a lot to be said for that sunshine."

I nodded, feeling foolish, feeling as if he were abandoning me.

"And you?" he asked. "Imagine my surprise." His eyebrows arched.

"It seemed funny-ish to me at the time."

He nodded slowly. Not a good Tim sign. "Excellent," he said. "It's all going according to plan. The plan being to one day live under an overpass in the Bronx."

"It is the new Brooklyn."

Tim yawned, then straightened his arms and pushed himself up off the chair, a thing he did many times a day, to keep his circulation moving. He had the arms of Hercules.

I stood to go. "You must be beat."

I walked over, leaned down, and gave him a hug. "Glad you're back."

"You okay?" he asked.

I nodded. "Just tired. Ashamed. Embarrassed. A Monday, in other words."

I stood at the door.

"Howard said I've given up on life," I blurted out, another of those times I didn't know I was going to speak.

"Bit harsh."

"I thought so. Well, not in those words. He said I was an obituary writer who didn't know how to live."

Tim said nothing, a habit of his in conversation, knowing that I would fill the void.

"I know how to live," I said. "I'm just . . . I'm in a transitional phase, according to the *Diagnostic and Statistical Manual of Mental Disorders*."

"That's one word for it. What else did he say?"

"Nothing."

"What else?"

He'd adopted a slightly different tone. Quieter.

"He said I stopped caring." I snuck a peak at Tim, to see his reaction. None.

I kept going. "He said that I needed to wake up."

"Well, I can't say I love his rom-com syntax, but he may have a point."

"I got an email last night from Jen," I added.

"Oh?"

"Her mother died. She sent me the obit."

"I'm sorry to hear that. How old was she?"

"Seventy-seven."

"Did you know her well?"

"Not well. But I liked her. She was very kind to me. She actually . . . She called me a month or so after the divorce was final. Just . . . checking on me."

"Sounds like a nice woman."

"Wake's tomorrow night."

TIM

The first time I met Tim he was lying on the ground in a snowbank, his wheelchair on its side. It sounds worse than it was.

I was with a real estate broker named Ken who spoke while staring at his phone. We had come to look at an apartment in Tim's town house.

Ken had shown me three places earlier that day and I had been considering putting a deposit down on one I didn't really love when he asked if I wanted to see one more place. I didn't. It was the day after a snowstorm, many of the sidewalks hadn't been shoveled, and I was tired of Ken and the sadness of empty apartments layered in thick coats of yellowing paint, hissing radiators, the vague smell of cat. But I went.

"Can I give you a hand?" I asked Tim.

"I'm good, thank you," he said, as if taking groceries from the car. "It happens. Turns out being paralyzed is not as glamorous as I thought it would be."

We then watched him right his chair and muscle his way into it, a remarkable physical feat. It was cold, windy, the temperature hovering around freezing. Tim was sweating from the exertion and yet kept a smile on his face. He wore an old Carhartt jacket and beat-up leather gloves, khakis, and leather work boots. He looked like a carpenter.

Once upright, he extended his hand, removing his glove. I did the same. "Tim Charvat," he said.

"Bud Stanley."

"I'm sorry," he said. "But have we met?"

"Jesus," I said, remembering. "We have. A few years ago. Jen Bennett."

"Of course." He nodded, doing the math, me looking for a place on my own. "I heard a rumor she was moving to London."

"I've heard that too. I heard her new boyfriend is hot."

He grinned. "Go have a look at the place. Then we can have a chat. Unless I freeze to death in a snowbank first."

Ken and I made our way upstairs. A slow walk-through revealed a kitchen in a gorgeous time warp. Beige linoleum floors with small daisies. A vintage Norge refrigerator. The faint, pleasant smell of cleaning products. The floors in the small living room were wide-planked oak stripped to a sun-faded blond. In the back there was a bedroom and a small office next to it. Out the windows the late-afternoon sun cast shadows on the wall of the building in the back. It was covered with ivy, which was now covered in snow. Birds came and went. There was a large ash tree in his back garden, taller than the buildings around it. The sounds from a wind chime could be heard among the chatter of the birds. It was perfect.

"Who lived here?" I asked Ken.

"Older gentleman."

"Why'd he move?"

"I'm not one hundred percent sure. Great light, right?"

"Yeah."

"Do you read much?" Ken asked.

"Some. Why?"

"Tim . . . when you talk with him . . . a lot of people are interested in this place. He's looking for a certain kind of tenant."

"One who reads?"
"One who . . . you'll see."
"So wait. How many people have you shown the place to?"
"Fourteen."
"And they weren't interested?"
"Oh no. All of them want it. This street, this place?"
"How many does he like?"
"Zero."

"Do you like Ethiopian food, Bud?"

We were in Tim's living room, two floors below the apartment for rent and a world away architecturally. Someone had spent time and money renovating this space, bringing it back to its original state. The same wide-plank oak floors sanded to a light blond and left unvarnished, the wood smooth with age. Ornate area rugs in places. A lived-in couch, side chairs, a wall lined with books, the highest shelf within reach of someone seated in a wheelchair. Firewood stacked on either side of the large fireplace, a fire going. In the corner of the room, hugging the ceiling, were several brightly colored balloons.

"You know I'm not sure I've ever had it," I replied.

"There's an Ethiopian restaurant on Court Street," he continued.

He nodded and saw me glance at the balloons.

"My birthday a few days ago. Just turned fifty-eight."

"Happy birthday. You don't look fifty-eight."

"From the waist up, perhaps. Fifty-eight for someone in a chair is pretty damned good. Anyway. Mr. Tilahun enjoyed it. Ethiopian food, I mean. The former tenant. He was Ethiopian. Wubashet Tilahun. He was a philosophy professor at Brooklyn College for many years. Remarkable man.

"Oh. Wow."

I sensed he was unimpressed with "Oh, wow." So I added, "And he moved?"

"Well, that's one way to put it. He died."

"Oh, I'm so sorry."

"Yeah. It was not unexpected at his age."

"How old was he?"

"He was eighty-one. A spry eighty-one, but still. He died at home. And that's important."

"Home, like, here?"

"Yes."

"So . . . in the apartment?"

"That's right. Did Ken not mention that?"

"No."

"Yeah. He was making bread and apparently he bent over to open the oven door and that was it."

"That's . . . very sad."

Esther brought a tray with tea and cookies.

"Esther, this is Bud," Tim said.

Esther forced a smile. "You fell in the snow?" Esther said to Tim after she'd placed the tray down.

"I did."

"Well. Always clever to go out in snow as a cripple." She hit Tim in the back of the head and left.

"Thank you, Esther," Tim said, smiling.

One couldn't help but notice how extraordinarily handsome he was. His gaze, open and smiling, held you. "So you're an obituary writer," he said, fixing his tea. "That must be fascinating."

"Oh. Well. It can be."

"Tell me."

I assumed we were making small talk. I would come to realize Tim didn't do that.

"Well," I began, unsure what words would follow. "It's . . . interesting. It's hard. It can be. It's people's . . . lives . . . their whole lives . . . but you only get, maybe, a few hundred words. I mean . . . in a way, that's the beauty of it. This brevity forces you to make choices about what things to focus on and care about."

The words surprised me. They seemed to please Tim.

"Like life itself," he said.

"Yes."

"Great to have work you love. Where did you grow up?"

"Outside Hartford."

"Family?"

"An older brother."

"Are you close?"

"I can't stand him. But of course I'd do anything for him."

"Ahh, the New England Irish," he said and smiled. "Where does he live?"

"Shanghai. Banker. Rich."

"Bespoke suits? Fat ties?"

"You've met him." I smiled. "Most of his life he was known as Gerry. Moved to London for this British bank, before the Shanghai transfer, and he became Gerald. He now speaks with a slight English accent. English colleagues. Plays badminton competitively. Apparently that's a thing. I still call him Gerry, as I know it annoys him and I'm mature like that."

Tim sat, smiling, waiting, a thing I would come to learn he did, in no rush. It made me want to fill the silence.

"I guess there might have been a time when he and I got along," I said. "But I don't remember it. Maybe it was the six-year age gap, never going to the same schools, never being interested in the same things. Maybe it was that my parents—especially my mother—saw Gerry as the perfect child. In many ways he was."

Tim sipped his tea, old friends catching up.

"They had married late, my parents," I continued, surprised that I was still talking. "Later than their friends, I mean, their generation. I heard whispers over the years that my mother had difficulty having children. So, brother Gerry is the golden one."

"I hope I'm not asking too many questions."

"No. I'm just glad I know the answers. Wait until we get to state capitals."

You can fall in love with someone from their smile. He drew you in with that smile. *Be my friend*, it said. *Enter my rare and endlessly interesting world*.

"You?" I asked. "Any siblings?"

"A younger sister, Louisa. Love her to death. Lulu to me, but no one else. She lives in Los Angeles. Big job at one of those fancy talent agencies. She has phone calls with movie stars. When she calls and I answer the phone, I hear her assistant, 'Hi, Tim. Please hold for Louisa Charvat.' I love this. I love the strangeness of it. Apparently that's how agents place phone calls."

"I may start doing that," I said. "I'll call and say please hold for Bud Stanley and then I won't say anything. Just hang up."

"Parents alive?" he asked casually.

"Ahh, no. Mother died when I was young and my father passed away a few years ago."

Something about the way he asked these intimate questions, the way he waited so calmly, put me at ease. His manner, his voice, resonant and easy to listen to. He spoke a bit slower than normal. Sometimes he would stop, midsentence, a funny expression coming over his face, looking out somewhere, as if, perhaps, an idea had dawned on him.

"You?" I asked.

"No, I wish. My parents were one of those couples that still held hands after fifty-plus years. Dad was also a dreaded banker and was very good at it. But always wanted to be an artist. So he retired early and traveled the world and bought art. He painted but not well, which he knew. And that killed him. Not literally. A heart attack while sitting down to dinner with my mother one evening killed him. His last words were 'I think I might top off my drink.' My mother thought he was joking when he dropped to the ground. Joke was on her."

Here he looked out the window, as if remembering something. He opened his mouth to speak but said nothing.

"People can die of a broken heart," he said to the window. "She died six months later, my sister and I at her side. Have you ever sat with someone as they died?"

He asked this brightly, as if he were asking if I've tried the new Honey Nut Cheerios. I was tempted to ask if trying to force your way into the room as they died counted. Instead I shook my head no.

"It's quite something. Especially if they're ready . . . if . . . if they lived. Do you know what I mean?"

"Totally," I said. "Sorry. I lied. I'm not sure I understand."

He laughed. "I don't really know what I mean either. I guess I mean this. That at the end—and I've had the privilege to be in the room with a few people now, my parents, two friends—I think, and it's just a guess, but I think we let go of everything and the true nature of experience falls over us. This . . . miracle that is existence. Which we layer with so much. With anxiety and fear and greed and smallness and what's next and hurry up and I've got a meeting and all the . . . stuff . . . that gets in the way. I'm not saying we should all go live like a monk. I'm saying that if you haven't lived the life you want, if you haven't loved life, then at the end, I think a deep and very sad regret comes over you. But if you have, if you've lived well . . . friends and family and . . . if you've *lived* . . . then just as true is the peace you feel. I've seen it. Does this make any sense or do I sound mad?"

"You don't sound mad at all. Fine, maybe a little."

He liked that. "Thank you for indulging me. With all the questions, I mean."

"Of course." And here I thought we were done. Only I did that thing I do sometimes: speak without knowing I'm going to.

"I don't read much," I said. "Ask me about a book and I'll probably lie and say I read it but I also don't tell the whole truth sometimes. I just want to be up front with you. I'm not a very . . . cultured person. I like thrillers. Spy books. World War II. Left alone, which is most days, I'll rewatch *Tinker Tailor Soldier Spy*."

"The original or the remake?"

"Original."

"Alec Guinness," he said, nodding.

"Alec Guinness."

More slow nodding, the kindly smile.

"I mean, I used to read," I prattled on, a faucet I couldn't turn off. "I did. I was aware of who was writing, would buy new books, read reviews. Watched the Sunday-morning shows. I read *The New Yorker*. Fine, I leafed through and read the cartoons. Then I stopped doing that and let them pile up. It's just that . . . time has a way . . . of . . . weighing on you. I had three Oreos with my coffee this morning. That's a lie. I had four. I was embarrassed that I had four. I live in a city with art and music and theatre and except for the rare visit to the Frick, I mostly wander the streets for hours at a time on weekends. This is a new thing. Since the divorce, I mean. I'm kind of learning to be alone."

I realized I'd been staring at the carpet for a goodly portion of this soliloquy and now looked up at him wondering why I'd said any of it.

"Anyway," I added, standing. "Ken asked me if I read and said you're looking for a certain kind of . . . tenant. It is unlikely I'm that guy."

He stared for a time and then said, "Well, for what it's worth, the Frick is my favorite museum in New York. And I'm not sure I could ever really trust anyone who wasn't tempted by an Oreo for breakfast on occasion."

He extended his hand, which I took. "Thank you for coming by," he said, "and taking the time to chat. Forgive me if I don't stand."

Not long after I moved in, I would find handwritten notes in my mailbox. *Small concert this evening at mine. Would love to see you. T.*

The notes arrived on thick cream-colored paper, his name printed in a deep blue-black ink. He was, I would come to learn, fond of decorum, of small traditions. I would also come to learn that he surrounded himself with friends. Many of them were failed artists, these part-time poets and freelance oboe players, people who hadn't worked an office job in decades. Unpublished novelists and documentarians. A merry band of also-rans whom the world had passed by and for whom Tim's salon was a blessing.

And so he read early drafts of their manuscripts, helped photographer and painter friends get small gallery shows. He produced an independent film about the history of the Gowanus Canal. At one salon we watched a movie by our neighbor, Murray Eustis, about the waves of Coney Island. It was oddly mesmerizing if longish at eighteen minutes. Except that, quite unexpectedly, a naked man would run through the frame every few minutes. Tim had started a small theatre group that put on plays where the entire cast was made up of people in wheelchairs. He called it Remain Seated. He seemed to know everyone, and yet, when you were with him, you felt as if you were his best friend.

The story Tim told me was this—after I got to know him, after I got invited down, after we sat, long after the others had gone, by the fire, talking. (And please forgive the broad strokes. I'm trying to paint a portrait of an elusive person, one not easily captured by biographical details, but by sitting with him, listening, sharing his company. But it's a start.)

He was born in Manhattan but grew up mostly in rural Connecticut, in what he described as a "sheltered, well-appointed life." Both he and Louisa excelled at sports, loved hockey and soccer, swimming and skiing. Framed photos around his apartment confirmed this, told the stories of his youth. Summers on Cape Cod, smiling, sun-kissed faces at the beach on Sandy Neck, in Barnstable Harbor. Now in Vermont on the side of a snow-covered mountain, posing with Louisa.

After college (Kenyon, I think, one of those small, difficult-to-get-into places), his father offered to arrange a job at Sotheby's in New York. But Tim said he wanted something difficult. He suggested two options to them: the Marine Corps or the Peace Corps.

He was posted to the West African nation of Burkina Faso, where he took a crash course in French, taught reading to first graders, and helped build a school. It was two and a half years and he said he had romanticized the idea before going, that a few months in he was ready to quit, to come home, and take the Sotheby's job. He wrote a long letter to his parents pleading with them to get him out but ultimately didn't send it.

He said the days were long and draining. The images he had before he'd left, of making a difference, quickly evaporated in the harsh reality of profound poverty. During long, sweltering nights, when others went out drinking, he read. He read plays and poetry and William James and Dickens. He read biographies of Vermeer and Picasso, van Gogh and Pollock. He fell in love with beauty, he said. The beauty of people, of possibility, of art. He read and wondered about his life when he got back.

He moved up quickly at Sotheby's New York. He was a man about town, seen often in the galleries of the Upper East Side and the newly born galleries of then-bohemian Chelsea.

He said he dated casually. He was in no rush, enjoying life. It was, he said, an easy time to meet people. They were young and pretty and moving in the same circles, the same parties and galleries and summer houses. And then he was introduced to Esme.

Esme Kleinschmidt was twenty-six, had long, chestnut-brown hair, and was, according to the *New York Post*, the richest single woman in New York City. Her striking face—high cheekbones, Streisand-like nose, wide-set Jackie O eyes—often graced Page Six. She had, like her billionaire father, gone to Stanford and then dropped out of Harvard Law to move to Tokyo, where she got work as a photographer for *Vogue*. On the side she shot her own work, a world far from fashion.

She asked him out. A coffee that lasted all afternoon and that turned into a dinner that evening. That spring and summer, they were inseparable, traveling to Cape Cod and Martha's Vineyard and over to Antibes for a friend of Ezzy's wedding. He said they talked about marriage, about moving to London, to Los Angeles, to Prague. She would take pictures and he would paint, maybe write. Their children would see the world, learn French, learn Greek. He said that he didn't know it was possible to be that happy.

It was around this time, a Labor Day weekend at her family's house in East Hampton, that her father took Tim for a long walk and said that under no circumstances would he be allowed to marry his daughter. They were Jewish and Tim wasn't and that was that. While all that was true, the real aim of Carl Kleinschmidt was to pair his daughter with his longtime business partner's son, cementing a relationship in peril.

All this was news to Ezzy and she was devastated, threatening to cut ties with her family. She didn't. After long talks with her mother about doing the "right thing," she married that next spring.

One summer evening, a month shy of his thirty-first birthday, on his way from the Upper East Side to a gallery in Chelsea, on an old turquoise Vespa he used to get around the city, a cab that had run a red light hit Tim's back wheel, sending him and the Vespa into a midair tailspin, leaving Tim in a medically induced coma for five days, due to massive swelling of the brain.

When he awoke, his sister and parents were there, by his bedside, waiting, hoping to muster the words and the courage between their heaving sobs to tell their sweet boy the horrible news.

JUDY BENNETT, 77

Tim drove. It was one of his favorite things to do.

He sat behind the wheel of a 1984 Mercedes 300 Turbo Diesel. He bought the car from a high-end car dealer outside Boston after a long search. One previous owner, low miles, pristine. The only change Tim made to the car was to specially outfit it with a manual handle on the steering column that controlled both the accelerator and the brake.

We took the Brooklyn-Queens Expressway to the Brooklyn Bridge, then up the West Side Highway and through the Holland Tunnel into New Jersey.

We listened to the music of Tim's college years, his twenties. The La's, the Jam, the Replacements, the Smiths, Nick Drake.

"When's the last time you saw Jen?" Tim asked.

"When she took the furniture. Maybe a month after she left?"

"And her mother?"

"I don't remember. Maybe the Christmas before she left. They didn't get along, fought a lot on the phone."

"You'll get to meet her new boyfriend. Who I think is her husband now."

"Bad form that they didn't invite me to the wedding."

"This is going to be so wonderfully awkward I can hardly wait."

It was the day before my thirty-eighth birthday and I was on the train from Providence to New York to interview for a job. An older reporter at my paper, Warren Speckle, had dropped a job listing on my desk. *Obituary writer, United World Press New York.* "New York," he said, the two words heavy with meaning, the expression on his face suggesting it was the holy land.

The listing sat on my desk for a few days, a little siren. I was tired of small cities, of the occasional girlfriend, of the rootlessness. I also felt acutely aware of the rush of time, of my impending fortieth birthday. I felt like something was passing me by. Time, maybe. Opportunity. A life. I felt, like a million people before me, that something new, something better, was possible in New York.

I was standing in line behind her in the café car when she turned suddenly and spilled what I would soon learn was nuclear-grade hot coffee on my hip and thigh. My leg felt as if it were on fire. I heard a particularly high-pitched scream coming from what I assumed was a small girl. The small-girl scream turned out to be coming from me.

The conductor brought me to his office, urged me to remove my pants, and gave me a plastic bag with ice that he'd procured.

"I'm so sorry about your crotch area," she yelled from the other side of the metal door.

"You're not the first woman to say that," I shouted back.

She laughed. "I'm Jen, by the way."

Eventually the pain subsided and I pulled my pants on and we found a seat together. She kept apologizing and talking, a nervous talker, and I kept staring at her large caramel-colored brown eyes, pixie-cut brown hair. She was on her way back to New York, she said, after visiting friends in Boston. She said she worked in art curation at Sotheby's. We talked until Penn Station. I asked for her phone number.

It is hard to fully describe what it's like to arrive in New York City, to live there, still reasonably young. I walked too slow, looked up too much, a child among the grown-ups. The energy, the noise, the heat, the crowds. It was gorgeous.

I thrilled to go to Midtown, to the offices of this storied news company. I wrote obits but also helped out on small features, filling in. Howard would come by and ask if someone had time for a story on the anniversary of the Staten Island Ferries or a write-up on Gettysburg or a weekend feature on the history of the Iowa State Fair butter cow sculptures. (It's a wire-and-steel mesh frame, not solid butter, by the way. Still, it's almost eight hundred pounds of butter.) I always volunteered. I wanted to do more.

The people I worked with, whom I passed in the halls, saw on the elevator. Pulitzer Prize winners. I thought this . . . *this* is what I have been waiting for. This energy that is New York, this riptide you can't fight. This endless offering of life. *What do you want?* it asks. *Art? Music? Theatre? Drugs? Sex? Money? Dog parks? Good Korean food at 4 a.m.? Say the word and it's yours.*

And Jen.

After work I'd make my way over to the East Side, to her offices. We'd walk for a while, find a place for dinner. Often she had art shows to go to and I'd sometimes tag along. I know little about art and it was daunting and fascinating to stand in small galleries and studios downtown and Brooklyn and warehouses in Queens and try to take in pieces that sometimes blew my mind and sometimes looked like they belonged on the sidewalk on trash day.

On weekends we walked. We walked with no destination. We walked and found a place for coffee, for a late breakfast, sharing the *Times*. We took in a movie. We had a late-afternoon beer. Those early days, those dopamine-and-oxytocin-fueled early days, those best-selves days, the world around us surely as in love as we were.

There are 161 songs about New York City, more than any other city in the world. There is a reason for that. Despite the noise and the outrageous cost, the crowds and truly repulsive smells, it is unlike anywhere else. To move there, even at my advanced age of thirty-eight, was to be reborn, revitalized. If human beings are energy, what are eight million of us in those five boroughs?

I proposed nine months later. I didn't want to wait anymore.

I had come home one evening and washed up, changed shirts, a small ritual I had. I opened a beer and asked her what she wanted, a thing we did, at least for a time, before it all changed. We'd sit and talk about the day, put some music on, begin making dinner. Her parents had done it, she said.

"The baby and I will have a club soda," she said.

I was confused at first. I began reaching for a can of club soda. I thought of the movie *Dirty Dancing*. *Nobody puts Baby in a corner.* Who names their child Baby? Who would want to be called Baby? I was staring into the refrigerator when I understood. I turned to her and she was smiling.

"Wait," I said. "Are you . . ."

You change. I hadn't realized it, but you change because your world has changed. Because there is a new life now that you are responsible for.

We signed up at babycenter.com. It sent us updates each week, each phase, the growth. At week five, we learned, the embryo is a tadpole covered in layers: ectoderm, mesoderm, endoderm. Brain, spinal cord, nerves are forming. At six weeks eyes, nose, mouth, ears. At seven weeks the baby's brain creates 250,000 cells per minute. The baby is the size of a blueberry. We called her Blueberry that week. I thought girl. Jen, too.

Names. You think of names. Grace, Jen said. Anne, I said, my mother's middle name.

You don't tell anyone yet. I didn't know this. You wait until twelve weeks. This is something women know. But I told Tuan. He smiled. An honest-to-God smile. He said, "You're going to be a great dad." I had no clever comeback for that.

You change. How can you not? Jen with paint colors for the baby's room and furniture and clothes. Single-minded, preparing, a primal thing, the only thing, a mother. I wondered if we would stay in the city. Would we move to the suburbs? The idea of a small house, a leafy neighborhood. Back in Concord,

New Hampshire, I had covered local youth sports for a time. Saturday mornings at baseball fields, at hockey rinks, the parents gathered in the bleachers, chatting, sipping coffee, cheering the children on. It seemed lovely to be part of a community like that.

You wait for a reason. You wait because life is so fragile. Because to create it, to sustain it, well, sometimes it doesn't take.

A Sunday night and Jen from the bathroom trying not to cry and crying all the more for it.

"What?" I said, panicked.

She winced in pain, shaking her head.

"No," I said. "No."

Who would write that obituary?

I wanted to give her time. In hindsight I wonder if I was the one who wasn't quite over it.

"Should we try again?" I asked one evening, maybe six months after.

A forced half smile. "Maybe let's wait."

Are we ever fully honest with someone else? I don't mean to suggest outright lies, but do we really express those quieter, deeper feelings? Those amorphous, hazy things, core things that even we struggle to admit to ourselves. Do we share everything?

She had been in a relationship right before we met. I should mention that. One ignores these things at their own peril. But I did. They had worked together. She didn't like to talk about it.

She stopped laughing. That's when I should have known. I could always make her laugh and at some point she'd stopped, at least with me. She seemed to work later, go out with friends more.

"Have I done something wrong?" I asked one evening, rather pathetically.

"No. No. It's just . . . I don't know what's wrong with me. I just feel . . . different."

"About what?"

"I don't know. Life. Us. I just need some time."

"Us?"

She winced. "No . . . not . . . *us* . . ."

I knew she was lying. That's the thing about an affair. You know. Of course you know. But you lie to yourself. At least I did.

I did the worst thing you can do. I clung. I waited up for her. I asked too many questions. To watch someone slip away, get into bed at night, always tired, turn the light out.

Later, after it all came out, after the shouting and the anger subsided, after the long, brutal talks in the living room—her crying and me foolishly feeling sorry for her, praying she would come around—she finally had the courage to put an end to it all.

"I needed to feel better," she said, unable to look at me. "After the breakup. And you were . . . just so sweet. And I really did think I was over him. But I wasn't."

I remember standing. I don't know why. I remember she had bags by the door. I remember her wincing expression, how she was feeling sorry for me. I don't really remember punching the wall and breaking the plaster.

A pity for him (well, technically me) in that his name also begins with *B*. You would have thought she might plug his name in farther away from mine in her phone, under *Hot English Lover* or *Sex God* or *Cock-ney*. But no. She simply put it under Ben. Ben Finch-Atwell. English. What's not to loathe? Her boss, it turned out. I certainly got the sense from her text mistakenly sent to me that memorable Thursday afternoon that he was a superb lover (always good to learn) and a much-needed antidote to her current domestic situation (though not quite in those words).

Finch-Atwell was from a long line of Finch-Atwells, people who said the word *yes* by pronouncing it *ears*. I'd met him at a party in our apartment. That doesn't get one's imagination running at all.

The text ellipses sat, waiting for a reply. So I replied. **Wonderful to hear about the athletic lovemaking! But not sure this is meant for me?**

I watched the ellipses on my phone, waited, wondered what she might be feeling, thinking, typing.

Oh fuck! came the reply. Indeed.

She left, taking her things, which was most everything. I was happy for her. I was. In the way that someone can be happy for someone else but also sort of wish them dead. I would soon turn forty, and that number, that idea, rocked me. It wasn't possible. It felt like the end of something. My marriage, my youth. I was falling. What I didn't know yet was that a man in a wheelchair was waiting to catch me.

We parked in the handicapped spot next to the back entrance of the funeral home. I got out of the car and popped the trunk, taking Tim's chair out and setting it up next to the driver's door. It was a series of choreographed movements we had perfected. I placed a smooth oak board about two feet long and a foot wide in the space between the driver's seat and Tim's chair, to act as a bridge for him to shimmy over. Unless you have seen it done, it is hard to imagine. He has to raise his body up off the driver's seat and swing himself over to the board. Then another small lift and move into the chair itself. For the average person it would be difficult, requiring an unusual amount of upper body strength. But he also has to move to lower half of his body, the lifeless dead weight of his legs, with his arms. It was, he said, something that had taken time to master, lifting and moving his legs over. There were many falls. Now he did it like an Olympian on the pommel horse.

A small line of mourners waited at the back entrance to the funeral home under an awning. As we made our way up the ramp, a funeral director dressed in a well-worn black suit opened the door for us and suggested we could bypass the line. We followed. He walked with a slight stoop. Two tiny drops of blood dotted the collar of his white shirt, a shaving mishap, perhaps.

I said, "This is why it's imperative to travel with a handicapped person at all times."

The funeral director looked at me, eyes wide, and walked a bit faster. Tim shook his head.

Inside, the powerful smell of flowers. To our right, a receiving line, with Judy laid out, open casket, surrounded by large bouquets. To our left, a room with chairs where perhaps a dozen people mingled, speaking in hushed tones. I signed the guestbook for both of us and we moved to the end of the short line, waiting to pay our respects.

And there she was. My ex-wife. So strange to call her that, the distance between us now so complete. How bizarre, this stranger whom I once loved. Or at least thought I did. We showered together. We flew on airplanes and held hands and went to bars and restaurants, took in the mail, made grocery lists. She wandered the apartment half naked sometimes.

Jen was speaking to an older woman, holding her hand while she spoke. Next to her stood her older sister, Heather, who had been married for a time to a Saudi prince. We rarely saw her and the few times we did she never really spoke to me. And, standing on Jen's other side, a tall, thin man in what appeared to be a superbly tailored suit with a paisley pocket square. He stood with his hands behind his back and nodded slowly to the old woman who spoke with Jen. High cheekbones, pronounced nose. Surely it was Finch-Atwell. It was strange because I remembered him as far better-looking.

"Him?" Tim whispered as the line moved slowly. "You lost out to him? That's pathetic."

The line moved and we were almost up. *Run, Bud. Turn and run.*

Heather first. "Heather," I said, shaking her hand. "I'm so sorry."

A squint-eyed expression, scanning her mind for my identity. "Thank you, Doug."

"It's Bud, actually. Jen's ex-husband."

"Of course," she said.

"Heather, this is Tim Charvat, a friend of Jen's from the Sotheby's days."

Tim shook her hand.

Heather regarded us and looked as if she were smelling something she didn't care for. She turned to the next mourner in line.

"Tim!" It was Jen. "You came. My gosh." She reached down and hugged him, ignoring me.

"I'm so sorry, Jen," Tim said.

"You sweet, handsome man. Tim, I'd like you to meet my darling husband, Ben," she said, gesturing to the thin, well-tailored man next to her. My replacement. Maybe it was my clouded view of him, but he seemed to have an expression that said, *I find this wake and these people boring.*

Tim smiled and shook his hand.

"How *are* you?" Jen asked, in a new (to me, anyway) and overly dramatic manner. "You look so well."

"I'm good, thank you. How are *you*? Your mother."

"I know, I know. Thank you. That's *so* kind of you."

She seemed to have adopted the slightest hint of an English accent, a cadence that punched words. "She was older than her years, poor thing. A smoker, drinker. But who isn't?" she said, laughing quite suddenly.

The laughing stopped the moment she turned to me, replaced by a plastered-on fake smile.

"Bud," she said. "You're very nice to come." Although my sense, from her mildly nauseated expression, was that I was not nice to come.

"Hey, Jen. I was sorry to hear about Judy."

What ensued was awkward. What I thought would be a handshake, she thought would be an exceptionally brief and, if possible, contact-free hug. But upon seeing me stretch out my hand, she stopped the hug and extended her hand. Unfortunately, I had changed course and was going in for the hug, creating an image that, from a distance, probably looked like a man hugging a mannequin. Against the mannequin's will.

"Eow," she sighed, as if covered in cooties.

The fake smile was morphing into distress.

Jen said, "I saw on Facebook that you died?"

"Just on the inside," I said.

"Yes, well . . ."

"I—" But as I started to speak, she had started with "Are you—"

"Oh . . . sorry," I added. "You go."

"I was just going to ask if you were still in the obituary business."

Something about the way she said it. Also Finch-Atwell staring at me.

"God no. Private equity now. I want to make a difference in people's lives."

They both stared at me, the expression of non-native English speakers.

"I am. Just . . . taking an enforced sabbatical."

Slow nod, a kind of LED screen on her forehead announcing her thoughts, which were, *Thank God I put that loser in the rearview mirror.*

She reached for Finch-Atwell's hand.

"Sorry," she added. "This is Ben. Ben Finch-Atwell."

He was all smiles, happy in the winner's circle. His English charm on full display. "How are you, centurion? Heard a lot about you."

Centurion?

"I'm sure you have."

A small cloud passed over Jen's face. She squeezed her eyes shut, for just a moment, as if to erase the picture in front of her. I was holding up the line.

Tim saw an old coworker from his Sotheby's days. I walked out back to the parking lot, buttoning up my coat. I put my hands in the jacket pockets and felt a lone cigarette. I took it out and examined it. I turned to see a woman looking at me smiling. She had blue eyes made all the more pronounced by her flushed cheeks, like she had been outside all day. She looked to be late-thirties, maybe younger. She had on a vintage overcoat that stopped at her knees, high leather boots that looked well worn. Her hair was dark brown, held up in back by a clip, strands of hair framing her face.

"I don't really smoke," I said, rather unconvincingly.

She nodded. "Okay."

"How did you know Judy?" I asked.

"Oh, I didn't."

"Sorry?"

"I didn't know her."

"Oh," I said and nodded. "Okay."

I was still nodding. "Sorry, I'm confused," I said.

"I just . . . ya know . . . go to wakes sometimes. Funerals, too."

"Of strangers?"

"Yeah."

"Okay. Why is that?"

"I tried golf for a while. Doing this now." She shrugged. "Did you enjoy the wake?" she asked, as if she were a waitress asking if I enjoyed the salmon.

"Ahh . . . enjoy . . . I mean . . . I guess?"

"How did you know the deceased?"

"She was my former mother-in-law."

"Oh. I'm so sorry. It's nice of you to come."

We stood, smiling, nodding. I couldn't think of anything to say.

"Are you close with your ex-wife?" she asked. Perhaps it was the way she asked it, a bit of hope in her voice.

"Not so much."

"Your idea or hers? The divorce, I mean. I hope that's not too personal."

"Mine. Absolutely. Well, mine once she accidentally texted me thinking I was her boss with whom she was having sex. And, apparently, really top-quality sex at that."

She tried to suppress a smile. "So important to keep those names separate in your phone," she said.

"Totally agree. So yeah, as soon as she started having sex with someone else and told me she wanted a divorce, I put my foot down and . . . you know . . . granted it."

"You let her know who was in charge."

"I absolutely did."

"Is that her new husband? The thin Englishman in the nice suit?"

"Yes."

"This must have been awkward for you?"

"*Awkward* is my middle name. She's a perfectly nice person and I wish her and the English fellow well and don't at all wish they would drown on vacation in Capri."

She snorted.

An older couple passed us on the way to their car.

"Clara," she said.

"That woman?"

"No. Me. That's my name."

"Oh. Sorry. I'm a dope. I'm Bud. Bud Stanley."

"It's nice to meet you."

"Same."

She turned to go and stopped. "There's a funeral day after tomorrow. Green-Wood Cemetery. A doctor."

"Oh. Okay. Was he a relative?"

"No. Total stranger."

"Sorry," I said. "I'm still kind of confused about the going to the wakes of people you don't know."

"Also funerals."

"Have you tried going to, like, a movie or a play?"

She grinned. "You should try it."

"Really? Why?"

"It's hard to describe. It's Bud, right? I'm sorry, I forget names the minute I hear them."

"Bud, yes."

"It's just . . . There's something that happens. If you let it. If you're open to it. It's kind of . . . the secret to life."

She shrugged.

"I have to go," she added. "It was nice chatting."

She smiled and turned to leave.

"Dr. Gauss," she said, turning back as she walked away. "Green-Wood."

LIMBO

Things Tim and I did sometimes:

We swam at the Red Hook pool in summer.

We occasionally rode bicycles, Tim had a recumbent that he pedaled using his hands.

We shot baskets at the netless hoops in the playground behind PS 29.

We went to the Bastille Day celebration on Smith Street every July 14 and danced in the street in front of Bar Tabac. Fine. I didn't dance. I can't dance. Tim did.

We visited the doctor (Tim's). We went to a specialist who massaged his legs to keep the blood from pooling, to stave off the dangers of thrombosis, clotting and instant death.

And, on occasion, when the weather broke in spring, we played catch.

He needed to feel normal, he said. He needed to try.

It was still cool but the sun was out and the trees almost ready to bloom. We headed to a turf field not far from the house, a poor little ballfield wedged between the BQE and busy Columbia Street along the waterfront. District 78, Brooklyn's Little League, played their games there but today it was empty, a lone Parks and Recreation worker at one end, a woman throwing a tennis ball to a hyperactive dog at the other.

Tim slipped his hand into the old mitt, held it up close to his face and inhaled, the smell of aged leather and the memories of a thousand summer afternoons when he ran effortlessly around deep green grassy ballfields. He had played baseball in high school. Third base, he'd said. He still had a forty-five-year-old Rawlings glove, whiskey brown, with a deep, soft pocket, the leather heavy from repeated oiling. He had found a man on Long Island, a retired police officer, who restrung the leather webbing after it had frayed a few years back.

"I'm stiff," he said as we began throwing.

"You're also not a threat to steal if you get on base."

He faked a laugh. "What fun we have with crippled jokes."

"You can be canceled for using a word like that."

"Do you feel that you're being canceled, for your stupidity, I mean?"

As he got warmed up—even seated he had a stronger arm than I did—he motioned to me to move back with the flick of his glove.

"I need new sneakers," he said.

Tim took pride in his footwear. I realize that might sound odd. Most days he wore clogs that were easy to slip on and off. He had devised a system where he took a broom handle fastened with pincers at the end so that he was able to grip the shoes with the pincers and slip them on.

He found the clogs ugly, though. And when he left the house he liked sneakers in the nicer weather or a pair of old Red Wing boots he kept shined and well oiled. Today he had on the sneakers, a well-used pair of reissued green-and-white P.F. Flyers, high-tops, with Boston Celtics legend Bob Cousy's name on the side.

We threw in silence for a time, the back-and-forth rhythm a kind of meditation, the movement so natural, so mythic, American boyhood. The weight of a baseball such a familiar memory, the feel of it, so perfect at five ounces, 108 raised red stitches.

Traffic crawled along the BQE behind the outfield. Off the third-base line, on Columbia Street, traffic backed up at the light. People leaned on their car horns, eager to go, anxious to be elsewhere, to keep moving, keep going, a New York thing, impatient to stand still. But the more we threw, the *thwap* of the ball on a clean catch in the pocket, the more the noise of the city seemed to fade as the wind came off the water, a cool breeze that rattled the leaves on the handful of trees around the ballfield. We stayed for a while, in no rush.

And then there was the time with the chair.

I had asked him, foolishly, naïvely, what it was like one evening. We were sitting on the back deck. It was Labor Day weekend and the city was quiet, parking spaces on the streets, the energy different. Our faces were half lit by a string of small, sepia-colored lights that Esther and I had strung along the brick wall. A lone cicada and a firefly or two danced around the small back garden, a trellis with wisteria, the spring-summer bloom gone now. We sat and sipped from bottles of cold beer, long silences, the sounds of an ice-cream truck far off.

That day he had volunteered at the VA hospital in Bay Ridge, by Fort Hamilton. He'd go when they had someone new to life in a chair.

"What's what like?" he said.

"Day to day. In the chair."

He looked at me, and for just a moment I thought he was angry. Perhaps he was. It's a guess on my part, based on a look. Who's to say? But the look changed.

He had, to a great extent, eliminated difficulty in his home. Books and utensils, pots and pans, things within reach. He had redone his bathroom, widened doorways, put in a small elevator. He was, due to the money, able to control his world at home. Less so with the outside world.

He stared, a thin, forced smile. "I don't recommend it."

"I'm sorry. I didn't mean to be . . . dumb."

"You're not dumb. It's just . . . I'm not sure how to explain it. Obviously it sucks. But . . . that's just the surface thing. It's that everything is harder. Everything takes longer. If you walk out of the house and realize you forgot to lock the door, you go back. For me, it's seventeen extra steps. Back up the ramp, dealing with the door."

I nodded, pretending to understand.

"Do you really want to know?" he asked.

I had tried, to the extent possible, to see the world through his eyes. But there was really only one way to know.

The next morning. Sunday morning. Upon waking, I got up to pee. It was then I remembered what he'd said. "If you really want to know, go a day in a wheelchair."

He was waiting for me downstairs. Esther had gotten Tim's spare wheelchair out. These were not the kind of things you found in a hospital. These were titanium, aerodynamic, and weighed only nineteen pounds. These were the Formula 1 of wheelchairs. The minimalist, compact design allowed the user to move very close to a chair or a bed or a car door. No small thing when you're transferring the dead weight of half your body.

"You call this a way to spend a holiday weekend?" Esther said.

I sat. And the chair and I immediately fell backward to the floor.

"Oops," Esther said, clearly enjoying my misfortune. "I forgot to put the anti-tip lever on." A small steel rod that acted as a kind of kickstand for the back of the chair.

"You're a natural," Tim said, wheeling himself out of the house, down the ramp, to the sidewalk, to the world designed for walkers.

Our first stop was a diner a block and a half away, a two-minute walk. It took me sixteen minutes to get there. I stopped twice, once because I almost fell to my left on a slanted sidewalk. The other time because I was tired.

We sat at an outdoor table. I was sweating. My hands were sore. I kept lifting myself up to readjust my hips, which I could never quite get comfortable. Tim watched and said nothing.

I wasn't hungry. I sat with an iced coffee while Tim ate avocado toast and sipped an iced tea as if we were on a terrace in Portofino. If Cary Grant had used a wheelchair, he would have been Tim Charvat.

"At first," he said, "and for a long time, you're aware of how people look at you. The pity. You're self-conscious all the time.

But at some point you begin to accept the chair. It's not a foreign thing anymore. It's a part of you. A part of your body. You . . . You care about how you control the chair. Do you have good form? You were reaching way back, throwing your hands forward. Shorten your grab. Make small circles. They teach you this in rehab but it takes so long to learn to use the chair with grace, with ease."

We wheeled back down Court Street, the slightest decline in the road, the joy of not having to push. I found that even sitting while going slightly downhill, trying to control the chair, to keep it straight, was far more difficult than I'd thought it would be.

The door at Union Market. We sat and looked at it. This is a place I had entered a hundred times. Five hundred times. Just around the corner from our apartment. I'd never noticed the incline before the door.

I looked at Tim. He shrugged. "Give it a shot."

The trick was to wheel the chair up to the door, grab the door handle while keeping the chair steady, move the chair back slightly, muscle the door open, and somehow move the chair through the door. My first try resulted in me making it up the incline, until I took one hand off the chair to grab the door handle. The chair spun and I rolled fast into a parking meter. Two young women, heavily tattooed, asked if I was okay.

"Here," one of them said. She opened the door with ease, held it, as I struggled up the incline, Tim following.

The aisles were narrow, though they had never seemed so. A young man was stocking lemons, taking them from a large cart that blocked our way. Had I been walking I simply would have squeezed past.

The man turned and saw us. "Dude, I'm so sorry. Here . . ." as he moved the cart.

Tim grabbed lettuce—mercifully at chair level—and put it in his lap. Their house-made pesto was unreachable. But like Q in the Bond movies, Tim was ready, pulling a slim pair of long pincers from the side of the chair and deftly snatching a tub. Same with the pasta, high up on a shelf. A small cake from behind the glass case had to be brought out to us, not handed over the top.

To my left, a woman, maybe thirty, standing in line, looking down, everyone looking down, smiling, pure pity.

We paid, they bagged the items, Tim placed the bag on his lap, and we left, Tim leading, backing out, holding the door for me, a kind of gymnastics feat on his part.

I was tired, my hands raw, my hips screaming. It had been less than ninety minutes since we left the house.

Tim looked over at me, looked at my sweating face, took in my expression.

"I know," he said. "But thank you."

"So?" he said, throwing the ball back to me now.

"So what?"

"What's your plan?"

"Wait for the hearing, I guess."

"At which time they will . . . what?"

"Welcome me back with a spot bonus and a company car?"

"The phrase *limited horizon* comes to mind when I think about you." He faked a smile. "Breaking ball."

He threw and the damned thing curved. He saw my surprise and winked. I threw it back.

"Show me," I said.

He gripped the ball, held it up for me to see. Middle finger lined up with one seam, index finger snug next to it. Then mimed bringing the ball forward and down. Then he threw it and it curved again.

I tried. It didn't break an inch. Tim smiled as he caught it.

"You suck," I said.

"You're jealous of a man in a wheelchair. What does that say about your life?"

I watched as he paused, raised himself up off the chair a few inches, winced, readjusted his body.

"My arm hurts," I lied, walking over to him.

"That's the problem with you able-bodied people, always complaining."

I sat on the turf near his chair and we looked at the traffic, the cranes on the waterfront, the new building going up, the late-afternoon blue-purple sky under fast-moving clouds.

I put our gloves in a backpack and we made our way slowly back home, over the BQE.

"It strikes me that you're in limbo," Tim said. "Neither dead nor alive. Much like your writing, come to think of it. Are you familiar with the concept of limbo?" he asked. "In religion, I mean?"

"No."

"It's the place between heaven and hell. The person has sinned and died without God's forgiveness. They can't enter heaven without redemption."

"What happens if I can't redeem myself?"

"You go to hell."

"How does one redeem themselves?"

"There's the great question. It has a long and very ugly history, the paying of indulgences. But mostly it has to do with how you lived your life in the eyes of God."

I turned to see Tim looking at me.

"There was a woman at Judy's wake," I said. "She didn't know Judy. She goes to the wakes of strangers."

"Why does she do this?"

"She said it was the secret to life."

"You sure she didn't say living in Paris?"

"She mentioned a funeral that she's going to tomorrow."

"She's going to another funeral of someone she doesn't know?"

"Yeah."

"And you're thinking of going?"

"I don't know. Maybe. Is that weird?"

"I'm not sure *weird* is a strong enough word. I'm going to go out on a limb and take a guess that she's pretty?"

"Exceptionally."

"I see."

Tim stared at the sky. "I looked up this quote last night, after we got back from the wake. A Frenchman named Montaigne. He said, 'We do not know where death awaits us: so let us wait for it everywhere. To practice death is to practice freedom.'"

"I'm not sure I understand."

"I think you're onto something. I think we should go to the wakes and funerals of strangers."

"You know, when you say it out loud it sounds pretty weird."

"Heaven or hell hangs in the balance, my friend."

"Well, it's in Queens, so I think we have our answer."

DR. SAMUEL GAUSS, 86

We pulled into Green-Wood Cemetery, the funeral procession of cars already there.

"This isn't strange at all," Tim said.

I got out of the car to help Tim set up his chair and sliding board. As we were doing this, a man dressed in black whom I took to be a funeral director handed me a single-page pamphlet. *Dr. Samuel Gauss, 1933–2019*. Gracing the cover, a photo of a far younger Dr. Gauss, perhaps fifty. A smiling, cherubic face, too-large ears, wearing a white lab coat with a stethoscope around his neck.

We followed as the small crowd of mostly older people shuffled toward the grave. The day was cool, almost cold, a wind whipping up from nowhere, scattering old autumn leaves. Tim and I hugged the grass along the small, paved road, passing row upon row of gravestones. Past older ones, hand-chiseled names in the stone, the edges softened with age. Nathanial Beecher. Thatcher Merriweather. Cornelius Rutledge. More recent ones now. Baxter and Jones, Reiner and Drake. David Deruvo, born in 1919 and died in 2011. He was a staff sergeant in the U.S. Army in World War II. And Charles and Barbara Enright, an etching of a single-engine airplane under his name, Korean War vet, and a simple cross under hers. They died within a year of each other, well into their nineties.

Old-growth maples and elms and ash trees, slowly coming into bloom. There was a smell of freshly cut grass. Wind through the trees, the tall pines. It was quieter in here, the noise of traffic from the BQE faded. Instead, birdsong.

On a small rise to the left, many rows away, I watched a woman wearing an old-fashioned hunting cap rest her hand on the top of a gravestone and imagined its cold, rough surface. Who was she visiting? Father? Husband? Brother? Friend?

The intimate crowd gathered. The casket sat atop a bier over the grave, fake plastic grass covering the fresh dirt. Tim and I stayed to the back.

I turned to see a gravestone. Irene Gormley, 1935–2017. Below that, Walter Gormley, 1937, a dash, and nothing else. There was, however, a homemade sash with the words *Walter Gormley, Coming Soon.*

I watched the faces of the mourners gathered around Dr. Gauss's grave. They varied in age. The older ones sat on folding chairs while the rest of us stood. I tried to read people's faces. Some had their heads bowed. Some looked around. One man blew his nose aggressively while the woman next to him watched, a look on her face that suggested she wanted to harm him. There was the occasional yawn. A few people snuck a peek at their phone, checking a text from a colleague, perhaps, a lover, the weather, a fantasy baseball league. Did they know the old man well? Did they have fond memories of golfing with him? Or perhaps of how he was, in fact, a cheat at golf, kicked the ball to improve a lie? Did they have a note to call him and didn't? Did they feel that terrible longing for lost time, a thing not done, that wincing regret that keeps the mind in a hamster wheel of *I should have, I should have, I should have*? Were they not thinking about him at all and wondering if there was a toilet nearby? Can one pee behind a tree in a cemetery? Is that disrespectful?

A priest shook holy water onto the casket from a silver container that looked like a tall pepper mill.

"O God," he intoned, "who by the glorious resurrection of your Son Jesus Christ destroyed death and brought life and immortality to light, grant your servant Walter to your . . ."

A few murmurs from the assembled. "Walter?" I heard someone say. At the center of the crowd around the grave, wearing black, an old woman sat in a folding chair. She lifted her head, a confused expression on her weathered face, and shouted. "Walter? His name isn't Walter! It's Samuel!"

The priest said, "I am so . . . I am so sorry. I'm doing another . . . later on . . ."

He cleared his throat and started again.

Tim whispered, "I have to admit that this is more interesting than I thought it would be."

The priest soldiered on. "O God, who by the glorious resurrection of your Son Jesus Christ destroyed death and brought life and immortality to light, grant your servant Samuel to your never-failing care and love, and bring us all to your heavenly kingdom, through Jesus Christ our Lord, Who lives and reigns with you and the Holy Spirit, one God, now and forever. Amen."

I saw her, standing not far away. The woman from Judy's wake.

"That's her," I whispered to Tim.

"Who?"

"The woman from Judy's wake, who said to come to funerals."

"I want you to play that sentence back in your head."

She looked over and saw me, a slight smile. She walked over quietly. A dress below the knees and tall brown boots. Over it she wore what looked like a vintage wool jacket. It was too big, as if it was originally a man's jacket.

"Hi," she whispered. "Bud, yes?"

"Yeah. You're Claire."

"Clara."

"Yes. Sorry. My friend Tim," I said, motioning toward Tim. Tim smiled and they nodded to each other. We were trying to keep our voices down.

We watched the priest sprinkle more holy water on the casket. It seemed like a lot of water. He then stopped, a confused expression suggesting, perhaps, that he'd forgotten that he'd already drenched the man.

The old woman who had corrected the priest on the name, small and frail, seated by the graveside, slowly tried to raise her aluminum cane.

The priest said, "Mrs. Gauss. Please. I know you wanted to say a few words."

"Seventy-one years we were married. Seventy-one years. And he was a philandering, moody prick most of it. An absolute prick." And here, in a gesture of great gusto, she raised the bony middle finger of her right hand and forcefully presented it to the casket.

The priest waited, appearing unsure about how to proceed. Finally he nodded slowly and said, "Okay. Well . . . Amen, I guess."

Clara said, "Do you feel it?"

"Feel what?"

"You didn't feel it."

"I'm not sure what you mean. I certainly feel weird being here."

She nodded. "You need to feel it. Trust me. Mr. Kaminski. Brighton Beach."

Tim and I found a coffee shop in Windsor Terrace. We ate grilled cheese and soup. The waitress, maybe twenty-five, with blond tips and black roots, a small silver nose ring, refilled our coffee cups.

"We've never talked about it," Tim said.

"About what?"

"How you'll go. How you will present yourself to the infinite. Buried? Cremated? Funeral pyre?"

"Why am I going first?"

"It's just a sense I have. Plus, I'd love a new tenant so I could raise the rent."

"I'm not keen on being underground and I don't like the heat," I said.

"Cryonics? I read something about it. Pricey at two hundred thousand dollars, but you get the cold part, at three hundred degrees below zero."

"Tuan was telling me about a thing," I said. "You have yourself stuffed. I've seen photos. A man sitting in a chair, holding a can of beer. Stuffed. Dead."

"I like that for you."

"You could put me in the corner of your living room, a kind of novelty party fixture. I'm holding a glass of wine, a frozen laugh on my face, my index finger pointing, as if I just said, 'Good one!'"

"I love it. Or on the stoop, to ward off Amazon package thieves."

"And you?" I asked.

"Cremation. And then to a plot with my name on it, my sister, too, next to our parents, under an ancient, leafy oak tree in a cemetery in a small town in rural Connecticut."

"Does the underground thing bother you? Is that why cremation?"

"Not really. Also I'll be dead."

"Yes, but that's the quandary for me. I can't imagine a complete lack of feeling."

"You should read your own writing."

Tim motioned for the waitress.

"Do you have any pie?" he asked her.

"Pecan and pumpkin, pumpkin. Sorry. I just like saying that."

Tim smiled. She smiled back.

"Which is better?" he asked.

"Pumpkin. Hands down. I put a little whipped cream on it." She moved her hand in circles to mime putting the whipped cream on.

"Sounds great. Two please."

She turned and walked away.

"You and women," I said to him.

"You mistake their pity for attraction."

"You mistake their attraction for pity."

"No. I am the rare male who is no threat, quite literally. Sexless, short, seat-bound."

"New this fall on NBC."

The waitress arrived and placed the pie in front of each of us. Large slices, topped with big dollops of whipped cream.

"Enjoy," she said.

We both took forkfuls of pie. Tim raised himself up off the chair with his arms, winced, lowered himself. He watched a man in a white apron who had come out from the kitchen change the garbage bag in the trash.

Tim was talking to his pie. "I think, if we're going to do this bizarre exercise, invade these sacred spaces, we should maybe give it some thought."

He looked up at me.

"What do you mean?" I asked.

"I mean, someday someone is going to get up and talk about you, talk about me. What will they say?"

"I worry people will say, 'Bud who?'"

He faked a smile.

"Sorry," I said. "Bad habit. Go on."

"No, it's nothing."

"Tim."

He was finely calibrated, my dear friend. He rolled with my too-often asinine comments. But underneath he was always thinking, always trying to put the pieces together, to reach further, understand more.

"I was just thinking about this therapist I had. In rehab, after it happened, the accident. I'd gone through a few with my tirades and epic rudeness. I was just atrocious. Angry and lost. Except this woman, this new therapist, she knew me in sixty seconds. First session, she said to me, 'Do you want to live?' Doesn't say her name. Doesn't say hello. Just said, in this weirdly calm voice, 'Do you want to live?'

"And I said, 'No.'

"She nodded and said, 'Okay. Then there's nothing else for us to talk about.'

"She stood up, walked to the door, opened it. It was strange, the effect. I panicked. I thought, *They've given up on me. She's going to walk out that door.* My sister, Lou, had stayed in New York for three months but had gone back to Los Angeles. My parents visited, but I was absolute shit to them. And I said . . . I said, 'What if I did?' And she stopped at the door and looked at me. Didn't say anything for a minute but just looked and then said, 'Well, that would give us a lot more to talk about, wouldn't it.' I don't know why, but I started laughing. I laughed until I was sobbing. I wanted to die. I really did. But I also wanted to live, by just the tiniest fraction more. I just didn't know how. You remind me of that guy. This . . . person who refuses to step into his life, watching, commenting. Maybe we're all obituary writers. And our job is to write the best story we can now."

LEO

"This is how you hold a hockey stick."

It was Leo, my neighbor's son. He was sitting on his stoop as I passed by his home, his eighty-pound Rottweiler, Muffin, sitting by his feet. Muffin eyed me, a no-nonsense bouncer who allowed very few people into the club. Recognizing me, she put her large head back down. God bless the person whom Muffin didn't recognize who approached Leo.

Leo is seven but turning eight soon. That is how he announces his age. He likes to sit outside and count things. Cars, trees, planes that pass overhead. He counts the sirens he hears. He counts the number of street sweepers he sees. He has a notebook and he writes it all down. He draws pictures next to the numbers. I have seen it. He has shown me the notebook. He is a man who takes notebooks seriously.

I eyed him skeptically. "How do you know that?"

"Because I just said it."

He stared at me and then tapped the stairs ten times.

"Okay. But how do you shoot the puck?" I asked.

He mimed a shot of some kind, not remotely resembling hockey.

I nodded. He nodded and shrugged, as if to say, *I know, amazing.*

We waited, two guys in no hurry.

"It's late," I said. "Why aren't you in bed?"
"'Cause it's not bedtime."
"Mom and Dad home?"
"My mother is at a work dinner and my father is in Budapest. Did you know Budapest is a place?"
"I had heard that."
"There's a country called Turkey. Did you know that?"
"You're making that up."
"It's true. And Budapest is in a country called Hungary."
He looked at me, eyes wide, a skeptical look on his little face.
"It's madness," I said.
From my jacket pocket I took a few reporter's notebooks and a small box of pens pilfered from the office.
"Thanks, Bud," he said, as he took them and put them in a small bag he kept his supplies in.
He stood, causing Muffin to raise her head. "A group of penguins in the water is called a raft," he said. "On land they become a waddle." He sighed, the weight of his knowledge pleasing to him.
"Ask me what I'm going to be for Halloween," he said.
"It's April."
"A dinosaur who has like a blow-up fan thing inside and it blows it up with air and I'm in there too and I get taller than I am normal so I look like a real dinosaur. It's sooo cool and scary but I can't see good out of it, so I'll go with my mom."
"That sounds epic."
"It is. Was electricity new when you were little?"
"No. How old do you think I am?"
"Are you dead? My mother said you were dead."

"I was. I'm better now."

"Okay. Well, that's good. Bye, Bud."

And like that he was gone. Muffin followed, but not before she looked over her shoulder at me with an expression that—to my mind—suggested she was thinking, *You, sir, are a horse's ass.*

I met Leo about a year or so ago, when I was walking home and saw him sitting on the stoop, a little old man, making notes in the notebook that I would come to learn he carried everywhere, Muffin at his feet.

I stopped and was about to say hello when Muffin was up, barking, teeth bared, on her hind legs against the gate. I was close to wetting myself.

"Muffin. Shh," Leo said quietly, and the dog did as she was told. Leo kept his head down, making notes.

This replayed itself on other evenings until Leo said, "How many butterflies have you seen in your life?"

"I would say maybe about sixty-four," I said.

He nodded. He seemed pleased with the response. "I've seen 162."

The family had moved from Manhattan into a twenty-five-foot-wide brownstone a few doors down from Tim's smaller, thinner, three-story town house. The parents were elusive. What little I saw of his mother was when she left the house, phone to her ear, to get into a black Mercedes that waited for her in the mornings. She was known, a woman easily googled, maker of headlines and investor in companies, board member. A woman you saw and thought, *I know her from somewhere.*

The husband worked for one of the giant law firms. They were a very good-looking couple, though I almost never saw them together, occasionally loading a massive SUV, going, coming, in transit, on the move, flying somewhere, coming back, many-stamped passports, flyers of first class, wearers of remarkably good-looking handmade shoes, knowers of good restaurants, of the best hotels to stay at in Tokyo and Bangkok and Jerusalem.

I learned some of this from Benni, Leo's nanny, a woman of perhaps fifty who was originally from the Philippines. She wore thick glasses and had a gold crucifix around her neck that she fiddled with. She blinked a lot, a nervous woman who struck me as deeply kind.

When I would pass, if Leo was out on the stoop, we would talk. Sometimes it lasted for just a few minutes, sometimes longer. But I began to notice the tapping. He would tap the stairs and then stop. Once, he looked up and saw that I had seen him do it, an expression crossing his perfect little face that suggested he had done something wrong. He blinked repeatedly.

"You okay?" I asked.

"Yup.

"Can I ask you why you were tapping the stairs?"

"To make sure that a meteor won't hit the Earth."

He stared at me, as if trying to see if he could trust me.

I nodded, making a facial expression that suggested, *Well, obviously.*

"It won't really," he continued, "but I think it will and I have to do it but I don't do it really anymore since Rachel. Rachel says lots of people do things like that."

"Who's Rachel?"

At the top of the street a fire truck went by, siren blaring. Leo opened the notebook and jotted something down.

"My therapist," he said. "She asked me, she said, what would happen if I just tapped five times and I said I had to tap ten times but she said what if I just tried five times and if I did I would get a stamp in my good emotions passport which I still have and so I tried just five times and it was soooooo haaaaard. But I did it. And then you know what she said?"

"No."

"She said try tapping just two times. Can you believe it?"

"I can't," I said.

His socks were yellow and had smiley faces on them. Muffin was dreaming, making small noises. Without looking, Leo reached down and patted her gently and the noises stopped.

"And then one tap. And then . . ."

He looked at me, caramel-brown eyes impossibly large, mouth open, revealing little gaps where his Chiclet-like baby teeth had fallen out. His nose was running a bit.

"Tell me," I said, mimicking his wide eyes.

"It worked!"

"That's amazing."

"I know."

"Good for you."

"So what I do now is blink ten times. I haven't told her that part."

I tried to suppress a smile.

"I had a therapist for a while," I said.

"Did you tap ten times about things?"

"No. But I can understand wanting to do that."

"What was your therapist's name?"
"Judith."
"Did she use finger puppets?"
"I wish," I said.

A woman jogged by, headphones on, and Leo made a note in his notebook.

"What did you talk about with Judith?" he asked.
"Well, I had a wife for a while."
"What was her name?"
"Captain Velveteen Underpants."

Leo does a thing where he tries not to smile, hoods his eyes, tries to hold his expression, but you can see it start to spread. He laughed.

"That wasn't her name," he said.
"No. Her name was Jen."
"Was she nice?"
"She was. But then she met a man she liked more than me. I. *Me* or *I*, I forget which. And then she had to go so . . . it's not a very interesting story."

"No," he said. "It's not. Do you know how old the oldest tree in the world is?"
"I don't."
"Five thousand years old."
"You fibber."
"Nope. The Great Basin bristlecone pine in the White Mountains of California. I read it."

He blinked ten times and he saw that I saw. Benni called to him.

"I didn't see a thing," I said, winking.

He smiled, my new friend.

JAN KAMINSKI, 76

Howard said that the writing of an obituary is an ancient thing, a campfire thing. The remembering of the dead. Who they were and why they mattered. He shared some advice his father had given him. "You're not writing the story of their life. You're writing stories *from* their life."

Howard said that a good obituary should show readers some aspect of the deceased person's world—the sleep habits of a midnight-to-8-a.m. shift baker, the Christmas card collection of a neighborhood barber, the Kiwanis Club award of a longtime den mother for the Cub Scouts.

You drop into a life you knew nothing about prior to that morning. But you do your best to get to know them, to see them, perhaps, as others saw them, as they maybe saw themselves. I know it's not art. I'm no poet. But I did get it right sometimes.

A Columbus, Ohio, man who was a local legend for cleaning up a small park that the city had abandoned, keeping it clean for the neighborhood children. He was hit by a car coming home one evening from the park. I found out about his war service, about his time in Triple-A baseball for the Scranton/Wilkes-Barre RailRiders. That he played left field. About the memorial the city planned to erect in his name in the park.

Two elderly sisters who never married. Frances and Anne Kearney, longtime Hell's Kitchen residents who daily attended the 8 a.m. Mass at Saint Malachy's. Everyone called them Fanny and Babe, Irish spinsters who lived together their entire lives. They had worked in a munitions factory during World War II and later at Schrafft's, where they had their picture in *The New York Times* as the last waitresses at the last New York location on Fifty-Eighth Street. Babe died first. Fanny died six months later.

The best ones wrote themselves. I don't know how else to explain it. You began typing and forty-five minutes later, an hour, maybe more, the small yet enormous story of a life, a welling in your eyes, a desire to get up from your desk, to move, to leave the building, to escape death.

The dancer. I remember the dancer.

There was a mother and son from the Bronx. Francesca and Tony Iarratti. The son had finally come out to his mother, a strict Catholic who found homosexuality abhorrent. She and her son hadn't spoken for more than ten years, until the day he called to say he was dying of AIDS and she informed him that she was dying of pancreatic cancer. He moved back home to live with her and they took care of each other. This consisted of sitting next to each other on the couch, under an afghan she had knit years before, watching *Jeopardy!*, sipping chicken broth and nibbling on saltines and peanut M&M's. They made a pact. No sadness at death. No regrets. Whoever went first, the other would dance on their coffin. They laughed about it. They listened to Dean Martin records and, when the pain wasn't too bad, danced in the living room overlooking Arthur Avenue, the ancient Italian bakeries and espresso bars, the old men in the folding chairs talking about the weather and the Yankees, the twentysomethings hustling to the city, not a soul in the world knowing these two people were dancing in the face of death.

She went first, in her own bed, her own room, as she had asked of him, her son by her side, holding her hand, whispering, "Mama... Mama..." And later, at a neighborhood funeral home, the old women in black smiling and clapping, he kept his promise. With the help of friends and a step stool, he climbed atop the casket in his bare feet and somehow, this rail-thin boy danced in a way more graceful than people thought possible, laughing and crying at the same time.

Make those calls, the cold calls to the widow, the widower, the newly single mom, the serviceman's parents. Try that as your job. Call them back to make sure the facts are right, the names of the schools they attended, the branch of the military they served in, the number of the engine-and-ladder company. You can't get these details wrong. This is history for family and friends, a thing they will print and laminate, save and pass down.

The thing is, though, when you listen too carefully, too closely, day after day, to that pain, to that keening, it can take a toll. Because to really listen is to feel it, isn't it? Therapists are taught not to own the pain, not to take on the pain, but instead to simply observe it, at a distance. And you do, for a time. And then you don't. Then you begin to let it in, to live it, if only for a moment. How can you not feel it some days? There's a person on the other end of the phone and you're asking them to talk about the most painful thing that's ever happened.

Do that day after day and tell me you might not want to walk outside and bum a cigarette off someone, a thing you kicked long ago, taking deep drags, feeling the thick smoke in your lungs, the instant nicotine buzz, while trying to let go of someone else's death, wondering why the world doesn't stop when someone dies. Stand out on the sidewalk on Broadway, smoking, hating yourself for smoking, looking at the faces, all those lovely faces, all those lives and friends and families and loves and thinking you are all going to die one day and wondering what we are going to do with that knowledge we daily ignore.

In the late afternoon, Tim and I made our way to Brighton Beach. The weather had turned cold and windy with sideways rain. We took the BQE to the Belt Parkway, past the mammoth container ships waiting on the tide, past the Verrazzano Bridge, Coney Island in the far distance, the parachute jump dominating the skyline. Farther out, past an old Veterans Administration hospital, past two-story brick houses, past a high school with scaffolding around it, an asphalt playground with netless rims, not a tree in sight.

We drove along Brighton Beach Avenue, the occasional rumble from the B train on the tracks above us. I'd read once that Brighton Beach had been built as a resort in the late 1800s, named after the English seaside town. After the Second World War, it fell into disrepair and for decades it had been decrepit, poor, a place of single-room occupancies. But it changed when Eastern Europeans—Russians, Poles, Ukrainians—emigrated. Little Odessa, they called it. English was a distant third or fourth language. Even the architecture, the twenty-story apartment buildings, beige brick, poorly built, looked like something from the Soviet era. But what it lacked in charm it more than made up for in location, sitting along the Atlantic coast, a long stretch of beach and boardwalk, the older people out in all weather, a reminder, perhaps, of home.

Inside the funeral home, people gathered in small groups, speaking in hushed tones in what I took to be Polish. The smell of the flowers. The overwhelming smell of the flowers. It hits you as you enter. A funeral director spied us, came over and handed each of us a single-sided pamphlet with a photo of Mr. Kaminski and a brief bio in both English and Polish. The picture looked as if it had been taken many years ago. It appeared to be a passport photo, a headshot of a square-jawed, high-cheekboned handsome man with a buzz cut. The funeral director spoke in a low, barely audible whisper, in Polish, directing us into a space toward the front of the line. We hadn't planned on joining the receiving line.

We were five people back in the line.

The bio in the pamphlet said Mr. Kaminski was born in the city of Poznań but that he and his family emigrated to the United States in 1990, shortly after the fall of Communism, finding a community in Brighton Beach. He and a brother owned a garage together. It said his father fought in the resistance during World War II.

We were two people back, the line moving forward as family members greeted old friends, shook hands, accepted a hug. The mourners moved on to kneel at the open casket, their faces a few feet from the face of the dead. What do we do in those brief moments, so close to death that we can reach out and touch it? Maybe we say a little prayer, the rote memory from a thousand church services. *In-the-name-of-the-Father-and-of-the-Son-and-of-the-Holy-Spirit-Amen.* What do the words mean? *Our father, who art in heaven, hallowed be Thy name.* Do the words hold meaning after so many recitations or is it simply the cadence, the rhythm, that offers comfort? Maybe we steel ourselves to stare at the face of a person who just a few days ago was alive and talking and laughing and thinking about soup for lunch. Maybe we walk to the edge of the knowledge that this will be us someday. Maybe we live, for just a moment, in that rarified space when we are fully, terrifyingly, wonderfully alive. And then, in the next moment, we go find someone to talk to about our new car lease and how we got a complimentary roof rack.

I looked over at Tim, who had taken his phone out.

"We need to get out of this line," I whispered.

"Too late. It would be disrespectful."

He typed fast on his phone, then put it to his ear and then handed it to me.

"Listen," he whispered.

It was a Google translation of "I offer you my condolences," in Polish.

We were first in line, facing a man, midseventies, in an ill-fitting suit, who looked eerily like the deceased and who nodded slowly as he shook Tim's hand with his own large, calloused, powerful hand.

Tim repeated the line, sounding like a native Polish speaker. *"Składam ci moje kondolencje,"* he said.

The man's face changed, a slight smile.

Tim moved on, repeated it, rolled to the casket, and blessed himself.

My turn.

The man reached his hand out. I shook his hand and nodded, tried to remember the line, *"Składam ci moje kon..."*

The man looked confused. "What is that?" he asked, his accent heavy.

I said it again, a bit less sure this time, more of a question, the phrase having completely flown out of my head by this point. *"Konni..."* I stopped.

The man snorted and elbowed the woman next to him in the receiving line. He said something in Polish to the woman, who looked at me. They both began laughing.

He turned to me and said, "We don't laugh at you. It's just... you said, 'I offer you my horse.'"

"Oh... I'm... I'm so sorry."

"Yes," he said, still laughing. "But I don't want your horse."

He and the woman kept laughing, speaking Polish under their breath. The woman turned to the man to her left in line, closest to the casket, and said, "Maybe I would like a horse? I need ride home," causing the man to start laughing.

"I don't even have a horse," I said, regretting it immediately. It made them laugh harder.

The man in front of me felt the need to share this to the largely Polish-speaking crowd. He said something while pointing at me. The assembled laughed while looking at me. I nodded, smiling, not knowing what to do.

"I told them, 'You are the horse man,'" he said.

"I am the horse man," I said, forcing a smile and an awkward laugh.

Tim said, "How do you say 'horse's ass' in Polish?"
They liked that one.

Tim saw her first. We sat along the far wall of the large receiving room, watching the proceedings, the long line of mourners, the people chatting off to the side.

"Isn't that the woman from the funeral the other day?"

I felt as if I were in junior high, at a dance, the long walk over to a girl—Beth Creehan, in my case—to ask her to dance. (Beth said no and then I had the four-hundred-mile walk back, my friends laughing. Fortunately, these memories don't stay with you longer than seventy or eighty years.)

"Hi," I said. "Clara, right?"

"Hey." She grinned.

Under the work jacket she had on a black dress that looked as if it was from another era. Dangly silver earrings. Her hair a lovely swirling mass held up with a clip, strands falling out. I was briefly tempted to move one behind her ear. She was flushed from the cold and rain.

"I don't suppose there's any chance you knew Mr. Kaminski?" I asked.

"No."

"Okay," I said, nodding like a dope. "It's nice to see you," I added.

"Are you hitting on me?" she asked, grinning.

"What?! No . . . I . . ."

"You're hitting on me at a wake."

"No."

"Are you lying?"

"No. A bit. But if one can't find courage with a dead body in the room, then when?"

"Who said that?"

"Gandhi."

"Is that true?"

"No. I just made it up."

She stared at me as she removed Carmex from her overcoat pocket, squeezed some on her finger, and rubbed it on her lips.

"Just a guess . . . but I'd bet you're single," she said. "You don't date much. You have a guy friend you go drinking with. You rewatch the Bourne movies, *Mission: Impossible*. You tell yourself you're happy."

"How do you know that?"

She shrugged.

"And you?" I asked.

"It's not interesting. I was in finance. Then private equity. Sharpe ratios, standard deviation. Do these terms mean anything to you?"

"No."

"Not important. Anyway. I did that for a while. But then I kind of wanted to commit suicide."

"Banking. Who wouldn't?"

"No. I literally wanted to commit suicide."

"Oh."

"I mean, I didn't have a plan or anything. I was just . . . run down."

She said this casually, as if relaying the route she took to get here that evening. Then she winced suddenly. "I hope this isn't too weird. I'm just trying to . . . I don't know . . . be honest."

"Honest is good," I said, smiling, and her wince changed to a relaxed grin. She stared at me for a time. You can't kiss a stranger but you can want to.

She shrugged. "I went to a place out in the Berkshires, in western Massachusetts. It was more like a spa, but with mildly crazy people."

"Sounds great."

"I'm not sure *great* is the word I'd use. I'm also not really sure why I'm telling you this."

"How do you feel? I mean, are you feeling better?"

"You're sweet to ask. Most people don't. I'm trying to change my narrative. The voice in my head. What do you do, Bud?"

"I'm an obituary writer."

"Sexy. Are you here for work?"

"No. I published my own obituary one night when I was drunk and now I'm probably going to get fired."

"That's insane. I admire that."

She had an unnerving way of staring without blinking.

A very old woman, quite short, wandered close by, murmuring in what I took to be Polish. She looked up at me and spoke as if we were old friends. I nodded but of course didn't understand a word she said. At one point she reached out her hand and rested it on my arm, patting it. I kept nodding as she did this. She looked over at Clara, touched her arm, smiled, then back to me. Finished with what she needed to say, she wandered off.

"You speak Polish?" she asked.

"Not a word."

She grinned. "I like your face."

"Oh. Thank you."

We stood and watched as the mourners filed in.

"Can you swim?" she asked.

"Yes. Technically. Not well. But yes."

"You take a lot of words to say very little."

"You've met my editor."

"I swim. In the mornings. Around seven. At Jacob Riis. There's a lone, bizarrely twisted pine tree at the far end of the parking lot. Meet there." She shrugged again. "If you want."

"Swim in the ocean? At this time of year?"

Tim had come over. She looked at him, squinted, pointed, and said, "Tim?"

"Well done," he said. "And you're Clara. Nice to see you again."

Clara and Tim shook hands.

"I'm trying to change my narrative," she said, smiling.

"That's great," Tim said. "I love your dress."

"Thank you. I like your chair. It's cool-looking."

"Oh. Thanks."

"Would it be rude to ask you what happened?"

I stiffened.

Tim being Tim, he simply smiled. Perhaps, too, there was something about the way she asked it, almost childlike.

"Vespa accident," he said. "With a cab. The cab won."

"I'm so sorry."

"Me too."

"Do you swim?"

"I tend to sink."

Clara stared at him, smiling. "You're movie-star handsome."

"Oh. No, thank you."

"I have to head out. But it was nice seeing you both again." She turned to me. "Jacob Riis. Tomorrow. Bright and early."

And she turned and made her way out.

* * *

The crowd had thinned. Tim and I sat in the back of a small reception area off the main viewing room and watched as the number of people coming in slowed to a trickle. Small groups mingled, chatted, the occasional chuckle. Life went on, whether we wished it to or not.

Tim said, "You picked up a woman at a wake."

"I think it was more like she picked me up."

"You're meeting her at the beach?"

"God, no."

"Why not?"

"It's April and we're not in Saint Barts. Why are there no bars at wakes?"

I sighed. The smell of the flowers was giving me a headache.

"She's very attractive."

"She said she wanted to kill herself."

"My kind of gal. Go. What's the worst that happens?"

"Speaking of going."

"Not yet. I feel like we need a moment of some kind. A revelation. Don't you? If we're going to do this? What are we learning?" Tim asked.

"That an evening out at a wake isn't as fun as it sounds?"

I looked at the family in the receiving line, which had dwindled now. They waited, looked around, sipped from bottles of water.

"Not so much," I said. "The idea seemed—I don't know—bizarre, like an assignment, almost. Now it feels . . . sad."

"But isn't that the point?"

"Do you mind if we don't do life lessons right now?" I said. It was out too quick. There was an edge to my voice. Although maybe it was just in my head. I could feel Tim look at me. I ran my tongue against the back of my lower teeth.

A woman with a silver tray holding what appeared from a distance to be a bottle of vodka and several shot glasses approached the family. I watched them speak, though I couldn't hear them and certainly wouldn't have understood them unless the word *horse* was used. They laughed and cried and downed their shots, laughing afterward. The glasses were immediately refilled.

"What I mean," I added, "is that . . . I'm not sure what I mean."

I was finding it hard to breathe, as if I'd just sprinted fifty yards. My throat was dry. The damned flower smell was driving me nuts.

He stared at me, waiting me out.

"For what it's worth," he began slowly. "In my limited experience, I think we tend to flee pain. It's natural. Physical pain. Too hot, too cold. We fix it. Mental pain. Same thing. We . . . drink, take drugs, obsess about sex, about food. Trust me, as a half man. I've tried all of it. A smart person once told me to sit with it. To stay in the pain."

The family in the receiving line was sitting now. One of them was saying something. They suddenly started laughing. And the laughing changed to crying.

"Why would someone want to do that?" I asked.

"Because it's the only way to make it go away."

Again he waited. Then he said, "That must have been incredibly difficult for you. Sitting in a room like this, surrounded by flowers. When you were thirteen."

I had no words. At first my reaction was anger, blind rage, just for a second, maybe two. Then snippets of memory, of film. There, again, so clearly, watching everything, as if detached and yet somehow feeling it all.

"Hey," he said. "I'm sorry. We can go."

"Twelve," I said. "I was twelve."

I turned to look at Tim, forced a smile, and was saved by a mildly drunk Polish mechanic holding a tray of shot glasses with vodka.

"For the horse man and his friend," he said with a two-hundred-watt grin. "Please. Drink."

We did as we were told.

NO LIFEGUARD ON DUTY

Jacob Riis beach lay along the western end of Long Island's Atlantic coast, on the Rockaway Peninsula. In summer it acts as a kind of Hamptons to the rest of us, a hundred radios playing different stations, eighteen languages being spoken, far-too-small thongs barely covering sunburned bums next to a family of fully clothed Hasidim next to heavily tatted musclemen.

Today, the massive beach lay empty.

I arrived at around 6:30 a.m., mostly because I had been sleeping poorly of late, waking early, still tired. I drove through the vast, empty parking lot capable of holding almost five thousand cars. A depression-era brick building, a massive bathhouse, sat empty. Beach-sound silence, waves and wind and a cawing gull. Behind me, in the far distance, the skyline of Manhattan, a world away.

I drove slowly until I saw the tree and parked the car, sipped from a cup of coffee I'd stopped for on the way. I wanted to see the beach. I zipped up my fleece and walked out to the boardwalk, the beach spread out in front of me. To the right, half a dozen Canada geese stared at me, as if I had interrupted their morning yoga. It was April and cold and the light was changing from the dull grays of predawn to brilliant orange, a sliver of moon still visible.

I walked toward the water, as if pulled to it. The ocean stops me in a way few things do. I watched the movement of the waves, the wind over the sand, the distant horizon, sky meeting water, the teals and shades of blue, washed-out watercolors that were changing by the minute as the sun moved higher, shining light over the waves, over the sand, the world waking up again.

At the water's edge, I knelt down and put my hand in. A bracing cold. I imagined the feeling of stepping all the way in, the shock. I cupped the water and splashed it on my face, tasted the salt.

To my left, a group of sandpipers waited for a wave to recede and then ran to the ebbing surf, short strides, quick steps, like women in pencil skirts in a hurry, a peck under the wet sand, then just as quickly back, somehow, just before the next wave hit, little thieves, stoic, as if to say *Nothing to see here*.

I walked back to the car and sat inside, sipping my coffee, fairly sure I was being stood up by a person who went to funerals as a pastime. Though it dawned on me I was doing the same.

My phone buzzed, a text from Tuan.

Are you awake? he texted.

No, I replied.

My phone rang almost immediately.

Tuan had been reaching out, in ways that, for Tuan, were signs he was thinking of me. Which is to say he would text links to bizarre deaths from history. This was how he checked in. A few days ago he sent me a link to the death of Franz Reichelt. Apparently he was a tailor living in Paris in 1912 and claimed to have invented a parachute. He somehow obtained permission from Parisian authorities to test the chute by leaping from the top of the Eiffel Tower. People gathered to watch. A man flying, how exciting. Unfortunately, the chute did not do its job.

"There's a new intern in our area," Tuan said.

"Good morning, Tuan."

"The intern. I worry they're shopping for your replacement."

"With an intern?"

"Seems a fair trade," Tuan said.

"What does he or she do?"

"He. He's annoyingly handsome. Like someone from an Abercrombie catalog. Not that I have a collection of those. He bites his nails, then spits it out. He calls me bro. Every other word is *bro*. Sometimes *brah*. I don't understand."

"I don't think of you as a bro, Tuan."

"I'm most definitely not a brah. A sis, maybe. A Ms. or Madame on my best days. Apparently he's someone's son. Some CEO friend of a board member. He talks on the phone while he's doing his work, with his AirPods in, so that I think he's talking to me. At first I responded, until I realized he was talking to someone else. Kyle. His name is Kyle. He talks of women's body parts. Sexual conversations. In the workplace. *Rack. She had a nice rack. Bootylicious.* He says these words out loud."

"Are you saying you miss me?"

"He greets me by saying, 'What's good?'"

"I think that's something young people are saying now, Tuan."

"What's good? As if he's asking about a special at a restaurant. I mentioned Columbus Day to him and he almost had a stroke. 'Bro, that's like majorly racist. It's Indigenous Peoples' Day.' I wanted to say to him, how can a homosexual be a racist?"

"I'd love to hear the punch line."

"I'm worried for your job. Well, I'm worried in relation to myself, in that I don't want this bimbo as your replacement."

"I feel bathed in love, Tuan."

"Where are you? What are you doing with yourself?"

"Well, I'm going to the funerals of strangers. And shortly I'm about to go swimming in freezing-cold water with a woman I just met."

"I don't have words for how unraveled your life has become."

He hung up, abruptly, as was his way.

Another car pulled in and parked beside me. A 1970 International Harvester Scout, mustard color. Clara got out. She was wearing old blue jeans with a parka over a baggy sweatshirt and a ski hat with a big pom-pom on it. I got out of the car.

"Hey, you," she said, smiling. "I'm stunned you showed."

"Thank you. I already swam, so if you want to jump in . . ."

"Do you have your bathing suit?"

"Yes. I'm wearing it under many layers."

"Let's go," she said. "I'm really glad you came."

We walked to the beach, past the battered, shuttered buildings. The dawn had given way to a clear blue-sky day, the light dancing through the occasional fat white clouds, causing dappled sunbeams on the sand.

"Here's my advice," she said as we walked toward the water. "Don't think. Don't hesitate. Don't hold your breath. It's going to feel briefly like you're being electrocuted. It doesn't really feel like water."

"But then it gets better?"

"No. It gets worse."

"But you adjust at some point?"

"No. You simply go numb, starting in the extremities, arms, legs, restricted movement, and then you drown."

"Fun."

"But after, you feel as if someone injected you with a happy drug. Also they say it's good for the skin, inflammation, and the immune system. Also depression. Although I might be misremembering that. The Norwegians do it, and they're healthy and happy. Although come to think of it the suicide rate is pretty high in Norway. Anyway. Not to worry. It could also be that you have a sudden heart attack because of the shock to your system."

"What's the temperature of the water?"

"In April the low is about forty-three degrees and the high is about forty-six."

"Is this a good idea?"

"Don't be a baby."

We stopped shy of the water. It was strange to think Manhattan was just a subway ride away. Here, now, away from the eight million people, there was no traffic, no sirens, no *beep-beep-beep* from a truck backing up. She stopped and turned, looked at me.

"What?" I asked.

"Amazing, right?"

I nodded.

"Take off your clothes," she said.

"You could at least ask me out for a coffee. I'm not that kind of guy."

She ignored me but I saw a grin. She began removing her clothes. Coat, sweatshirt. On top she wore a skintight runner's shirt. She took off her ski hat, her hair bunched up in a bun, strands falling around her face, on the back of her neck. She unbuttoned her jeans and shimmied them down her hips, revealing a black bikini bottom.

It was strange to watch my reaction. Life as a divorced single man, the dormant sexuality I had kept in check during my largely monastic few years. Living in New York, it was impossible not to notice the endless parade of beautiful people, openly sexual, dressing to attract, allure. A dime-sized pink birthmark on her shoulder, and on her lower right hip a tattoo of a daisy.

Without turning around she said, "Stop staring."

I removed my jacket, sweater, shirt, khakis. Beneath I'd worn baggy trunks. The wind seemed to pick up but maybe it was my imagination.

"I forgot my towel," I said.

"You won't need it. The endorphins kick in and you feel like Superman."

She removed her shirt to reveal a bikini top and I tried not to look at her breasts, the shape of them, her cleavage, tried too hard perhaps. To the point where I was looking her in the eye and she at me.

"Ready?" she said.

"No."

She ran and I followed. She screamed when she hit the water. I screamed louder. It was worse than she had described. It felt as if electricity were hitting my body, the pain ferocious. I kept going, following her, pulled forward, against my will, and dove under.

We sat in her truck looking at the beach, the engine on and the heat cranked, sipping hot tea she had brought in a thermos.

"Have you given much thought to caskets?" she asked.

"I haven't. Do you know something I don't?"

A big smile and a sip from her thermos.

"Caskets are four-sided," she said. "I read this. Coffins are six-sided. And wider at the top. They make coffins in metal, wood, mahogany, oak. There are biodegradable caskets now, made from bamboo and seagrass. No heavy machinery is used. No carbon footprint."

"Who knew."

She said, "They can be really expensive, too. Titan makes a seventeen-hundred-dollar casket called the Going Home. Imagine that job, naming caskets."

"That would be amazing. The Bye-Bye. The I'm Outta Here. The Don't Wait Up."

She laughed, a full, loony cackle.

"So, I have to ask," I said. "Why the funerals of strangers?"

She shrugged. "After the whole thing with the hospital, I wasn't ready to go back to work. To *that* work. Finance. I was sort of like, what am I doing with my life?"

A car pulled up and the door opened and a large dog leapt out, followed more slowly by his owner, a heavily bearded man who quickly lit up a cigarette, following the dog bounding toward the beach.

"Some women meditate," she said. "Some do SoulCycle. They use the word *soul*. That's what passes for soul today. Rich white women listening to some asshole who thinks she's Gandhi while they play Diplo and yell bullshit clichés. *You go, girl!*"

"No offense, but aren't you a rich white woman?"

"Yes. But also no. I'm a working-class kid from Cincinnati who got lucky because I'm good at math."

"I'm confused."

"Wakes, funerals . . . They make me feel alive, remind me."

"Of what?"

"That this is it."

She looked over at me and shrugged.

"We're so afraid of death," she said. "Standing in that room. A wake. It's so awkward. What do you say to the person? *I'm sorry? What a lovely service?* I was in line behind a man at a wake a few weeks ago who, when asked how he was doing by the grieving husband, said, and I'm not making this up, he said, 'Well, I'm having a fantastic year business-wise.'"

She scratched her head, shook out her hair, shoulder-length, tangled, the color of whiskey.

"Sand," she said. She turned, a little grimace of embarrassment. "So what's going on with your job?"

"There's a hearing soon. In the meantime . . . against my saner judgment, I'm going to the wakes and funerals of people I didn't know."

"I love this. It's a pitch for a movie. The obituary writer who was afraid to die."

"I'm not afraid to die."

"Of course you are. Everyone is. Maybe you're afraid to live too? There's the movie-poster line. *Learning about dying taught him how to live.*"

Here she adopted the voice of the movie trailer announcer. "In a world where death terrified him . . ."

"I'm not terrified . . ."

". . . one lost middle-aged man must now face his greatest fear: life. Bud Stanley is himself in . . . *Bury the Lede.*" She cackled.

Maybe it was the warmth of the truck after the shock of the water, the heart-rate-doubling, body-shivering cold of it, the giddy high of being here now, warm, the smell of the old leather seats. Maybe it was the muffled sound of the ocean waves. Maybe it was her flushed face and unblinking eyes, neither of us with anywhere to go. I'd known her for a morning. I'd known her for a decade. So I talked. I told her about the obituary. I told her about the blind date and the woman who brought her boyfriend. I told her about Tuan and how impossible he is and how kind he was to me after Jen. I told her about Tim. I told her about my mother. I talked and couldn't seem to stop.

GERALD STANLEY, SR., 84

Prior to my new and bizarre pastime, the last funeral I attended was my father's, four years ago in Florida. It was a small affair on a sweltering hot and humid August day. He chose cremation and asked that his sons scatter his ashes at a local beach he was fond of.

My brother, Gerry, gave the eulogy. No easy task, but my memory of the brief speech was that it sounded like an awkward best man toast at a rehearsal dinner, peppered with frat guy jokes ("I think it's fair to say he liked the ladies"). I wrote his obituary.

Gerald Stanley, a career employee of Axium Life Insurance in Hartford, Connecticut, and two-time winner of the Insurance Underwriters Claims Settlement Award, died Thursday from heart failure. He was 84. Stanley had been recognized for his contributions in advocating best practices that enhance the independent agency. (I wasn't exactly sure what that sentence meant but had found it in a collection of files my father had kept on his middling career.) *His son, Gerald, of Shanghai, said, "My father cared deeply about life insurance. But he was first and foremost a family man."*

I floated the idea of adding a quote saying, *His son, Bud, an obituary writer in New York, said, "Death runs in our family."* Gerry nixed it.

My obituary for him was more of a brief biography, dates and events, rather than any nuance about our father's life. I found my father's obituary one of the harder ones I've ever had to write but not for the obvious reasons. I wasn't particularly grief-stricken. Sad, certainly. Surprised, in the way all deaths are surprising, even when you know they're coming. But not grief. I knew my father for my entire life but I can't say I knew him well.

Gerry, Sr. He worked for an insurance company in Hartford (insurance capital of the world) and, I think, never cared a wit about the work a day in his life. If it had been up to him, I think he would have spent his days wandering the house and yard, doing odd jobs, repairs, paint touch-ups, reading, making sandwiches, napping, going to the hardware store despite not needing anything at the hardware store. But that did not pay well. So he took a job. It was safe, easy, for life. Like insurance itself.

He lived for small pleasures, it seemed to me. For his evening reading, for one or two scotch and sodas upon arriving home, for wandering out to the small shed in the backyard, where he kept a radio, a small refrigerator with bottles of beer and Coca-Cola lined up in neat rows, his tools hung from a pegboard, each with their name in his small, precise script underneath.

On weekends in the summer, while his friends from work golfed, he tended to our yard, pushing a lawn mower, emptying the bag of grass clippings, the smell of it intoxicating, a deep marker of seemingly endless days. Perhaps later, as the heat of the day waned, he'd open a can of Narragansett and wash the car. I always helped, more often than not standing by, watching. "Here," he'd say. "Do it like this." And he'd take over, humming. Sometimes I wondered if he remembered I was there.

It was my brother, Gerry, who got the attention. Understandably, too. He had all the gifts. Smart, confident, handsome, a superb athlete. His friends talked about how funny he was, but I never saw that side of him. When I would overhear my parents talking, it seemed to me, anyway, they talked of Gerry. Of his good grades and how well he was doing and football and where he might go to college. It didn't bother me, though. I thought Gerry was amazing too. I didn't believe I deserved the attention.

In the fall, after one of Gerry's football games, my father enjoyed putting on a pair of old khaki pants and well-worn leather work boots that he shined himself, treating them with a waxy waterproofing, an old sweatshirt, and work gloves, and gathering the brush, working until dusk, until the temperature started falling.

In early spring, he would get a permit from the fire department and have a burn, the collected branches and leaves in a large pile in the far corner of the yard, asking me to bring more from the pile he'd added to over the winter months. Gusty winds blew the smoke one way, then another. It seemed to follow me, smoke causing my eyes to sting and water. Those cold early-spring afternoons, the wonderful, earthy smell of woodsmoke staying on my clothes for days, a deep comfort I can't name.

My mother would come out to pitch in or simply bring him hot tea, standing and talking while he sipped, her arms held tightly around her chest, never quite warm enough. I can see it so clearly, this nothing moment, this core memory. Why? Why remember that when I've forgotten so much of my life?

On those quiet family evenings when my mother was doing the dinner dishes, humming and maybe watching a small TV or listening to a radio program, my father would sit in the living room and read from arcane books, sipping at his scotch and soda. If I happened into the room, he would look up from his reading—the *Hartford Courant*, perhaps, or a book on woodworking or maybe a back issue of *Popular Mechanics* magazine—stare at me for a moment as if trying to place me, nod and smile, and then continue on.

Much later it would dawn on me that he was less of a father and more a man I happened to share a house with.

Not long after Jen left, I visited my father. His third wife had just died. Many years before, he had sold our home in West Hartford and moved to Delray Beach, Florida, after a brief visit there to meet up with friends from our old neighborhood who had relocated. He visited in February, every Florida real estate agent's great hope for northeasterners, and was, of course, smitten. The warm sun on his old bones, the smell of orange and lemon trees, honeysuckle and oleander. The bright colors, ocean blues and manicured green grass. Surely the perfect salve to cold, slate-gray Hartford. He moved that year.

And then he changed.

It was partially cognitive, as he began to forget things. But it was the shift in his personality that threw me most, one that was unrecognizable to me. His sole focus seemed to be the company of women.

He married a second time to a woman a few years his junior who had once been a waterskiing champion in Palm Beach. They seemed happy, though the marriage was cut short, just three years, when, while grocery shopping at their local Winn-Dixie, she stopped at a display of fresh peaches, cut by a young associate and stuck with toothpicks, tried one, and promptly choked to death.

The obituary (I didn't write it) was both poorly written and factually inaccurate, stating that she "passed during an unexpected incident with a kiwi in the aisle of a local supermarket." (I thought this unfortunate wording, as it sounded to me like an untoward tryst with a New Zealander.)

His grief passed quickly and within a year he was married again, this time to a woman named Connie who was passionate about golf. He picked up the game, though he had never shown the slightest interest. They played, they ate lunch at their club. He said he was having the time of his life. (On both occasions he called me after the event to let me know that I had a new mother. His words, not mine.)

Connie's demise came moments after she had just holed a superb chip shot from a challenging lie in deep rough on the eighth hole of the Kings Point par-three course in Delray Beach. She'd gotten into the golf cart and begun to drive over to my father when she collapsed, a lifelong hypoglycemic. Sadly, her foot remained pinned to the accelerator and she and the golf cart tumbled over the lip of a particularly steep sand trap, the cart landing on top of her. Doctors assured both my father and Connie's grown children that she'd felt no pain. She was seventy-nine.

In a decision that later caused a rift with Connie's children, my father played the ninth hole after the ambulance had left, stopped for lunch in the grill room, before finally going on to the hospital to fill out paperwork. After Connie's service, my father apparently asked Connie's sister to dinner, unaware that her sister's husband was standing next to her at the time.

As requested in a letter left for his sons, Gerry and I took our father's ashes to his favorite spot at the end of a boardwalk. The Boynton Beach Fishing Pier, which is in the next town over from Delray, juts out perhaps a quarter of a mile into the ocean. It was late afternoon and low, dark clouds had moved in, rain threatening. The pier was a popular fishing and sightseeing spot, but the weather had held off tourists. We walked the length of the pier, Gerry hiding the urn in a travel bag he had brought. I sensed he was as tired as I was and wanted to go home. Gerry had flown in the night before, arriving late. He had a flight back to London that evening to stop in at the head office.

We reached the end of the pier and looked down twenty-odd feet to the water, the waves crashing into the wooden supports. Gerry removed the urn from the bag and tried to gauge the wind.

"We should say something," he said.

"Okay."

"Any chance you've prepared something?"

"No. Was I supposed to?"

"You're the obituary writer, for God's sake."

The feelings his annoyance elicited in me. I was suddenly twelve years old. How is it we never escape family?

"Next time one of our parents die, let me know what you'd like me to do," I said to him. "Jesus."

The wind had picked up, and as he spilled the ashes they blew everywhere, some back in our faces. My eyes were closed against my father's ashes when I heard Gerry say, "Shit." I opened them to see his empty hand as he looked down to the water, the urn having slipped. We looked at the water far below and then at each other and laughed.

Gerry walked over to a fisherman and handed him a $20 bill and came back with two cans of ice-cold beer.

"To the old man," Gerry said, lifting his beer. I toasted him.

We sipped our beers and watched as the skies cleared, the near-daily afternoon Florida thunderstorms having passed. The heavy heat of the day was gone and it was soft winds now, a salty breeze off the bay. Fishermen dotted the pier, baiting with shrimp, with minnows, with whole chickens. The sound of seagulls, the low sound of someone playing a radio and a person singing in Spanish.

"How are the kids? Claudia?" I asked.

"All good. Getting big. You're nice to send presents on birthdays, by the way. No small thing to Claude. And me."

"And how's living in China?"

"It's a weird place. We're in a bubble of expats and clubs. I travel a lot but we also get to go places, take the kids for long weekends. Thailand, Vietnam, Japan. It's a good posting. Another year or two and then back to London. That's home now."

I watched him talk, watched this face I once knew so well. He had more lines around his eyes, his mouth, a dusting of gray on the sides, but still the square-jawed handsome guy he always was. He looked like our mother.

"You?" he asked. "The job? The . . . Jen thing." That was Gerry-speak for *I sort of love you, I kind of care about you*.

"Good," I said and nodded. "All good."

I couldn't bring myself to say more, though I wanted to.

Gerry turned and looked at me. Maybe it was my imagination but I felt he knew, felt he knew everything, knew I was ebbing confidence, that I was lost. It seemed to me he was trying to decide whether to say something. Instead he reached his arm around, hit my back, a kind of pat, his hand resting briefly on my shoulder, my big brother.

"Meet someone," he said. "Have some kids. They're the only things that keep me sane. Look," he said, taking out his phone, scrolling through, showing me photos of his children.

We sat for a while, sipping our beer, talking about not much, finding an ancient connection, brothers again, relying on each other, if only briefly, just as our parents had hoped for a long time ago.

WE LOOK FORWARD TO FIRING YOU AGAIN IN THE FUTURE

The email from Human Resources requested that I arrive promptly at 2 p.m. on the twenty-ninth floor. There were, they said, some papers to sign.

Tuan called as I walked into the building. He was waiting in the lobby but hadn't seen me yet.

"Where are you?" Tuan asked.

"Disney World. I'm nude, running from Goofy, who appears erect. It's a nightmare."

"Sounds quite wonderful to me."

I tapped his shoulder and he jumped.

"You're a cretin," he said. He then looked me up and down, a sour look on his face. "And you're wearing Dockers?"

He turned and I followed him to a waiting elevator. We stepped in, Tuan swiped his security card, pressed twenty-nine.

The doors closed and we stared at our reflections.

"Work busy?" I asked.

"Several obituaries today. Your departure is not making my life easier."

"My apologies."

"There is an issue with the bro."

"What happened?"

"He asked me what I was writing. I told him an obituary about a man who wrote the definitive history of jujitsu. He said—I wrote it down—he said, 'Is that like an Israeli religious thing?'"

"Oh my."

"And then the little shit refused to write an obit."

"What do you mean?"

"A former CEO of a big tobacco firm died. The bro refused on the grounds that the man was morally reprehensible. His words. Frankly surprised he knew the word *reprehensible*."

The elevator doors opened on twenty-nine. We stepped out.

"What did you say?"

"I told him to talk with Howard."

"What did Howard say?"

"Well, and here I quote the bro: 'Dude, your friend Howard is harsh. He told me to write the damned obit or leave. That is just not how I roll.' End quote. I wrote it down, as it was too rich to leave to fickle memory. Give me a drunken, middle-aged writer over a millennial any day."

Tuan left and I announced myself to the receptionist and waited on a couch, watching as my former colleagues hustled by, on their phones, on their way to a meeting, on their way, perhaps, to interview a new obituary writer.

A bearded man who I'd seen around the office before—Gary?—walked by, talking on his phone. He looked over at me and did a double take. "Hey man," he said to me, still holding the phone to his ear. "I heard you were dead."

I couldn't tell if he was kidding. I'm fairly sure he wasn't. I wondered what the person on the call was thinking.

I said, "You can't believe the news these days."

***

We were in a conference room. I sat on one side of a long, polished table, my back to the windows that looked out over Midtown. I faced a glass window looking out onto a hallway and cubicles, the offices of HR and Accounting. On the other side of the table sat Howard and, a few empty chairs away, Beth Liebling, head of HR. Next to Beth sat a man in his late twenties.

"Buckley," he said to me, smiling like someone about to ask for money, stretching out his hand. "He/him/his."

"Sorry?"

"My pronouns. He/him/his." He slashed the air with his hand, as if he were slicing bread or putting in a forward slash. "What are yours, Bud?"

"I don't think I have any. Maybe he/him/who?"

Beth jumped in.

"Bud. Thank you for coming in on short notice."

Buckley, eager to play a role, said, "I am so sorry, Beth. Bud, would you like water? The bottles are on the credenza over there and I don't want to assume able-bodiedness, so I will walk over and get you one."

Howard's head dropped forward, a small death. "You saw him walk in," Howard mumbled. "Obviously he's able-bodied."

"I find your tone hostile, Howard," Buckley said.

We had to take sensitivity training. It started a few years ago. A team of experts came in for three days of seminars and exercises. We took part in role-play. I was, at different times, a gay man, a nonbinary woman, and a hearing-impaired person in transition. Tuan was my partner during much of this and I said to him how much I would love to actually be deaf as his office mate. Unfortunately for me, the instructor heard me say this and was unable to find the humor in it. I was forced to leave the class and have additional one-on-one training with a woman who I felt loathed me on sight and asked me why I thought it funny to make a joke about a hearing-impaired transgender woman. I said I believed what had happened was a misunderstanding and that I could explain. She held up her hand as if she had been badly scalded and said that my attempt to mansplain in the context of my white, cisgender privilege was repugnant to her and that she frankly wasn't sure that even an immediate apology would erase the trauma my words had caused but that if I wrote an essay asking for forgiveness for my tone-deafness to the LGBTQ community as well as people of color, minorities, and the non-able-bodied, that might be a start.

"So, Bud." Beth forced a smile. "We have a . . . situation."

She spoke slowly, carefully, and occasionally looked at a pile of paper in an open manila folder on the table.

"Your obituary triggered . . . We're talking about a company with more than six thousand employees worldwide . . . triggered a series of . . . unpredictable . . . unstoppable . . . steps in the company's computer system and its vast employee . . . files."

Beth was having difficulty finding the words.

"The files," she said, forcing a laugh.

I didn't see Beth often, but when I did we chatted briefly, caught up on recent vacations, on how her now-college-aged daughter was doing, how she couldn't believe we were both still here after all these years. She appeared to be in her early fifties, though I am not good at judging ages. Hair the color of faded wheat, cut short, gray roots. She wore oversized designer glasses. She blinked often.

Beth looked as if she was about to continue when Buckley, unable to help himself, said, "I think what Beth is saying is that we had hoped to terminate you today. *Terminated* is probably the wrong word, considering."

Howard sighed loudly. "Beth. Please."

Beth, after a quick turn to Buckley, a look that said *I will harm you*, said, "Buckley. For the love of . . ."

She turned back to me, faked a smile, and said, "We can't fire you because you're dead. According to the system. The company's system. You're dead."

Beth cleared her throat and took a deep swig from a can of Diet Coke.

"Let me back up," she said. "As I think you know, we are—like so many companies—one that is automated. Helen from Accounting? Helen's gone, Bud. She's dead. Not literally. But she doesn't work here anymore. The new 'Helen' is a bot that doesn't bake brownies or talk to you about her grandkids or bring the card around every time it's someone's birthday. But the bot also doesn't make the mistakes the real Helen used to make. The old Helen made on average sixteen errors on a batch of one hundred accounts payable. This Helen does nine hundred accounts payable a day with zero mistakes. No brownies. Guess what? Brownies are bad for you. You want a birthday card? Call your mother. What's my point?"

The forced smile seemed plastered onto Beth's face. She struck me as someone desperately in need of a vacation.

"I've been with this company for thirty-one years. Thirty-one. And this is the first time the system has told me that we cannot technically terminate a dead employee."

"I'm sorry," I said. "I'm a little confused. I'm not dead. Or I am and heaven really sucks."

Buckley, eager to answer: "For all intents and purposes, you are dead to the company. Which is why you have rights."

"But if I were alive?"

"You'd be fired and we would end your COBRA due to negligence on your part."

"So I'm better off dead?"

"Certainly in terms of health and dental, yes."

Howard looked as if he were about to have a stroke. Beth cut in.

"Obviously there is a glitch in our system. We've not . . . We've not had this happen before."

Howard raised his voice. "No one's ever been stupid enough to publish their own obituary before."

Buckley, looking at Howard wide-eyed, said, "Your language is violent, Howard."

"Sorry. I should have said 'epically fucking stupid.'"

The possibility that I might not be fired stirred a joy that surprised me. The past several days had seen a newfound lethargy even for me. The prospect of a new job, at forty-four. Who would hire me? Who was hiring at newspapers, anyway?

"So . . . am I fired?" I asked.

"No," Beth said. "Legally we can't fire a dead person."

Buckley butted back in. "But we are very hopeful that you will be found to be alive."

Beth stood abruptly and gathered her papers, handing two sheets to me. "Sign here, please."

"What am I signing?"

"You're signing a document that says you are not legally dead."

"Is that really necessary?"

Buckley now. "It is. We need it so that we can then feed that information into the system to make you alive again so that we can fire you."

"Moron," Howard mumbled, looking at Buckley.

"I'll file a complaint, Howard."

"I'm sorry about this, Bud," Beth said, ignoring them both. "I'm late. I have to lay off four people from Accounts Receivable."

Howard walked me to the elevators.

"Howard," I said. "I don't understand what's going on."

He sighed. He looked tired. "What's going on is that I'm trying to make a case to keep an employee who by all rights should be fired. But then you appeared dead in the system."

The elevator doors opened and Howard got on.

"What do I do?" I asked.

"Try out being dead. You seem cut out for it. To be honest, at this point, I'd love to be dead to the system."

THE HIERARCHY OF HUMANITY

I met Tuan at a Pret a Manger near the office. We had to specify which one, as there was another Pret a Manager directly across the street. It was a little after three in the afternoon and the place was largely empty, less a disheveled man who was dressed as a penguin from the waist down.

Tuan was sitting at a small table in the corner by the window. In front of him was a large coffee with cream and three empty sugar packets. He nibbled on a brownie bite, one of two he had in front of him. Opposite Tuan, a tuna sandwich with cucumbers in its wrapper and a bottle of club soda, my usual lunch.

"You're a sweet man, Tuan."

"Tell me," he said, looking out the window. "I heard a wonderfully macabre rumor from Buckley, who's so gay he annoys gay people, that you're dead to the system."

"It's true."

"I couldn't love this more."

The sandwich—cold, soggy—tasted wonderful. I realized I hadn't eaten yet that day.

"Any good deaths?" I asked him.

"Two stand out. A man in Wisconsin who once protested the Vietnam War by standing naked on a small platform atop a twenty-foot pole in his front yard for four days, making national news. And a Tacoma, Washington, man, seventy-nine, who, fifteen years ago, was in a car accident, sustained a head injury, and inexplicably spoke with a French accent for the rest of his life. It's called foreign accent syndrome. Exceptionally rare. His wife, Barbara-Ann, who survived him, said she enjoyed the accent, as it, and here I quote, 'spiced up their marriage quite a bit.'"

I smiled and Tuan snuck a peek at me, proud of the quote.

"That's good stuff, Tuan."

He smiled out the window.

"Have you heard of Cotard's syndrome?" he asked.

"No."

"It's a rare psychiatric disorder where a living person believes that they are dead."

"Interesting. Course the funnier version is the other way around."

"Funny," Tuan said without smiling. "Next you'll tell me that an anagram of *funeral* is *real fun*."

When Jen's affair came to light, I mentioned it to Tuan. I assumed he'd take some weird Tuan-like joy in it. Instead, he was quiet for a time and finally said, "Sorry to hear that."

For a long time after, when I got in in the morning, I'd find a coffee on my desk with a roll or a donut. At lunch he'd drop off a sandwich (at 11 a.m.). He would casually and awkwardly say that he was going to see the new such-and-such movie that evening and did I want to come. Sometimes I did. And sometimes we would get something to eat after, me half comatose, him chatting about the dangers of dehydration or the time he stood next to Liza Minnelli on a street corner on the Upper East Side.

On the occasional Sunday morning, a long, lonely stretch of day ahead of me with nothing to do, Tuan would call to say he was heading to Brooklyn and would I like to have brunch. I was unaware at the time, unable to really understand what he was doing. I was too involved with my own pain. It's a strange thing to have your life upended, to go to lawyers and pay a lot of money and not speak to this person you were once married to. To part with half of your life savings. To become bitter and angry and no longer trusting of people.

Ten months into my malaise, with Judith's counsel, with Tuan's quiet, daily support, I managed to book a trip to the Mayan Riviera. I slept late, swam, read two books. We get better. We heal.

I brought back a bottle of Don Julio 1942, Tuan's preferred drink. When I gave it to him, in the office the morning I returned, I found it hard to speak.

"I just wanted to say thanks," I said.

And then, unaware I was going to do it, I hugged him and he reciprocated by not moving a muscle.

"Well, okay then," he said. "Let's never do that again."

And that was that.

"Where do you see yourself in the hierarchy of humanity?" Tuan asked.

"I don't understand the question," I said.

"As a cisgender white male, I mean. Where do you stand, do you think?"

"I'm eating, Tuan."

"Let me tell you where I see you," he continued. "But let me start at the top of the social food chain. Lesbians. I see lesbian couples as up here." He held his long, thin arm straight up. I noticed that the nails of his slim fingers were painted turquoise with small black hearts. "Women are life-givers. They don't start wars, commit murder. Lesbian couples are almost perfect. Their Achilles heel, of course, is an almost laughable attempt at fashion. Think a female college basketball or lacrosse coach. Culottes. Second . . ."

"Tuan . . ."

"Second would be gay men. Natch."

"Maybe let's never say *natch* again."

He ignored me. "While not technically life-givers—despite argument from radical segments of my own people who believe that gender is meaningless in the birth process—imagine a world without us. Clothing, interior design, hair, makeup, choreography, art, theatre, food, topiary. Basically, you'd be left with the gray, ugly world of Eastern Europe during the Cold War or, worse, the soul-crushing blandness of, say, greater Westport, Connecticut."

"Third I'm assuming would be Republicans?" I said through a mouthful of tuna.

"Third would be closeted gay men in a marriage of convenience," Tuan said. "Fourth would be any trans person, either single or in a relationship."

"Tuan, they're closing in, like, three hours, could you speed it up."

"Fifth is a straight couple, the saving grace being the woman. And a distant last is . . . you."

"Thank you."

"So what have you been doing?"

"I told you, going to the wakes and funerals of strangers."

"How incredibly weird. Like *Harold and Maude*. If memory serves, Maude took her own life at the end of the film."

"Let's hope I'm Harold."

"If not, maybe I can have your office chair?"

Tuan sipped his coffee, checked his phone, sighed. "I should go," he said to his phone. He looked up at me, the worried look of a parent. "And if they fire you, what are you going to do?"

The man in the half penguin outfit stood, grabbed his large penguin head off a chair, and shuffled out.

"That could be you in six months," Tuan said.

I didn't know I was going to say it out loud but I said, "I keep dying. In my dreams."

Tuan looked out the window. It was easier on him to talk this way.

"Explain," he said.

"Like, I'm killed or I die. I fall or get shot."

"I have those sometimes," he said. "It's the job."

"This is different though. I wake up and can't get back to sleep. I've had dreams where I . . . that recur, you know. Bridges. I'm trying to get across a high bridge, over water. And I have to get down on all fours and crawl and then I fall. Most of the time I don't really remember my dreams. I stopped having sexual dreams years ago. If it is sexual, it's with an elderly coworker trying to be sexy but then she removes her hair or her hands fall off. What does that mean?"

"It means you're super-healthy emotionally."

"That's what I thought, too."

"So listen," he said. "I have a friend in Minneapolis. At the *Star Tribune*. He's an editor there. And I emailed him and said he should talk to you. So . . . you know . . . if you want to call him."

He stood and slipped into his coat, buttoning it, looking out the window. He turned to me and said, "And please don't mistake this as affection or friendship."

He stared at me, the hint of a smile, then turned and walked away. Which was just as well, as my eyes were tingling and I was finding it difficult to talk.

When I got close to home, I saw Leo sitting on the stoop doing a Rubik's Cube. He moved it with the fluidity of a master, yet he seemed to be making no progress. I patted Muffin's giant head.

"Know what the world record is?" he asked.

"A year and a half?"

"Two-point-nine-eight seconds."

"That's a lie. You lie."

"It's true."

"Who did it? Kourtney Kardashian?"

"I don't know who that person is. It was Max Park. He beat Feliks Zemdegs."

"Now you're just making names up."

He shook his head. "I'm not."

"Hand it over," I said.

He looked at me skeptically but gave it to me.

"I was, as a youth, a master at math," I said. "Some say a genius. Not my words, theirs. Time me."

"It won't be official," Leo said. "We need a clock."

"Say ready, set, go. Then count. I'm going to blow your mind."

"Ready, set, go."

I rotated the sides of the cube as fast as I could.

"One . . . two . . . three . . . four . . . five . . . Okay, you don't know how to do a Rubik's Cube."

"This is a defective cube."

"What?"

"Defective. Broken. Not an approved cube. I can't work with this."

"You're just not very good."

He blinked ten times. I blinked ten times back. He grinned.

"Fine," I said. "I lied about being good at doing a Rubik's Cube."

Benni came to the door.

"Dinner," she said to Leo. "Hi, Bud."

"Hi, Benni. Is Saturday a special day at all?"

"I think it might be," she said, with a conspiratorial smile.

Leo closed his notebook and stood. "It's my birthday! Max and Dylan and Finn and Rachel are coming. Rachel is the fastest runner of all of us. You're coming, right?"

"Unless I get a better offer. I'm a very popular person."

"You're not."

Benni kissed the top of Leo's head. "Nice to see you, Bud." To Leo, "Don't be long." She went back into the house.

He was quiet for a time, looking at the pages of his notebook. He said, "How do you start a conversation?"

"You just did."

"Yeah, but I know you."

"Who do you want to talk with?"

"Max. But he's always with other kids and I want to say something but I can't think of anything."

"Maybe ask if he likes Rubik's Cubes?"

"He doesn't. He likes sports. I don't know about sports."

"Movies? You like movies. Everyone likes movies. Maybe ask if he's seen the Minion movies."

"That's good. And if he says yes, what do I say?"

"Maybe ask what his favorite part was. And then he might ask you what your favorite part was. And then you're just talking."

He was writing this down. He looked up quickly. "What if he's bored?"

"How many times have you and I talked? Like, a million? Okay, not a million but a lot. And you know what? I've never, ever been bored once."

He wore flannel pajama bottoms with the characters from *Paw Patrol* on them and oversized slippers in the shape of sheep.

Leo looked up, sighed. "So . . . I finally decided what I'm going to be when I grow up."

"Tell me."

"Well, it's either a spy or a marine biologist."

"I think you'd be a great spy. You see everything. You make notes. But how are you under interrogation?"

"I don't know what that is."

"Marine biology. Also fascinating."

"Except one problem?" he said, holding his little arms up.

"Tell me."

"I can't swim."

I watched him. He looked up, scanning the sky for a helicopter in the distance, trying to spot it. He looked down, jotted something in his notebook.

"Have you seen a dead body?" he asked.

"Why, did you lose one?"

"No. I just mean, like, at a funeral."

"I have."

"Yeah. Me, too."

"You have?"

He nodded.

"Who?"

"My sister Lucy."

Children can hold a stare, not blink, not flinch.

"I didn't know that. I'm so sorry, buddy."

"Oh, it's not your fault. It was a loooong time ago. Like maybe three years and eighty-one days. But I talk to her all the time, so it's okay."

He stood and put his pen in the spiral metal coil at the top of the reporter's notebook.

"You do?"

He nodded. "Oh yeah. She's always with me. I tell her about everything. She knows about you and Tim. She likes you guys."

I stared, unable to speak.

"Do you know that the American copper butterfly lives for just two weeks?" he asked.

"I didn't."

"The mayfly lives for just twenty-four hours."

I watched him make a note.

"What if this is a dream?" he said. "What if we're asleep right now?"

"Where's real life then?"

"That's the mystery."

He waved, turned, and walked into the house.

PROFANITY CITY

It was a Wednesday evening and Esther put out cheese and crackers, charcuterie, several baguettes, along with wine and beer. Our neighbor, Murray Eustis, was finally ready to share his new film. It was time for a small salon.

Esther, myself, Tim, Julia Felder, and Francisco the baker at the French place were in attendance. The French place was a bakery around the corner with an elaborate and hard-to-pronounce French name that everyone just called the French place. It was fronted by a dashing but enigmatic man from Marseille named Luc who didn't know his way around a kitchen but who was very good at PR. The bakery had been named best baguette in Brooklyn three years in a row, in large part because of Francisco. "Quintessentially French," said *New York* magazine. "No one but a French baker could do this." Francisco was from Mexico.

We chatted. We nibbled. I stood talking with Murray.

"What on earth was I talking about?" he asked.

Murray was standing too close to me and looking up over my head somewhere. He'd been talking for some time. A confused look passed over Murray's lined, handsome face. I didn't know his exact age but I'd peg it at late sixties maybe. Five foot ten, perhaps, but a bear of a man, broad shouldered, wild, unkempt hair, more silver than black now, the look of a Bolshevik.

"The state of the news," I said.

"Right. I think the relentless bad news—pings, alerts, *this just in*, breaking news . . . I feel I'm lost in my own sentence, but you know what I'm getting at."

"Absolutely," I lied.

"For me a deep fatigue has set in," he continued, staring at the bookcase. "An exhaustion full of questions. Why are we here? To make children? To love? To eat and sleep and defecate regularly?"

He moved his drink to his mouth but stopped.

"Is there a God?" he asked. "What if there isn't? What are we to do with that? If it's just lights-out, eternal darkness, a world that goes on as if you had never existed, disappeared, like an ocean wave over a footprint in the sand."

"How's the motivational speaking going, Murray?"

He ignored me.

"Cognitively I know that life is precious and beautiful and blah blah blah. Can we agree on that?"

"Absolutely," I said.

"But I no longer feel it. The Hallmark cards and TikTok posts and insipid beer commercials tell me to feel it, plead with me to feel it. Do I most days? Alas, no. Freud spoke of ordinary unhappiness as something to hope for. I understand this completely now. An evening under the duvet, with a pint of Häagen-Dazs, watching reruns of *Law & Order*? I'll take it."

He was drunk, bonkers, and made complete sense to me.

Murray had worked as a copywriter in advertising for many years before leaving to pursue writing novels. Early promise from his first novel, *A Penny for Your Thoughts Is Too Much*, never materialized. He ended up an English teacher at SUNY Queens, where his Introduction to the Essay was a popular class.

"Do you think this is a male problem, Murray?" I asked.

"Absolutely. Women are vastly more intelligent emotionally and frankly that's the only intelligence that matters. I can list every world capital and details of America's involvement in the Pacific Theater during World War II but can't mention to the occasional lady friend why I weep when I watch a Subaru commercial."

"The one with the dad and the school bus."

"You know the one."

We clicked glasses, two depressed, emotionally unstable men.

He looked at me, as if remembering he was speaking with me, and said, "Sorry to hear about your death. Best thing that could have happened to you, old boy. And now I desperately need to find a toilet or I shall wet myself and I try to do that only once a day." He kissed me on the forehead and was gone.

We gathered around Murray's laptop computer.

"The film is called *Profanity City*," he said. "I've been working on it for some time. I've had a lifelong fascination with so-called bad words. I think this is due in large part because I have a Proustian madeleine-like memory of my mother saying that only unintelligent people curse. And New York, to me, is really the epicenter of great cursing."

"Why do you think that is, Murray?" Julia asked.

"Difficult to say. Density of population relative to space, maybe? One thinks of Mexico City, with a population roughly the size of New York. And yet it's almost twice as big landwise. Also, there are about seven hundred languages spoken in the five boroughs. *Putain*, in French. A versatile word that means *fuck*. Forgive my French. Or take *cabrão* in Portuguese. Literally means *billy goat* but is used to mean *motherfucker*. *Kingina* in Tagalog, the common language of the Philippines, means *mother's vagina* . . ."

"I think we get the picture, Murray," Julia said.

"For me, the real genius comes when we arrive in Staten Island. The creativity, the sheer vulgarity, is really top-notch."

We watched as people swore. It was far more entertaining than it sounds.

Later, Francisco the baker played the violin, an instrument he had learned as a child. Still in his baking whites, he played, accompanied by Julia Felder on piano. She had suggested Pachelbel's Canon in D, she told me, as it never failed to make her emotional.

They began, but hit a snag. Francisco winced. Julia looked over at him, smiled, a mother's smile. *All is well.* She took in a slow, deep breath, drawing her hand up along her chest, as if asking Francisco to mimic her. Francisco did the same. Then, in a quiet voice, she said, "In one, two, three . . ." And they began again.

Francisco read the sheet music, a thing that remains Greek to me. What a strange and wondrous thing, I thought. A single, universal language.

Tim turned the pages for him, following along. At one point, white flour dust, ultrafine, gossamer, fell gently from the arm of Francisco's tunic.

They played and we sat in silence as the music, composed three hundred years ago, was made new again, here, in this living room, among this small band of friends, reaching out across time, a distant past, fully alive now.

MOLLY DONNELLY, 43, AND EDDIE DONNELLY, 6

Clara had given us only the name of the funeral home, LoPresti & Sons, in Tottenville, a small neighborhood on the far southwestern end of Staten Island, just across from Perth Amboy, New Jersey.

It was late afternoon and the sun dipped behind high, fast-moving clouds. The weather had turned cold, the wind coming in gusts. As we made our way along the Belt Parkway and up onto the Verrazzano, icy New York Harbor 230-odd feet below us, snow squalls appeared as if out of nowhere. The wind shook the car, seemed to move the bridge.

"Do bridges scare you?" Tim asked.

"How do you know that?"

"Just a guess. Apparently I hated them when I was a kid. No memory of this but my parents told me. I'd hide in the back seat. Gephyrophobia."

I looked out the window to my right, the vast expanse of the water below, the enormous cargo ships waiting on the tide, the jagged skyline of the city in the distance.

"There's a bridge in Michigan," Tim said. "The Mackinac. Almost as long as this one, also very high off the water, over one of the Great Lakes, I guess. They have a service where someone will drive you across, for free. The Timid Driver Program. Apparently they changed the name."

"Seems judgy. So you're timid. Timid driver. Insecure driver. Emotionally stunted driver. Sexually awkward driver."

"The Chesapeake Bay Bridge is the Stephen King of bridges. Something like four miles long. Narrow lanes, no place to pull over. I read an article that said as you drive, a gentle curve makes it look like the road ahead just disappears."

"The urinating-from-fear drivers program."

"Elegance is not your strong suit."

Despite arriving well before the 4 p.m. start time, there was already a long line down Amboy Road leading to the funeral home. We waited, shuffling forward slowly as the line moved. I noticed the weird silence, how mostly it was gusts of wind through the trees, almost no one was talking. Very few cars passed down the road.

Inside, I could see the line snake to the main room, see the older couple standing by the caskets. There were two. I didn't understand at first. I looked around, at Tim, who was unable to see that far from his vantage point.

On a small table I saw the folded pamphlets. I picked one up, opened it, and saw their names, *Molly and Eddie Donnelly*. There was a photo. It looked as if it might be at the beach. He was sitting in her lap wearing oversized swim trunks, holding up a small plastic shovel and grinning broadly. She had her arms around him, on his bulbous little belly. Her head was tilted. Same grin. Sunglasses up on her hair, beautiful auburn hair. Freckles along the bridge of her nose, her teeth very white. I kept staring at the photo, at the two of them smiling.

When I turned the pamphlet over, a paragraph about a car accident.

I needed more information. I looked around. Behind us, two women, late thirties perhaps. I'm not good with guessing age.

"I'm sorry," I said to them. "What happened?"

"That accident on the Jersey Turnpike. The tractor-trailer truck that jackknifed, from last week. It was in the news."

I'd seen it, paid little attention to it, to the names of these strangers, to the accompanying photo, as I scrolled past, scrolled on.

"It was just the two of them," one of the women said. "The husband was gone."

"She cut hair," the other one added. "Molly did. Down at Elegance, near the Dunkin' Donuts." She was pointing.

"They were always together. It's almost a blessing they went together."

The women nodded.

Someone touched my shoulder. I turned to see Clara, who had come from the inner room. She put her hand on my arm, held it briefly. She forced a smile to Tim, then looked at me. She reached up and touched my cheek, then turned and left.

What is it we remember of a life? From those 28,000 days if we are lucky enough to live that long? Those 960 months? What was Molly Donnelly remembering as she drove home that afternoon? Surely our days are measured in small things, small connections, small thoughts. It's not meetings and deals closed. It is our children. Talking of the day, of lunch, of coloring, of nonsense, the parent listening, half listening, not listening, because this is a thing we do, we daily do, morning and afternoon, the little holy rituals that make up a day, a life, drop-off and pick-up, an expected thing, a known thing, a wave to the crossing guard, to a mom friend, to Ravi and Angie and Brandon, little school friends. My, how they've grown. New lunch box? New backpack? Good day? Hold my hand, sweetheart. Listen to your mother. A shared smile with the other mothers. They know this world. Can you believe this new principal? Did you hear so-and-so got laid off? The deli charges $5 for a half a gallon of milk now. Ineffable feelings. The best kind. Words overrated. Time to go home now. She puts him in the car, in his car seat, buckles him in, burying her face in his neck, a little kiss. We'll go home and have a snack and play and then dinner and a bath and bed. A story. *Frog and Toad* again. Fishy kisses. Super-tuck. He asks for a super-tuck. That's what he calls it. Night, Mom. See you tomorrow and tomorrow and tomorrow. We have time. Of course we have time. Please dear God.

There was traffic on the way back. We inched over the Verrazzano. At one point we were stopped. It was dusk and the wind whipped and the bridge seemed to move in the wind, deciding whether it wanted to stay up or not. We sat in midair. To the right, east, out toward Coney Island, the sky was blue-black. Move your head slowly left and the light became a spectrum, all the colors, lighter as you moved west. I rolled down the window a bit, to feel the wind, the cold. It stung my eyes, caused them to water.

"I don't know what we're doing," I said.

A strong gust rocked the car. The clouds seemed just above us, moving fast.

"Honoring the Donnellys," Tim said.

"How?"

"By remembering. By living."

The traffic began to move.

THE LIST

"You can change the way you think." So said the therapist.

This was about two years ago, shortly after Jen left. Howard and Tuan suggested that maybe I talk with someone. Apparently they had noticed some changes in my behavior. A more comatose demeanor, arriving later to work, questionable hygiene, a disheveled nature to my dress and general comportment that concerned them. I drank a lot of coffee and kept a package of Keebler Fudge Stripes in my desk. I started smoking again, a habit I had long ago kicked. The duct tape that had been holding me together of late had begun to lose its grip. I felt I was watching myself, not really in control of the script. I thought she might come back. That's what I told myself. But she wasn't coming back.

"What would you want to change if you could?" she asked.

"Well, I'd like not to be me."

"Ha-ha," she said.

"No seriously. I can't stop the record in my head. It's the same songs, the same voices, the same stories over and over and over."

"We can change that together. Rewrite your story."

Judith. Her name was Judith and I chose her from the company's health plan based entirely on her address and her photo. She looked to be in her midseventies and had, to my mind, a remarkable mane of silver hair, which, most days—and certainly in the photo—was done in a chignon, held by a heavy silver clip that I have no doubt had a story behind it. She lived on Fifth Avenue, in the nineties, in a limestone building just across from the park. I couldn't have picked a less convenient location from Cobble Hill. But I was smitten.

"It's not a story," I said. "It's a list."

"Tell me," she said.

"It's embarrassing."

"No, it's not," she said, smiling. "This is therapy. To be vulnerable is to be strong."

"Isn't it strong not to be vulnerable?"

"Not in the new world."

"I don't cry. Well, rarely."

"Most men say that, but they do."

"No, I'm serious. My mother's death, father's death, my hopes for my brother's death. I think the tear ducts might not actually work."

She nodded slowly but had a look on her face that seemed to say, *This guy may need to come here three times a week.*

"Feelings are hard," she said, "especially as we get older. We learn to read, we learn to write, we learn how to drive a car. But we never really learn how to deal with our feelings, unless our parents taught us or we figured it out. Unfortunately neither has happened with you. Read your list, please."

"I worry it makes me sound whiny and pathetic. Which are actually two of my better traits."

"Sarcasm is a defense, Bud. One we usually outgrow in our teens. But no matter. I think that's the old voice. It speaks to you in cognitive distortions. Let's change the station. No one wants to listen to that station anymore. It plays bad music. It's a crap station. Shoo. It's gone."

She said everything changes when the heaviness goes out of living, that I needed to put down the heaviness. I nodded but I didn't understand.

She said the cause of suffering is fear and avoidance. Don't run away, don't escape. Embrace it. I didn't like the sound of that.

She quoted someone and said, "We need to open to life as it is, rather than how we want it to be. And how we want it to be this constant state of painlessness, of ease and safety."

This last part caused me to look up and stare at her and say, "Yes," without realizing I was going to say yes.

"The problem, of course, is that that state doesn't exist," she added.

"Have you tried scotch?"

"More sarcasm. How wonderful. Would you read me your list?"

I couldn't stop the voice in my head. After the divorce. The reality that it had happened, that life sort of . . . exploded. It was as if I was watching myself and narrating it.

I told Judith this. I said, "Is it just me, or do we all have this voice in our head most every moment of every day that is, like, not our friend?"

"It's just you. But go on."

"He likes to kind of beat the crap out of me, review conversations I've had. In about twenty minutes, after I leave this office, my little voice will tell me how terrible I was in this very conversation, how I sounded like a complete buffoon. And it will again urge me to go over everything I said. The same voice beating the hell out of me every day. The same regrets, the same I'm-a-stupid-fucking-asshole-who-never-amounted-to-shit. After a while you believe the voice. And that's one of hundreds of examples throughout the long day . . . and those are the good days. The voice is having the time of its life."

My homework had been to make a list, to write down what I would want to tell my voice, what I would want to change.

"It's not in any order," I said. "It's just . . . you told me to write, random, stream of whatever."

"Bud. The list."

I read.

"I wish Jen hadn't left. I wish she would have told me . . . what she was feeling. I wish I had been the kind of man who she would have wanted to stay with. I wish I'd had courage and believed in myself. I wish the baby hadn't died. I wish I was a real reporter. I wish I was a correspondent in London. I wish I hadn't stayed in obits for so long."

I stopped and looked up at her. "It's whiny. It makes me want to slap myself."

"It's not whiny," she said. "Maybe a little whiny. Ha! That's a fun therapist joke! Go on."

"I wish I rebounded faster after she left. I wish I'd met someone. I wish I hadn't fallen into this . . . person I am now. I wish I didn't have a loop in my head about the things I wished I'd done. I wish I could call my mother."

"Talk more about that," she said.

"I'm not sure there's much to say."

"Try. What would you say to her?"

"I don't know. Let's not do this."

"What would you say?"

I winced hard against the noise in my head.

"I feel like . . . it's like I've been driving, okay?" I said, yet again unaware of the words coming out. "That my life is this long road trip. I thought I was doing okay. Things felt pretty good. Job, wife, future. And then it was like someone changed the script on me. Changed where I lived and who I lived with and what the future looked like. This new script was crap. I had a very bad part in this script. I was cast as middle-aged lonely guy. I don't want that role. But here I am. And I feel like somewhere along the drive I passed a marker, a signpost, a spot along the road. I didn't notice the spot. It was a nothing spot. But once I passed it, I crossed into the second part of my life, the part where youth and a fair bit of possibility are in the rearview mirror. And this voice, this person who told me about the signpost, I ask him where it's all gone, and he says, *Oh, it's at the last rest stop. You drove away, thinking there was nothing but time.* And I say, why the hell didn't you tell me?! And he says, *I tried. Like, a million times. Every day. Every word you wrote for your work. Every fucking moment that passed that you let go without doing something to make it matter. Every season that passed, every holiday you didn't spend with anyone. A million times I tried. But you didn't listen.*"

I was breathing heavily and staring at the carpet. I looked up at her and she stared at me.

"Important women in your life leave you."

"Yes."

"And you blame yourself."

"No. Maybe. Yes."

"You ask, 'What's wrong with me?' Worse. You doubt yourself. You no longer try."

I watched her. I refused to nod. I didn't have to. She seemed to know what I was thinking.

"The story forms," she continued. "The women leave. You're to blame. So you retreat, don't trust, perhaps begin to loathe yourself like they must have. The story hardens. What was once merely a thought, a fleeting, fact-less notion, is now a bedrock truth."

"Let's stop for today maybe," I said to the floor.

"This is where the fear comes from."

"The fear comes from opening my eyes in the morning."

"You turn forty-five next year," she said.

"Yes."

"Okay."

"Okay what?"

"I believe your mother was forty-five when she died?"

"Yeah. That's crossed my mind."

AVA GUTIERREZ, 41

I'd slept poorly, jolted awake around three thirty by a dream of falling. I lay there, awake and tired at the same time, yawning but unable to get back to sleep, to find a comfortable position, to quiet the runaway freight train of thoughts. No job, no prospects, far too little savings, far too much regret, a wonderful little pity party. Wind outside, in gusts, some rain against the window. Dark gray city light outside. Never fully dark, far too early to get up. You look for something to hold on to in those empty hours, those lonely hours. Something. Anything. The thoughts random, seemingly running on their own. Leo's birthday party. Clara's voice, her face. My brother. What was he doing this moment, somewhere in a bank in China? The Cardinal parade, when I was a boy, maybe six, dressed in white, white bucs, a red kippah, with the other boys and girls of the Saint Theresa School on a cool spring day. Freshman football, being put out to catch a punt, catching it, dropping it, and being hit by several opponents. My mother. That last time. That last day. I remember the light changing, hearing the birds, when I finally fell into a deep sleep.

Tim said he had come across a funeral that looked as if it should be on our list. He seemed adamant about it, so we drove north, toward the Bronx, late afternoon, the sun over our shoulders, between the skyscrapers, casting long shadows.

We drove down off the Triborough onto Willis Avenue and into Mott Haven. The names of the stores told the history of New York. Rosenzweig Lumber. Sean Coakley Plumbing & Heating. Iglesia De Dios Food Distribution Center. Kim's dry cleaner. I stared off out the window at the faces of the people on the street as we moved along slowly in traffic. A kind of theatre, a play, this unending parade of humanity. Pio Peruvian food next to Jalisco Tacos next to China House next to El Viejo Puerto Rican Café next to Famous Original Ray's Pizza next to Fat Albert and Hollywood Discount Furniture. It made no sense. The history of the world is tribes banding together behind large walls, going to war against one another, rejecting other religions, other ways of life. And yet here, on these crowded streets, the world came together. A bit of Spanish overheard here, a bit of Mandarin over there. Farsi, Yiddish, Italian. And yet somehow it worked. Food was ordered, diapers were bought, a flange was sold from a picture someone brought to a hardware store, neither person sharing a language. A neighborhood, a city, held together by a kind of societal duct tape, a New York shoulder shrug, a who-am-I-to-judge?

Tim made a right onto 138th Street. Halfway down the short block, we saw the hearse and the black limo in front of Saint Luke's Church. He pulled to the curb at a handicapped parking space. I grabbed Tim's chair from the back and set it up. We made our way along the sidewalk, past a firehouse across the street, one of the doors open, three fighters testing a chain saw but who stopped after one of them pointed out the hearse, the funeral that would be going on.

We entered by a ramp on the side, leading us into the back of the church. The service was underway and a woman, perhaps forty, stood at the lectern speaking in a quiet voice. A sister? A friend?

I sat in the last row, by the far end of the long pew, Tim in the aisle next to me. The first ten or so rows were full. I opened the pamphlet we'd been handed as we entered.

Ava Gutierrez, 1978–2019. She looked younger than her years, at least in the photo in the pamphlet. Long, dark hair, large brown eyes.

The woman who had been speaking sat and a priest stood and put his hands on either side of the lectern. He looked to be in his mid-fifties. He had thinning brown hair he moved over, across his head, with his hand.

"We look for words at times like this. As if they hold answers. I'm not sure they do. We say, *I'm sorry. I'm sorry for your loss.* We shake hands, we embrace, we heave with sobs. The clichés, while all true, are meaningless. Yes, she was too young. Yes, it is profoundly unfair. Yes, the world, for the Gutierrez family, is fundamentally changed."

He moved his hand over his hair again and looked down at what I assumed were notes.

"Before I came here to the Bronx," he continued, "I was at a parish in Hialeah, Florida. One of my duties was last rites."

I looked in the program. On the back page was printed the priest's name. Father Thomas Barry.

"The loveliest place to be is with someone who has lived. I can't honestly stand here and tell you I knew Ava well. But I did have the great privilege to sit with her, in her hospital room, after her long illness, her great strength and courage, her unending optimism. I sat with her husband, Daniel, and mother, Abril; her sister, Camila, and her daughter, Elana, and son, Hector. I watched the Yankees with her, her passion. I learned some new swear words in Spanish when the Yankees lost."

Laughter from the assembled. The tension broken a bit. He looked up, a slight smile.

"'I'm not afraid,' she told me at the end. 'I don't want to go yet, but I'm not afraid. I wouldn't change a day of my life. I'd just like more of it.'"

He paused and looked down.

"Do you honestly think, on days like today, that I'm not angry with God, that I'm not compelled to doubt, to swear and scream as I put these garments on? I am. And may God forgive me. Until I see her family's faces. Know that she lives on through them. That she wills us, urges us, to live. Right now. Because this is it. The thing we've been waiting for? It's right here, right now, in front of us. Do it now. Whatever it is. Do that thing that honors life."

We watched as the casket was led out, as her family followed behind it. I watched the husband, this widower now, this young man of forty or so years old, the world going according to plan only months ago. I watched his daughter, maybe seventeen, and son, maybe fourteen, heads down, unsure of the new world that awaited them, perhaps thinking it all unreal, not happening. I watched as the other pews emptied, one at a time, as people filed outside, the organ playing haunting chords, until just Tim and I remained, until the music stopped, leaving a deep and empty silence.

Something had happened here just moments ago and now it was over and soon she would be buried. People would go back to her home, drink coffee, sit together, eat sandwiches that neighbors had brought. And after a time, they would leave, go back to their homes, their lives, leaving the Gutierrez family alone, lives changed, trying to make sense of it all, to go forward, when all they really wanted to do was go back, to change it, to have it never have happened.

An usher collected stray pamphlets with Ava Gutierrez's smiling face on them. He left, the front door closing with a creak. An older woman came out from the wings and walked to the entrance to the sanctuary. She knelt and blessed herself, then walked up onto the altar and took a long brass candle snuffer and put it over the lighted candles. She left as quietly as she had appeared, kneeling again at the steps of the sanctuary.

Now we were the last ones in the church. I waited for Tim to move but he didn't.

"Should we follow to the cemetery?" I asked.

"Do you mind if we sit for a bit?"

I didn't. I was tired. The deep quiet of the empty church a welcome respite.

For a time, my family attended church each Sunday for the 10 a.m. service. My mother insisted that Gerry and I wear a sports coat and a tie. The rituals, the smells of wood and flowers and incense. It always scared me, the proximity to others, but I never really looked at them, until it was time for the sign of peace, which always made me anxious. I would watch as my mother bowed her head, closed her eyes. I sat, half listening, little of it making sense. The occasional word or phrase sticking.

He is seated at the right hand of the Father. What kind of chair? I'm not sure why I wondered that. In my mind it was large, red, crushed velvet, and Jesus's feet dangled from it like a child's. *We look for the resurrection of the dead and the life of the world to come, Amen.* How does the sentence not stop you?

My father would give Gerry and me each a dollar so that we could put it in the collection basket, which was always held by an old man with gnarled hands and prominent nose hair. The basket itself was made of wicker and had a long handle. Inside the basket, a green flannel lining held checks and dollar bills, the occasional $5 bill, coins. It looked like so much money. The old man would slide the basket down each row, and with each extension his wedding band would make a train-track *clickety-clack*, back and forth, out and back.

We continued going for a time after she died, but then less often, until my father rarely suggested it again, with the exception of Christmas.

After Jen left, during too-long lunch breaks from work when I would walk aimlessly through Midtown, up into Central Park, back down Eighth Avenue, I would sometimes find my way to Saint Malachy's on Forty-Ninth Street. I would go in, dip my finger in the holy water, bless myself, out of ancient habit, respect, a nod to my mother. I'd sit in the back, kneeling and blessing myself again. Most days it was older women sitting close to the altar, closer, perhaps, to God. The noise of the city was largely muffled by the thick stone walls, the heavy oak doors. The smell of incense, of polished floors. How do you pray? What are the words? How do you not make it sound selfish? Is anyone listening? Somewhere in the stained-glass-diffused light floated the ancient prayers, the words sometimes said at speed, rote, but always as a fervent plea, *Lord, have mercy on me.*

Now a late-afternoon fatigue washed over me. Another bad night's sleep the previous evening. My head hurt, a pounding in my right temple.

"What happens when we die?" Tim asked.

I wasn't in the mood to answer, to consider it. I wanted to leave, to go home. I stared instead at the daily missal and a copy of the Bible in the shelf on the back of the pew in front of us.

"Do you go to heaven," he asked, "and see your family, your friends, your old dogs? Is it lights-out, total nothing? Is it another form of energy where we become plants, soil, myna birds? Is it Buddhist reincarnation?"

I felt him looking at me, waiting for a response. "Ahh," I began. "We wake up in a Costco, unable to find the exit? I don't know."

"We're energy, though, right?" he asked, ignoring me. Perhaps it was the last wake. Maybe it was all this death. Maybe, too, the realization of what I'd done, the imminent firing, this impending new start that awaited me at midlife, the clock ticking, my options dwindling.

"I guess," I said weakly.

"I think about it more lately. Death. And not just because of . . . this."

I turned to look at him. "Why?"

"Because I'm a guy in a wheelchair. Because when half your body is dead, you don't live a long, happy life."

He raised himself up off the chair, readjusted.

He added, "We don't talk about death much, as a society, do we?"

I stared straight ahead, at the altar. I felt that if I closed my eyes, I might fall asleep.

"We learn science and chemistry and Shakespeare and history," he said. "But no intro to death. Isn't that strange?"

I closed my eyes. "Is it?" I asked. "Why would we need to learn something we already know?"

"But do we know? I mean really know?"

I was hearing a tone in his voice that may or may not have been there.

"That we're going to die?" I asked, annoyed.

"I'm not so sure. I think a lot of us live like we have endless time."

"You sound like a Hallmark card," I said, opening my eyes. It came out mean.

"Gee, thanks."

The image of Ava Gutierrez's husband, her children. Their old life gone. Day one now of a new life. *They should give you a pamphlet*, I thought. When you leave the funeral, they should give you a pamphlet, a link to a website, something that tells you how you're supposed to live now.

"You seem annoyed," he said.

"Just tired. Not sure I'm really . . . enjoying these."

"I don't think that's the point."

I do a thing when I'm overtired, in a bad mood. I speak without thinking, the words tumbling out too fast.

"I'm honestly not sure what the fucking point is."

"Calm down."

In my experience, when someone says "Calm down," it usually has the opposite effect.

"I'm not uncalm," I snapped back.

I could feel him looking at me.

"I know we die," I said. "Okay? I write about it every day. And what I thought would be . . . I don't know. I sit here and mostly I feel foolish and just want to run."

I kept going. "I'm just . . . kind of wondering what I'm doing here. I'm about to get fired. The . . . divorce and . . . I can't seem to get out from under this . . . I don't know."

"Your mother's death," he said.

"What?" I asked.

"I try to imagine you at that age, just three of you in the house. That must have been very hard."

It was as if he was trying to push me. At least, that's how it sounded to me.

"It was fine," I said.

"Was it?"

"It was what it was. You adapt."

The woman who had put the candles out reappeared, walking from one side of the church, at the front, to the other, disappearing in the back, behind the altar, where God lived.

"Did your father talk much about her?"

It was interesting to watch my reaction. A cocktail of anger and frustration and annoyance. I rubbed my face.

"No. I don't know. No. It was a different time. He was suffering, too."

"But you were just a kid."

The church bell chimed, startling me. Five times, five o'clock. I sat forward.

"What do you remember? About that day, the funeral?"

I was having trouble looking at him. I just stared straight ahead.

"Actually, I couldn't make it that day. I had tickets to *Cats* so . . ."

We forget so many details of our life. Weeks and months where events, moments, banal and meaningful, blur and then dissipate. And then there are the snippets that live on, forever sharp and alive, always there, waiting to be replayed. I remember smells. The flowers, of course. The little tree air fresheners in the Cadillac that drove us to the cemetery, how it gave me a headache. How people looked at me and faked a smile and looked away. How cold it was. How it wasn't real, couldn't be real, would be made better . . . later.

"I remember people left," I said. "After the reception. They left and we were alone."

The woman was back, at the altar table, carefully replacing a long cloth.

"And today?" he asked.

"What about it?"

"Is it . . . hard?"

Now I turned and looked at him, a confused expression on my face. "Hard? No. No. Because I don't feel a thing."

He stared at me and nodded slowly. Which annoyed me.

"I wonder if that's the problem."

"Oh, *Jesus*, Tim." It was too loud. "Please don't diagnose me, okay? Do I feel sad about my mother for a moment at the . . . these wakes and . . . and here today? Yes, of course. For a minute. But it's not . . . I can't . . . I can't go back . . . I can't live like that—"

He cut me off, too calm. "Like what?"

"Like a fucking Buddhist monk constantly in the moment or whatever." I didn't like the sound of my voice.

The woman at the altar shot us a look.

"Can *I* make an observation?" I asked. Even as I was saying it, another part of me said, *Stop, don't.*

"Sure."

"You do a thing," I said. "This . . . preachy thing. This Sermon on the Mount thing. Sometimes. Lately. My mother's death is ancient history. Okay? Let's not go there. I'm not a child afraid of the funerals of women. You want to go to one? I'll find us one tomorrow."

I closed my eyes. I hated that last sentence.

He just stared at me.

The woman looked at us, the angry squint of a Catholic schoolteacher from forty years ago. "Shhh!"

"Shush yourself!" I said, immediately regretting it.

Tim looked at me, a look of confusion and disgust. "You just shushed an old woman who volunteers in a church."

"Let's go," I said, standing. But his chair blocked the pew.

"What are you doing?" he asked. "Seriously. Like, with your life. You watch the world go by. This . . . spectator. Never fully engaged, because why do that? You're like a critic. You watch. You comment. But you don't engage. Because to do that takes courage. It takes vulnerability. The chance we might get hurt. But you've had enough of that. You're so afraid."

"Fuck off." It was out too fast. I meant it for me, not him.

He spun his chair and I followed, out the side door, down the ramp, to the front of the church and the car. It had turned cloudy and cold. We went through the motions of getting him back in, this practiced thing we did without needing to say a word. After he slid into the driver's seat I folded the chair and placed it in the back.

I opened the passenger door to get in and stopped. "I'm going to walk for a bit. Take the subway."

"Probably best. Esther's home so . . ."

He shook his head, a look of confusion, of disappointment. Neither of us said anything for a time.

"One more thing," he said, sounding angry. "And I hope it's not a Tim lesson. But this whole thing . . . It isn't about death. It's about the privilege of being alive. How do you not get that at this point in your life? And fuck off too."

SEVENTY-FOUR WORDS

I've lied to Tim three times. Once when I told him I had experience as a plumber and tried to fix his sink. Once when I told him I spoke conversational French and he seated me next to a friend of his who was visiting from France, an elderly woman who spoke no English. And the third was when I told him that I had never touched a dead person.

My mother. I'm not sure what there is to say. I wasn't going to include this.

In the evenings, she and I would sometimes take the dog for a walk after dinner, after the dishes were washed and put away, after any homework, in those soft, lazy hours before bed, when nothing much happens in a family, a bit of laundry, a TV show, a few innings of a ball game, my father reading or perhaps out back smoking a cigarette, puttering around the shed. Our dog was a twenty-five-pound rescue named Group Captain Lionel Mandrake, after my father's favorite movie, *Dr. Strangelove*. We called him Captain.

We would walk the side streets of West Hartford in the dark winter evenings, the clean smell of cold, of wood smoke, of the possibility of snow, and, too, on summer nights, the sound of crickets and the smell of freshly mowed lawns, sun-kissed children in bed, baths taken, a day of sprinklers and bike riding, the freedom of a summer day, the endless joy of it, no cares, a few quarters for a Coke and a bag of chips and the possibility of anything. But now just the sleepy quiet of suburban life and she and I and Captain walking, me talking, telling her stories, nonstop, the questions, the almost desperate need for her attention.

It was a Saturday morning and she had made scrambled eggs and toast, coffee for my father and tea, as always, for herself. She'd put me in the living room with a bowl of Lucky Charms and a piece of toast with jam to watch cartoons while she and my father sat at the small, whiskey-colored kitchen table, the one my mother always wiped clean of imaginary crumbs. The table sat by a large window that overlooked the yard. The local radio station was on low and my brother was upstairs packing his duffel bag, getting ready for a football game, a senior in high school now.

It is a piece of film I can replay anytime, something so clear and vivid, the dark green couch I sat with my back against and the plush mustard-colored rug that I could run my hand back and forth across, the color changing slightly when I did.

Mighty Morphin Power Rangers. Inspector Gadget. Reruns of *McHale's Navy* and *F Troop* and *Hogan's Heroes* on the UHF channels.

My brother came downstairs with his gear, half dressed in his football uniform, and dropped his duffel bag by the door. He walked up to me, slapped me on the head, and, by way of greeting, said, "Idiot," before taking my toast. He grabbed his bag and shouted to our parents that he was leaving. My mother appeared and asked if he could sit down for a minute first. My brother, even then, was quite sure the earth revolved around him and so made the face an annoyed prince might make to a servant. But my mother had the ability, without words, to persuade. He sat.

"Buddy B," my mother said. "Turn the TV off for a minute please?"

I did a thing, apparently, when I was younger. She was, my father would say with a smile, not a very good cook. But each evening, during dinner, I would react as if I were dining at a Michelin-starred restaurant. I would then, after dinner—I would have been six, seven—go to my room and write her a thank-you note. I did this until my brother said I was "being an idiot." Even then he had the earmarks of a career in finance.

"I have to go into the hospital for a checkup," she said to Gerry and me. "Today. Your father is bringing me in today."

Children do a thing. They watch their parents in a way others can't, at close range, unnoticed, day after day. Keen observers, they know a parent's moods, know the meaning of a prolonged sigh, can decipher a clenched jaw, a change in intonation. It was the second *today*. It was too bright, too forced. She seemed to falter.

"Why?" Gerry asked.

"It's just a routine checkup. Nothing to worry about."

"For like, what, a day or something?"

"Might be a day. Might be two. You know hospitals," she said with breezy casualness. We didn't know hospitals. "Tests take time to come back."

Gerry thought about this and nodded. "So, like, will you and Dad be at the game today or what?"

"Of course."

She turned to me. "You're awfully quiet, mister."

"Do you feel okay?" I asked.

It was here when it started to scare me. Because it was here, looking at me, that I saw her eyes begin to fill. But she smiled, blinking it back, quickly wiping her eyes, and laughing, said, "I feel fine."

"Go," she said to Gerry. "And good luck. Play well."

She watched him pick up his bag, then awkwardly steal a kiss from her, pecking her on the cheek, as if on a dare to himself, the desperate need of it, even at eighteen, as if it were somehow a weakness.

I watched her watch him go out the door. Her firstborn, her strong, handsome son, athlete, popular with the girls, college scholarship to Penn. Her arms wrapped tight around her chest, unaware of being watched. Thick brown hair that tended toward wavy, up in a bun now, the delicate jawline and high cheekbones, doelike brown eyes. She turned and saw me watching her, waved her index finger at me, a small hello, a thing she did, and then walked back into the kitchen.

It wasn't a day or two. It was twenty-six days, during which my father said it was all fine, that things were going to be fine.

On Sunday afternoons he would bring Gerry and me in to visit her. The tips of my fingers tingled from the anxiety of being there, in a hospital, the smell of a hospital, as we walked from the elevator to her room, past other rooms where people lay, no visitors, the look on their face as we passed, having heard the footsteps, hoping maybe someone was coming for a visit.

We would sit in her room, my mother propped up by pillows, having put on lipstick, combed her hair. She asked us about school, about my father's cooking. We'd take a walk to the cafeteria. If the weather cooperated, we sat on benches in a garden area out back. We asked when she was coming home.

Those first few Sundays she looked and acted like herself. She seemed fine. And then she didn't.

One Sunday, we walked to the solarium at the end of the hall. Except she needed Gerry and me on either side of her, holding her arms, this fit forty-five-year-old woman who never smoked, rarely drank, the occasional Irish coffee in a fancy cup she bought at a thrift store, who went up and down the stairs doing endless laundry. Now she shuffled like an eighty-year-old.

The last Sunday in October my father parked in the hospital parking lot and told us to wait in the car for a bit, that he'd go ahead, check to see if she was up for a visit. That was the day we knew. The day I knew. Gerry, too, I'm sure. We did as he told us, listening to a Patriots football game on the radio. I should know who they were playing but I don't. Maybe Gerry does.

My father had a beeper for work in those days. He wore it on his belt but always took it off when he got into the car. The beeper went off, a phone number appearing on it like a coded message. Gerry thought it mattered, that my father needed to know. And so he got out of the car, slammed the door, and ran to the hospital. I followed.

"Stay there!" Gerry yelled.

I kept running, trying to keep up. We went inside, took the elevator to the seventh floor, and jogged down the corridor to the right, past the nurses' station, and saw our father by the door to my mother's room. He was backing out, a nurse gently pushing him. At first I was confused. Was my father at the wrong room? But it wasn't the wrong room because as Gerry and I got closer we could see in, could see her, if briefly, because the door was closing and another nurse appeared and was trying to move us away, back toward the waiting area, by the chairs near the large windows because we were not supposed to be in the room right now, can't be in the room right now. But we don't move and my father is saying in a scarily calm voice, *That's my wife in there,* and the nurses are trying to hold him back as my father reaches for the door handle. The nurses stop him, pushing him back, saying *Please, please.*

My father stares straight ahead, never looks at me and Gerry until Gerry, all six foot two of him, lowers his shoulder and pushes the door open, pushing one of the nurses back, and the look on my mother's face, the surprised look on her face, because we were never supposed to be there, to see her like this, heaving for air, the doctor over her with the paddles and for a moment, for just a moment, she sees us, looks at us, her left hand rising up just a bit, trying to reach out. I think. I'm not sure. How can I be sure? But there is a look on her face, her eyes wide. She's trying to say something. And then a kind of a jolt, like she'd been shocked and the nurse at the door saying in a voice too loud *Please step out* but we don't. Instead we watch as her eyes close and her head falls to the right, her lovely hair falls over to the right, and the doctor stops what he was doing and so does the other nurse by the bed and the other nurse by the door. They stop because they know what we don't quite yet.

Just a second ago she was alive and now she's not. And I don't understand. Which is when Gerry howls, a wounded animal howl, and my father puts an arm on Gerry's shoulder and for a moment I am sure I am invisible and that maybe I have died too and in that brief moment a fear I have never known comes over me. And I think *Please, please, please wake up* and I watch her and nothing happens and no one says anything for what seems like a long time until they lead us out of the room and I am the last one out and as I go I look over my shoulder and still she hasn't moved and I wonder why there isn't a rule that says that you cannot watch your mother die.

After, they brought Gerry and me to a small room, where they brought us two bottles of Coca-Cola and a small pack of cookies, both of which went untouched, while my father did whatever you do after your wife dies. Identify the body, fill out papers, take possession of her things.

Outside, when we got to the car, Gerry made two fists and pounded on the roof, a primal scream coming out of him, the roof dented from the ferocity of the pounding. I watched him, terrified, then looked to my father, who just watched, said nothing, before getting in the car.

People came to the house that evening. Neighbors, friends, my mother's dementia-cursed father, who kept asking where she was. I watched as women brought food, handed out cups of coffee. The men nursed glasses of beer.

My father sat in a chair in the living room, people leaning in close, talking with him. He would look up from time to time at me and force a smile. Gerry was in the kitchen with his girlfriend and a few friends from high school.

I felt removed from it all. So I watched. I watched their faces, how they cried, hugged, sat together. How they talked, the low hum of serious conversation, but also how it turned from my mother to asking about other things, other topics, the intensity of death too much to sustain for too long, how after a deep sigh, a look around the room, people said things like, "How's Ginny? She's married now? Isn't that wonderful." How someone else talked about their car being in the shop, a valve job that was going to cost a fortune. How life went on. I didn't want that. I wanted it to stop, for the world to stop, to recognize this death and this moment. Pay attention to this. They did, briefly. And then they didn't, slowly filtering out, to their homes and lives.

After a while I went upstairs to my room and closed the door and kept the light on, as I always did, and went to bed.

A few numb days later, as we pulled into the funeral home parking lot, I saw that the line of mourners stretched down the street. It was raining lightly and all these people stood, waiting. They led Gerry and my father and me to the room with the opened casket and there she was. Good Catholics, we were to kneel and say a prayer. My father went first, his head falling forward, a man ruined, his shoulders hunched and shaking. He eventually stood, keeping his back to us, gesturing with his arm for us to do the same. We knelt on the hassock, Gerry bowed his head, and I looked at her, her face two feet from mine, this wooden stranger. I don't know why I did it but I reached out to touch her arm. And in the moment before Gerry pulled it back, in the moment before he hissed, "Don't!"

I felt her leaden, lifeless arm, felt how her body was no longer hers. Where was she? Her, I mean. Her essence? Where did it go? How does it just disappear?

Later, and for hours, we stood near the casket, in a receiving line, and shook the hands of friends and neighbors and people I had never met, listened to the words that meant nothing to me at the time, nodding, smiling, not knowing what to do with my hands, what expression to make. The flowers. So many flowers. The smell of the flowers. I stopped listening, stopped feeling.

Why *wake*, I wondered. Wake up? *Wake up. It's just all a bad dream.* It means vigil. To stand vigil over the dead. It said so on the back of the pamphlet from the funeral home, the one with my mother's badly xeroxed and pixelated photo on the front.

From time to time, after someone would shake my hand in line, say something, as I would watch them quickly look away, the pain of this boy in the badly fitting suit coat and clip-on tie too much to bear, as they moved on to my father and I stood and waited for the next person, a brief lull, I would look to my left, to the casket, to all the flowers that stood around it, the gold crucifix on the silk bunting, at her face, at her sewn-together lips, at the heavy powdered makeup, and wonder who was in there. Because it wasn't the woman I knew. *Sit up!* I wanted to shout. *Smile! Wink at me!*

What no mourner ever said, what I wished they had, was the truth that this would be the day that would define the rest of your life. I would come to learn that much later.

The point is that my mother's obituary was only seventy-four words long. I counted.

I counted when I saw it in the newspaper. I didn't understand how her life could be reduced to seventy-four words. Words that made no mention of how she loved the beach or how she did a little hip shake when a song she liked came on the radio in the kitchen or how she hummed when she was happy, how she leaned over the toaster on cold winter mornings as she waited for the bread to pop up, the warmth on her face, the smell of slightly burnt bread, turning to me and smiling, raising her eyebrows twice, our little secret.

How was there no mention of that? Of the details of a life? Instead, it was a few facts, where she went to high school, the names of people she was related to. She wasn't famous. She had never had her picture in the newspaper. She was one of the 164,000 people who die each day in the world, names we would never know.

I remember being angry. This wasn't fair. I wanted to rewrite it. I wanted to make it right. I just didn't know how.

VINCENZO "VINNY" MARCHETTI, 63

The weather had changed its mind and turned cold again. A dusting of snow that had fallen the previous evening had largely disappeared in the brilliant sun with temperatures only in the twenties.

Clara had texted and asked if I wanted to go to a funeral. The way one does. She told me to meet her at the Beverley Road subway stop in Brooklyn. She was standing in front of a bodega as I came up the subway stairs, looking through the viewfinder of her camera at two elderly women waiting for the light to change on the other side of the street. When I reached her she held out the camera to show me the photos. I looked at the screen on the back of her camera as she clicked through the photos of the beautiful old women. I turned to look at her as she looked at the photos.

"Cold," she said, looking at me, smiling.

We ducked into a bodega for two cups of coffee.

Holy Cross Cemetery is bordered by East Flatbush and Little Haiti, a rare patch of green and trees in the borough. I followed as she walked in straight lines, row by row, careful not to step over a grave. She wore a vintage overcoat, a black cashmere hat, and a pink scarf wrapped around her neck.

"Bowling would have been nice," I said. "A movie."

"This is better. It's quiet. How many spaces in New York are quiet? Listen."

She stopped and looked up. In a tree somewhere a bird called out.

"Plus," she said, "there's a gangster buried here. Louis Capone. And he wasn't even related to Al Capone. What are the chances?"

"Do you do this a lot?"

"Visit cemeteries? No. It's a new thing. I have a bad habit where I get into something and become obsessed. I got into golf two years ago. Bought clubs, got up early every Saturday to play. Joined a league. Until I realized I hated golf."

"No one likes golf. Even golfers don't like it."

"It's amazing how the words flow out of your mouth but mean almost nothing."

She stopped at a gravestone, took off a glove, and put her hand against the wind-worn stone, wiping away aged, sun-bleached lichen. *Jed and Sarah Mayhew.* He died first.

Clara said, "What were you like, Sarah Mayhew? What did you do for fun? What was your best day?"

She talked about the funerals she had been to. She talked about how many people look at their phones during the service. She talked about a funeral she read about where the husband of the woman to whom he had been married for sixty-three years had died during the funeral.

"Do you believe in God?" she asked.

"I swear for a second I thought you said, 'Do you believe in golf?'"

She tried to suppress a grin.

"My office mate, Tuan, asks me the same thing sometimes," I said. "Seems unfair to ask me that here."

"That's not an answer," she said, looking at the names and dates on the stone.

"I don't know."

"You're standing in a cemetery, atop the souls of hundreds of people. You're middle-aged. You must have thoughts."

"I'm only forty-four."

"That's almost fifty. The best years of your life a distant memory."

"You should be on morning TV. You have that upbeat vibe."

She grinned as the wind blew strands of hair across her face and she moved it back, behind her ear. *Don't move*, I thought. *Stop time. I want to remember this, whatever this is.* She stared and waited for my answer.

"I don't know," I said, more quietly than I'd expected. "I want to, but . . . I don't know."

She continued to stare, a look on her face that was open and curious.

"You?" I asked.

She wiped again at the gravestone and said nothing for a time.

"When I read the news, no," she said. "When I see small children, yes. When I listen to talk radio, no. When I fly on a plane, yes. When I take Amtrak and go through North Philadelphia and see how people have to live, no. When I sit in my kitchen in the winter with coffee and watch the sunrise, yes. When I volunteered at Memorial Sloan Kettering in the children's unit, no. When I see the parents who sleep next to their children for weeks at a time in that unit, yes. When I make the horrible mistake of glancing at the *New York Post*, no. When I see some tough-looking kid on the subway who I've mentally judged based on how he looks give his seat up for an elderly woman, yes."

She stared at me. Perhaps that's how it starts. Just a look, a nothing moment where you see someone a bit differently, maybe feel something that catches, that seems fully alive, not the rote day-to-day.

We walked, looking at the names and dates.

"What have you lied about?" she asked near the grave of *Margaret Kelleher, wife, mother, friend.*

"When?"

"In your life."

"I try not to lie," I lied.

"That's a lie. We all lie. Little ones. All the time."

"I don't lie."

"Are you lying now?"

"Yes."

"C'mon. One lie you tell, have told. Little fib."

"It's embarrassing. It's so dumb."

"I understand. That's why I'm asking."

"I have . . . I don't know why . . . but I have, on occasion, told people that I tried stand-up comedy."

"And you haven't."

"God, no. I'm not funny enough and don't have the courage."

Ann Mosley 1931–2012.

"But you liked the idea of being perceived as funny and courageous."

"Well, when you put it that way."

"Isn't it weird how we live lies all the time?" she said, kneeling to pick up an empty plastic water bottle that had littered someone's grave.

"I'm not sure I understand."

"Well. They did this thing in the nut bin. They said we should ask ourselves, when the thoughts get weird, is it true? Is the thought true?"

"Then what?"

"Ask what happens when you believe that thought. Then ask who you would be without the thought. The thoughts, the stories and narratives . . . they're lies. But we live every moment as if they're true."

Fredrich Baumgartner 1960–1991.

"What have you lied about?" I asked her.

She picked up an empty Doritos bag by a tree.

"I tell people I've been to Spain," she said.

"Why?"

"Ah, because I did, Mr. Stand-Up Comic."

Artemis Byrde 1922–1944.

"Insecurity, I guess," she said. "At my old job so many people had traveled, done a year abroad in college, were so much more worldly. So I just said it one day. The problem is they started asking questions. Where I've been, what I'd seen. Horrible. I had to study Spain to keep the lie up. I know a lot about Spain, in the event I ever go. Though I've been telling the lie so long I feel like I have been. I may actually cross it off my list."

I noticed two crushed beer cans and picked them up.

"Do you ever visit your mother's grave?" she asked.

The question surprised me.

"No. Not for a long time." Something about it, here in this place, made me feel guilty.

"What was her name?"

"Louise. Louise Stanley. Why?"

"I read this thing. I think it was the ancient Egyptians. They believed you died twice. First when you died, and second when people stopped saying your name. So, then. Louise Stanley."

"I like that."

"Joseph Darrell," she said.

"Who's that?"

"My father."

"Oh. When did he die?"

"Last fall."

"I'm sorry. I didn't know."

A quick fake smile. "It's okay. Yeah. So I was away for work. And he went into the hospital. It all happened fast. Except I waited to go back because I had this . . . big meeting. I waited two days because I thought . . . you know. Anyway. He died while I was in the air, flying back. All because of a meeting. With a bank. About some fucking deal."

She looked around at the gravestones, as if looking for something.

"Joseph Darrell," I said.

She looked at me and swallowed hard. She looked as if she wanted to say something but didn't. "C'mon," she said. "We're late."

We entered Saint Catherine of Genoa Church, the service already underway. We held the large wooden door so it would close softly, but still, mourners turned. The faint smell of incense. Rows of smooth wooden pews mostly empty, the memories of a million prayers, pleas, hopes.

We took a seat in the back of the church. The echoey silence was broken by the occasional cough, a creaking pew. The first five or so rows on either side of the church were full and a man who looked to be in his sixties stood at a lectern. In the center of the altar, sitting in a large chair, a thin and very young-looking priest. And at the entrance to the altar the casket sat upon a bier.

The speaker wore a boxy suit. He was short but broad-shouldered, barrel-chested, a meaty, nervous right hand constantly gesturing, the left glued to the lectern. He consulted notes awkwardly, sniffed loudly, unaware of the microphone's closeness. He seemed well into a story.

"So my grandmother, she goes into the bathroom the next morning, right, and what does she see but Vinny, lying in the tub, surrounded by her soup. She screamed, not expecting to see a grown man passed out in her tub. Or her soup for that matter."

He smiled as others chuckled.

"He was so drunk that he didn't see the soup. Now, why my grandmother made soup in a tub is a whole 'nother story, but what do you want from someone from the old country."

The laughs petered out and the speaker paused. His right hand made little circles, as if urging himself on.

He cleared his throat.

"We liked cars, me and Vin. And in the summer, when we was teenagers, after high school, we both worked at this garage in Bay Ridge. Best job. He had a sixty-four Pontiac GTO with four on the floor . . ."

Here he paused, as if he forgot for a moment that he was standing there, in the church, on the altar. He scratched at the back of his head.

"Me and Vin, we had our issues, you know? Families do, I guess. But he was my brother. My little brother. And I wonder what he thought about in those final moments, in that hospice, before he died."

He cleared his throat, moved his hair from his forehead. He was telling the story to himself, to his brother. I looked over to see that Clara was looking at me.

"I'd bet a dollar it was those summer afternoons. Those were the best days of our lives. Working at that garage and driving cool cars and listening to the songs we loved, the radio always on. Duke and the Drivers and the O'Jay's and Bill Withers and Grand Funk Railroad. I'd bet it's summer. In his mind. It's a summer afternoon and he's driving us home. The smells of axle grease and tire rubber and tobacco smoke on his fingers from a day working at the garage as he takes a drag on a Marlboro and turns up the radio and bobs his head, no rush to get home, plenty of time before six o'clock supper, Mum waiting on us. We pass the guys in the neighborhood hanging out on stoops, waiting for their fathers to get home. A horn tap to Jumbo Esposito standing on the corner near Saint Teresa's talking to Kevin Ahearn, Jumbo smiling, a little head wave, Kevin too, Jumbo giving him the finger still smiling. We'll see them later. Maybe drive up to Todt Hill and watch the planes coming into LaGuardia, one after another, car trunks holding Coleman coolers with bottles of Miller High Life, kids showing up, hanging out, the heat of the day gone and if you sit and listen to the crickets and swig a cold Miller, well, what else is there? I'd bet that's what he was thinking. No pain now, for my little brother. A morphine haze."

And here his voice cracked, just a bit, and he wiped at his face, his eyes.

"He's thinking about the perfect day and he's smiling. That's how I imagine it. Thinking about walking in that door and Mum telling him to wash his hands and Shake 'n Bake in the oven, our father sitting at the table reading the evening newspaper. Mum asking about our day but really talkin' to Vin. She lit up when he walked in a room. Her baby. We ate fast, wanting to be dismissed, to change into a clean shirt and a pair of chinos and put in a little Brylcreem and splash on some of dad's English Leather aftershave and we were gone. Back on the streets. The radio on. Time for one more cigarette. Push the lighter in, switch the radio dial, deep drag, elbow out the window, one hand on the steering wheel. Driving. My little brother. The music fading. It was time to go home."

Tears streamed down his cheeks. He wiped his face with his hand.

There was a long silence, and then applause.

"Oh," he added, almost as if he had forgotten. "I promised him I'd do something. I apologize in advance, Father."

He took out his phone and tapped at it, then held it up to the microphone, a grin creeping across his face, as the pure electric chords of the song . . . one everyone knew, had heard a thousand times, and yet so out of place here, now. A man's voice. Gravelly, rough. The unmistakable voice of Ronald "Bon" Scott, partial to performing shirtless, dead at age thirty-three, as he sang AC/DC's "Highway to Hell."

ASYLUM SEEKERS

Clara lived on the top floor of a brownstone in Fort Greene, a place she had bought six years ago after leaving Manhattan. White walls populated with large photos of trips she'd taken, of people and places. A gorgeous five-year-old girl at a train station in Delhi. An old man in the marketplace in Marrakech. The beach in Santa Monica. Green leafy plants sat on windowsills. Over the mantel was a large oil painting of a beach and rolling dunes. Behind the dunes, by a lone road, a cottage looking out over the beach. It looked like an Edward Hopper.

"I love that," I said.

"Yeah. Me, too. I used to pass this gallery in Chelsea every day, when I worked over there. I'd see it in the window. I'd never bought art before in my life. I mean, I don't know anything about art. But it just stopped me every time. So."

She walked to the kitchen and washed her hands.

"Beer?" she asked.

"Please."

She took two bottles of beer from the refrigerator and handed me one. We cracked them open.

"To funerals," I said.

"To living," she said.

She sipped her beer.

"I don't have much in the house," she said. "Pasta okay?"

"Sounds great. What can I do?"

"Make a fire."

She took down a large stainless-steel pot hanging above the stove, filled it with water, and placed it on the stove while I placed three logs in the grate and began to crumple newspaper.

"Hmm," she said, watching. "Mind if I . . ."

She came over and opened the flue.

"I was getting to that part," I said.

"Sorry," she said. "Anal."

She rearranged the logs into a triangle, stuffed the newspaper under the grate, and lit the paper from a box of stick matches. She blew gently on the paper a few times and up it went, the paper burning, the dry logs catching quickly.

"Kiln-dried. Has to be kiln-dried," she said to the fire, her back to me.

"I feel less manly," I said. "Is there something I could carry, something you need butchered?"

"Dice the garlic. Pretend it's a bear."

Esther had taught me how to use a knife in the kitchen. She had seen me mangle an onion when I tried to cook for Tim once.

"No, no, no," Esther said then, annoyed. "Is like you're a blind man. Like village idiot." She took the knife from me, took out the honing steel from the wooden block holding the knives, sharpened it with alarming speed, and took my hand. "Hold like this," she said. And with her other hand she covered both our hands and pumped the knife quickly, mincing the onion.

Clara took down a saucepan from the rack. She placed it on the stove, turned the heat on, and poured in olive oil. I could see her watch me dicing out of the corner of her eye. "Not terrible," she said of the minced garlic. I slid it into the pan.

I washed my hands in the large English farm sink. "Your place is great," I said.

"Thank you. I did a lot of work to it. Now it seems silly to me."

"Why?"

"I don't know. It cost a lot and I'm not sure who I was trying to impress. The old floors were fine. The kitchen was weird but fine. The bathrooms were ugly but fine. I feel like this is a new thing. Going into a house and gutting it and making it . . . perfect. Farm sinks. What the hell."

"You have a farm sink."

"That's my point. That sink cost two thousand dollars. I'm an idiot. It's a sink. The sink in my parents' house was just a sink. It worked. It did what sinks are supposed to do. All I did was blow two thousand dollars."

"It's a nice-looking sink."

"This isn't even the longest conversation I've ever had about sinks."

"We should maybe end it," I said. "Before it goes further down the drain."

She shook her head.

I watched as she fried the garlic in olive oil and diced cherry tomatoes and put them in a bowl with olive oil, cooking and talking.

"My parents visited when it was done," she said. "I don't know. I think I wanted them to be impressed. They nodded. Mostly I think they were embarrassed."

She poured the fried garlic into the bowl and let it sit. She pulled down a wooden bowl and put arugula in, made a dressing from olive oil, Dijon mustard, and lemon.

"Alexa, play Vince Guaraldi," she said.

"It's Bud. Bud Stanley."

"You're a moron."

We sat facing the fire as we ate. She opened a bottle of red wine and poured me a glass and a small glass for herself. Somehow I had gotten around to Jen. I was talking to the fire, long after we had finished eating, after she had poured me more wine, had made herself tea, brought out a bar of dark chocolate.

"I ran into them once," I said.

"No," she said, excited. "Where? What happened?"

"It was maybe six months after she left. I was in a superb place in my life. I was like Tony Robbins, only with stains on my clothes and the look of someone experiencing electroshock therapy. Tuan and Howard were concerned, let's put it that way. Tim, too, but I didn't know him that well then. Anyway, they drag me out one night. Dinner. One of Howard's favorite places. Café Luxembourg."

"Love."

"They know Howard there. We get a great table. It's a New York place."

"Totally."

"Howard orders a wonderful bottle of wine. We eat. Tuan is a spectacular lightweight with alcohol and starts telling tales of hookups when he first came to New York. I don't know why he had them, but Tuan produced, from his large handbag, three plastic tiaras. He put one on me, one on Howard. It was ridiculous. But I hadn't felt that good in a long time. Tuan suggests a nightcap at a piano bar he knows of. We walk to the door and there she is, at the bar. Howard and Tuan are walking ahead of me. They don't see her. But I know the hair. Brown, big crazy curls. She's leaning in close to a guy."

"Details. Making out? Canoodling?"

"*Canoodling* to me connotes something innocent. They were quaffing what appeared to be champagne, she was laughing, and then they would slobber each other."

"What did you do?"

"I was brilliant. The words just seemed to flow and I cut them both down to size. In the movie version, I mean. In the real version, I mostly just stood there, Howard and Tuan were already out the door. It was crowded and people were waiting at the bar. The Englishman, her boyfriend, was ordering something from the bartender and she was watching him. The way she was looking at him. I was going to tap her on the shoulder but I didn't. There's a mirror behind the bar. This old, like, speckled mirror, and she looked in the mirror, at herself, and saw me. Her whole expression changed, like she was seeing a ghost or something. It was that look. The one that went from adoration to . . . this wide-eyed dread. So I left."

"Wait. So she probably turned and you're not there?"

"I guess. I didn't stick around."

"You literally haunted her. I'm sorry, but that's the greatest burn I've ever heard."

I told her what happened with Tim, in the church.

"Well that's intense," Clara said.

"No . . . I mean, I don't know, it just annoyed me," I said.

"Why?"

"Let's say hypothetically you're insecure. Well, when someone calls you on your insecurity, points out a fault . . . you get angry at yourself, but if you're immature, you take that anger out on them because you know there's some truth in it."

Wind must have blown down the chimney flue. A hint of woodsmoke wafted off the fireplace. I looked up, suddenly embarrassed. She touched my knee and smiled quickly.

"Keep going," she said.

"There's this . . . distance, this gap I can't close. I sit there and I know the meaning of this thing, this event. I watch the faces of the people in the church, in the line at the wake, around the grave. And words appear in my head. *Sad. Awful. Tragedy. Loss.* But I can't feel those words. It's like if you said, 'Alexa, explain tragedy,' she'd define it. But it wouldn't explain the feeling of tragedy. Is this making any sense?"

"Of course," she said. "You're on the outside, looking in. I know the feeling."

"Tell me."

"You're waiting to live."

She broke off a piece of chocolate and handed it to me. She broke off another piece and ate it. I hadn't noticed it before but she had, on the bridge of her nose, toward her left eye, a slightly raised freckle.

"Can I ask about your stay at the place in Western Mass?"

"Yes," she said, smiling. "I'm not ashamed of it."

"I didn't mean . . ."

"I know." She reached over, touched my knee. "So, the long version is that it started with me having an affair with a married man. Not a good idea. He was very persistent and I fell for the flattery and was naïve enough to believe him when he said it was over with his wife. Which it wasn't. He eventually called it off. Left the firm. Did I mention that? I worked with him. So that was smart. I worry I'm boring you."

"I am a long way from bored. Go on."

She blew on a cup of chamomile tea.

"It's just . . . looking back . . . that wasn't me. It wasn't the person my father had raised. So, I just threw myself into work. Work, running, repeat."

She looked over at me. I got the sense—but who really knows—that she was trying to decide how much to share.

"And I'm on a business trip one day. My mother calls. *Your father is in the hospital. You should come home.* And I . . . go to this . . . meeting . . . leave two days later . . . and . . ."

She forced a smile.

"I couldn't get the noise out of my head. It just kept beating the crap out of me, telling me how horrible I was. I'd had something similar happen halfway through my first year in college. This was worse, though."

She shrugged.

"It was a six-week program. It wasn't, like, locked doors and things like that. No horror-film screams. It was modern-day depression. Clean and medicated and antiseptic. We slept. We lay in a fetal position on a couch in a common room staring at *Wheel of Fortune.* Crippling anxiety. The inability to get out of bed. To change your clothes. The heaviness of your arms. The heaviness of blinking. This . . . absence of any hope. I'm fun. Aren't I fun?"

She sipped from my wineglass and then stuck her tongue out at me.

"I had a therapist there," she said. "This amazing older woman. She liked to do the sessions outside, walking around the grounds, these beautifully tended grounds. She smoked. She said, 'There are three secrets to a happy life. Unfortunately, no one knows what they are.' Then she'd cackle. She'd walk, smoke, not say anything for long stretches. No rush. 'Look at the daffodils,' she'd say, smiling. 'Aren't they lovely?'"

She looked at what remained of the fire, red-orange coals now.

"Do you know about the monarch butterflies?" she asked.

It was something Tim would say.

"No."

She smiled, putting her hair behind her ear.

"They migrate between Canada and Mexico. It's an incredibly long trip. No one generation makes the whole trip. So they lay eggs at different stages through the journey. And yet every year, as if by memory, they fly over the same lake in a strange pattern. They fly south and then turn east and then turn back toward the south. No one knew why. Until some scientists wondered if maybe, a long time ago, there had been a mountain, a really huge mountain, in that area. The monarchs wouldn't have been able to fly over it, so instead they would have veered around it. This was their path, year after year. Except they kept doing it, even after the mountain was gone, because that's what they knew."

She had been talking to the fire. But now she looked up at me. "The script is unfinished. But we believe the story we've been telling ourselves about who we are and where our life leads. The story isn't written yet. Your life. You know?"

I didn't want her to stop talking.

"For a while," she continued, "I kept waiting for some . . . answer, some big, life-changing answer. The secret, right? I'm not sure it happens that way. The . . . That therapist, at the place, she gave me this quote. *The great revelation perhaps never did come. Instead there were little daily miracles, illuminations, matches struck unexpectedly in the dark.*"

"Who said that?" I asked.

"The Spice Girls." She grinned. "Virginia Woolf. We can change. Now maybe it's just a bit. But that little bit is . . . everything."

She reached over and stroked my cheek with her fingertips.

"Grab your coat," she said.

The rooftop of the building faced downtown Brooklyn, over the new, too-tall towers, over lower Manhattan and beyond. Maybe it was the cold, but it seemed like more stars than normal, so rarely visible in the too-bright New York sky. Now, though, it looked like a child's black construction paper, pinpricks, light behind it. When the wind turned we could smell woodsmoke from her chimney.

She pointed. "Polaris. Ursa Major. Ursa Minor. The Little Bear. Or Little Dipper."

I turned and watched her watch the sky.

"How do you know about this?" I asked.

"My father. In the summers we would go camping." She looked at me. The mention of her father taking her away for a moment. She continued. "The light we're seeing is gone already. It's . . . in the past."

"I can't wrap my head around that."

"Try this one. The visible universe contains about one hundred billion galaxies. Each one of those galaxies contains around one hundred billion stars. That means the visible universe contains something like ten thousand million, million, million stars. That means there are more stars in the visible universe than there are grains of sand on Earth. NASA can now see two billion stars. Which is less than one percent of the stars in the Milky Way."

"There were a lot of numbers in there."

"They come easy to me."

"How easy?"

"I used to tutor seniors in calculus," she said. "When I was a freshman."

"SATs in math. What'd you get? I got a 510."

"I did better," she said, staring at the sky. "But then, most of the nation did better." She was smiling.

We made our way back down and I stood at the door to her apartment.

"Well . . . thank you for dinner," I said. "Another funeral sometime?"

"So the thing is . . . I'm not going back to my old job. I want to . . . to do something else."

I nodded.

"I was thinking about teaching," she added.

"That's great."

"Have you heard of Bhutan?"

"Sure. I'm not sure I could find it on a map, though."

"Find India. Go north and a bit to the right."

"Good to know."

"They have something called Gross National Happiness. They don't just measure, like, the economy but people's well-being."

"I like that."

"I'm going there. To Bhutan."

"Really? When?"

"Five days." She nodded.

"Wow. That's . . . wow. For how long?"

"A year."

It was strange to watch my reaction, the stomach-dropping news of it, the mild panic. Can you feel mildly panicked? Whatever that space is, that feeling, where you're shocked, frozen for a second or two. That not accepting of it. *Run, Bud. Leave.* I took a step back.

"I'm sorry," she said. "I should have said something. It's just . . . I didn't expect to like you."

I forced a smile and nodded.

"Five days," I said.

This cocktail of disappointment and unfairness.

"Okay, my turn. How much do you know about mayflies?" I asked, a little gift from my buddy.

"What?"

"Mayflies," I said. "A friend of mine told me a mayfly's entire lifespan is just twenty-four hours. That gives us, like, five lifetimes."

She smiled. "I'd like that."

OFFICER AND LAUGHING GIRL

I woke early and showered, a newfound energy and lightness. I made coffee and sat in the kitchen looking out over the tall ash tree. Sunlight diffused through large clouds. It had rained the night before, the thunder waking me briefly. It was still quiet enough to hear the birds. No garbage trucks yet. No sirens. No helicopters.

I texted Tim.

Frick? Lunch? On me. Well, my portion, anyway. I'm an idiot. I'm sorry.

The clouds had cleared and the sun was out, but still cool. We couldn't bring ourselves to go inside quite yet and so we strolled east on Seventieth and then up Madison. I defy you to not feel a thrill on this island, on the Upper East Side, walking past the door-manned buildings, the high-end boutiques, the small shops that have been here a hundred years; stationery stores and cobblers, florists and dry cleaners.

Sometimes I wondered what people saw as we passed, if they saw us at all, this poorly dressed middle-aged man in need of a haircut and his boyfriend in the wheelchair.

* * *

As we always did whenever we made a visit to the Frick, we stopped in at the Three Guys diner on Madison and sat at a booth by the door. The schoolkids at the counter in the back, the girls in uniforms, gangly fifteen-year-olds, giraffe legs, unused to their new height, hunched forward, huddling and giggling in groups of three and four. The boys, shirts half untucked, neckties askance, pretending not to see the girls, but stealing looks, not fully sure yet what this magnetic effect was.

We stared out the window, the giddy, infectious energy of a Manhattan day. So much was possible. The lunch, the museum to come. We watched people walk by on the street, come in and out of the diner, overheard snippets of different conversations:

She clerked for Beyer. Now she's home with twins.

I've been to Mustique, Anguilla, and Saint Barts. Like, where's the next hot place?

He assumed the threesome would be with another woman . . .

We ate the wondrous food of small children. Grilled cheese, french fries, black-and-white milkshakes.

"I keep dying in my dreams," I blurted out.

"That's fun."

"What do you think it means?"

"It means you're impotent. Go on."

"I fall from a tall building. From a high bridge. I feel the fall. I'm aware of the danger and I think, *No. No, this can't be it.*"

He waited for me to say more but I didn't.

"And then?" he asked.

"I can't explain it clearly. It's hazy. But I'm aware that I'm . . . dead. And I'm just so . . . sad. And then I wake up and it takes me a minute to realize it was a dream."

Tim ate a french fry and sipped from his milkshake. "What do you think?"

He shrugged. "Maybe you are dying, in a way. Jen, the job. Maybe it wasn't just a whiskey-induced accident that you wrote your own obituary."

"You're saying I'm dying?"

"In a way. We all are."

"You should come out with a line of sad greeting cards."

"We die and are reborn all the time. We just ignore it. About three hundred thirty billion cells are replaced every day. You're different today than you were yesterday."

"I like that idea. But I feel the same."

"You're not. You're just thinking the same."

A group of girls came in, four or five, talking at once, laughing, sleeves pulled over their hands.

"I just . . ."

He waited, the careful listener.

"It's just that I . . . I want to be forgiven."

Tim look confused. "For what?"

"Everything. Jen. The obituary. The other day with you. My . . . thoughts . . . my failure . . . just . . ."

"Whoa. Hey. Look at me. All of that . . . It's just thoughts. Lies. Ain't real."

"The divorce? The obit? The shit I said the other day? I can't shake this feeling that I am just . . . crap."

"You should go with that feeling," he said.

I snorted.

"For what it's worth," he said, "I think the divorce was a gift. For you, for a new life. And, if I'm selfish, for me. The other day doesn't mean shit. There's just today. Okay? One day. What would you do?"

"Get a one-year gym membership."

"Genius. One day. Go."

I hesitated but I knew the answer. "This," I said.

He looked down.

"You?" I asked.

"Is walking an option?" He forced a smile. "I'm doing exactly what I want to do," he said, a real smile this time.

It was not uncommon for us to go to a museum, a gallery, an art opening. Though over the years he enjoyed it less. The crowds, the scene, the posers. The Frick was different. It was small and intimate and mostly on a single floor.

We wandered the quiet rooms for a time and then sat looking at the fountain in the garden court. It was a Thursday and, save for the occasional tourist and the sleepy docents, we had the place to ourselves. Around us were flowering plants, large palms, the sound of water from the fountain and, playing low, a woman on the cello in the corner. Tim told me that this used to be an open courtyard for cars. We were lulled into a quiet by the falling water, the smell of the flowers.

"About the church and what I said the other day," I said to the floor. "I'm sorry."

"It's okay."

"It's really not."

I looked up and he forced a smile.

"I'm sorry too," he said.

"Why are you sorry?"

"Because I'm a didactic douche sometimes. So much so that I just used the word *didactic*, which is such an annoying word. Sometimes I hear my own voice and I hate it," he said. "I hate that I think I know something about how to live."

"I think you know a lot."

"I think I'm a pontificating jackass a lot of times."

"You're not. It's just . . . it's hard to be like you."

"You think I'm better than I am. Because of the chair."

"No. It's because you're the best person I've ever known."

He looked at me and I could see the effect of the words.

"Many lifetimes ago," he said, "after I finally got out of the hospital, I went through . . . a lot of shit." He laughed. "Ugly shit. Rage. My life gone. Sex . . . gone. So I . . . I did stuff."

"Like what?"

"Oh, life-affirming things like vodka. A lot of vodka. Vodka and cocaine. I smoked crack, which is quite wonderful. The first time. Less so later, when your friends stop calling you because you're so fucked up and you're raging at them and you have no memory of how horrible you were. So that was good."

He looked over at the cellist and watched her play.

"I was losing friends. Lou flew in, gave me a talking-to, told me I was killing myself. Which I was. Begged me to stop, get help. I was numb, even with her. I just kept . . . pushing, to see how low I could go. Oh. Forgot to mention that I watched people have sex. In hotels. I hired sex workers. Had them come over, get undressed. Watched them. A guy beat the shit out of me once. Left me on the floor, drunk, out of my mind, bleeding. Stole money. That was a proud moment."

He forced a laugh and looked up at me.

"But Lou, Esther, my parents . . . they just . . . they stayed by me. Cleaned up after me. Cleaned *me*. Fed me. Sat with me."

Here his voice broke, just a bit, and he was forced to take a deep breath.

"So . . . if I overstep, if I give advice and sound like I know what I'm talking about, it's because you matter to me. That's all. I have a hard time seeing the people I love unhappy."

I ran my tongue against the back of my lower teeth. I blurted out, "So, I'm almost forty-five and I don't really know how to live."

Tim stared at me, unblinking. "Then I would say you are officially a citizen of the world."

"I'm just . . . I had this vague sense of how life might go. At least I think I did. College. Magically find a career. Marry. Kids. Lately it feels like someone else is writing the script of my life. I don't love this script."

I looked up, forced a little grin. Tim had a pained look on his face.

"Want to know the secret?" I asked. "The pure-shame, can't-ever-say-it-out-loud secret?"

I felt my throat constrict.

"I'm afraid," I said.

"Of what?"

"Dying. Because I'm not sure I've ever really lived. And I don't know how."

"And the wakes? The funerals?"

"I hate them. They fucking terrify me."

Two older women walked through the gallery. One said, in a heavy accent that I guessed to be German, "Look at the pool."

"What?" the other asked in native English.

"Pool. There's a pool."

"Yes."

"As a girl I swam nude!"

"You did what?"

"Nude!" She laughed and they walked on.

We'd both been watching them. Tim looked at me, his face in full laugh, covering his mouth.

"I'll shut up now," I said. "Just know I'd be lost without you."

He looked at me for what felt like a long time.

He paused, looked down, and then said, "Show me someone who is great with death and I'll show you a sociopath. I know a little bit about fear. All I can tell you is that it's a lie. It dares you to look it in the eye. Because when you do that, when you stare straight at it and don't flinch, you own it. These . . . wakes and funerals? That's you looking fear in the eye. There is another side. I know it. And what's waiting for you there is everything."

We stared at one of the two Vermeers at the bottom of the main staircase, where, legend has it, Henry Clay Frick himself had hung them and where they had remained. *Officer and Laughing Girl*. Tim's favorite.

"There are only thirty-seven Vermeers in the world," Tim said. "I think I have that number right. A handful in museums, some in private collections. The Met has five. And the Frick has three. I mean . . . his hand made those marks more than three hundred years ago. His face as close as ours is to it now, breathing on it, trying to get it right, to find the right color, the right shading, off by a fraction and stepping away and feeling like a madman because he can't get it right, wondering why he hadn't become a carpenter where he could just measure and cut and build instead of a painter, trying to capture the ethereal, the impossible, trying to re-create life on a two-dimensional surface. And then doing it."

"How old was he when he died?" I asked.

"Forty-three. Write me the lede sentence in his obituary."

"Gary Vermeer . . ."

"Johannes . . ."

"Johannes Vermeer, widely considered a seminal figure in the Dutch baroque period and man about town in Delft, and who once met Scarlett Johansson on the set of *Girl with a Pearl Earring* . . ."

"You're an idiot. Why is the girl laughing? Look at the painting."

"It's a nervous laugh. He just made a bad joke, said something embarrassing."

"Like what?"

"He just showed her how he could burp the alphabet."

"You don't deserve Vermeer. Look at the painting. Pretend you're not you. Let the picture speak to you. It wants to speak to you. It's speaking to you across hundreds of years. This is its power. It's trying to tell you something, a universal thing, a thing that has no boundary in time. Why is the girl laughing?"

I stared at the painting. I waited. It seemed too obvious.

"Because she's happy?" I said.

Tim turned to me and smiled. "Yes."

"That's it?"

"What else is there?"

BLOCK PARTY

As if on cue, a directive from whatever benevolent force might rule the universe, the day dawned sunny and warm for Leo's birthday party. The first soft breezes of spring.

Tim and I sat in the middle of our small street. Someone had put sawhorses at either end to block traffic. There was a mom painting faces, a bounce house, chalk drawing, a cotton-candy machine. Ten little seven- and eight-year-olds ran around like drunk people, shouting, laughing. An unidentified parent had dressed up as a dinosaur and wandered slowly around, waving his arms, making the children laugh and scream. There was a buffet of Leo's favorite foods. Macaroni and cheese, hot dogs, seaweed, grapes, pizza, Cup O' Noodles, a large bowl of dry Lucky Charms, and four dozen Dunkin' Donuts. Music played through speakers on a windowsill. Pharrell's "Happy." ABBA's "Dancing Queen." The Doobie Brothers' "Listen to the Music."

Parents mingled, many seeming to know one another from their children's schools. They were uniformly attractive men and women. They didn't look like regular people. They looked better, like people from New York. The men, youthful in appearance, possibly having squeezed in a quick 10K that morning, had superb hair. The women wore clothes seen in magazines on famous people. These women hadn't been invented in my childhood. Back then, women wore housecoats, oversized dresses, Keds with a hole cut out of the side for their bunion. These women didn't have bunions. I wanted to ask them what their secret was, how they had achieved what appeared to be success, wealth, self-confidence, deep happiness, and an appearance, at least, of total togetherness. It would have been awkward conversation had I approached them, as my face was painted like a baboon. (Tim's idea. He chose meerkat. I noticed that Tim and I were the only adults who had chosen to have our faces painted.)

We watched Leo get his face painted like a cat, surrounded by other children. By a long table piled high with presents, his father stood talking to two other men. He was a tall man, dark hair pomaded, combed back. He looked tanned, fit. He wore an expensive-looking cashmere sweater. Leo's mother was on her stoop, on a call that, if her expression indicated anything, seemed to be important. She'd been on the phone the entire time we had been there, which was about an hour. We thought we'd stay until they cut the cake.

Leo skipped over to us.

"I like your baboon face," Leo said.

"I hope you're referring to his face paint," Tim said.

Leo thought about this for several seconds and then laughed.

Tim and Leo were on the same eyeline, the same height. When Leo talked with Tim he absentmindedly fiddled with Tim's chair, with the rubber on the tire, with the handle. Tim sat, mother hen, watching him.

"How's it feel to be eight?" Tim asked.

"I'm not really afraid of the dark anymore," Leo said.

Tim nodded. "I get it. Although you know I'm almost sixty and there are nights I like to leave a light on. I think that's okay, don't you, Bud?"

I nodded. "Absolutely. I do that, too."

Leo's eyes seemed particularly large, unblinking, taking this in. I had a bag by my feet that I handed to Leo. Inside were several wrapped presents.

"Should I open them?" he asked.

"It's your birthday," Tim said. "You're the king."

His small, bony fingers unwrapped the first one. Leo being Leo, he opened the wrapping carefully, gently removing the Scotch tape, a man in no hurry, as if purposefully delaying the surprise.

"No way!" he shouted.

Six Rubik's Cubes, all different shapes.

"I love these!" he said.

"There's more," Tim said.

I handed him the small hockey stick and the bag with the jersey in it.

"This is a real hockey stick," he said, eyes wide. "Did you play hockey?"

"A bit. I wasn't very good, though. My older brother was really good."

"Can he skate backwards?"

"Sure can."

"Wow. I can't. Actually, I can't really skate forwards, either."

"There's time."

He opened the last present and pulled out a Hartford Whalers jersey.

"When I was a boy," I said, "there was a team called the Hartford Whalers. They were my favorite."

"I love whales!" he said.

"Look on the back."

He turned the jersey around to see his name, Leo, in large block letters. His mouth fell open.

"The pros have their name on the back of their jerseys," I said.

He pulled the jersey on, the shoulders too large and the arms too long. I rolled the sleeves up.

He grinned. "Thanks, Bud." He wrapped his arms around my waist. He stepped over to Tim and put his arms around his neck. "Thanks, Tim."

"Happy birthday, pal."

He skipped away, toward his classmates, toward the bounce house.

Tim wheeled over to talk with someone he knew, so I walked slowly down the street, past the kids, past the neighbors, all of whom Leo had invited. He had delivered handwritten notes to each house on the street. Only a handful could make it, but I watched as they stood and chatted, sipped a drink, ate a slice of pizza. Diminutive Julia Felder was talking with two women I recognized from the neighborhood but didn't know. The sun was shining and the trees had sprouted lime-green leaves and flower boxes perched on windowsills held pansies and daffodils. The sounds of traffic on Court Street and the occasional siren and too-loud helicopter faded in the chatter, in the children's screams and laughter, in the sounds of the Doobie Brothers telling us to listen to the music.

"How do you leave Brooklyn?" Julia had asked.

I saw Leo's mother and father talking with Tim and joined them. I had seen her on television. Brown, shoulder-length hair and wide-set green eyes. A large Roman nose and teeth that were slightly crooked but remarkably white. She was stunning.

"Bud, I've heard about you but never met you," she said, smiling and wincing. She extended her slender hand and I shook it. Her eyes didn't leave mine and I don't know if it was a practiced thing, but it was powerful, this ability to pull you in close.

"Seth," Leo's father said, extending his hand. "Leo is a big fan of yours."

"And I of him."

Sarah's phone buzzed. "I'm so sorry. Excuse me."

She stepped away to take the call.

"We're setting off some balloons in a bit. It's something we do on a family birthday. This . . . little tradition. For Leo's older sister, Lucy, who passed away three years ago. Hope you can stick around. I know it would mean a lot to Leo."

"Wouldn't miss it," I said.

I had invited Clara, thinking she'd never make it. But there she was, watching a group of small girls draw in chalk on the street. It was difficult to tell what, exactly, they were drawing. It was either a camel or the Brooklyn Bridge.

"Hey," I said.

She turned. "Hey, yourself."

She had an old denim jacket on over a yellow sundress and high-top sneakers. Her hair was down and longer than I'd remembered, thick, with small waves toward the ends.

"I'm so glad you came," I said.

"Your street is amazing."

"Come say hello to the birthday boy."

I spotted Leo.

"Dude," I said. "I want you to meet my friend Clara."

New people were tough for Leo. He stuck out his hand to shake hers but stared at his feet. Clara took his hand and they shook briefly. Except she didn't let go. She started moving their hands back and forth. I saw Leo smile.

"Have you seen the Minion movie?" he asked, looking up quickly and then back down.

Clara knelt down on one knee, eye level with him.

"That's such a great question!" she said. "I have."

Leo looked up at her. "You have?"

"Yeah. Who's your favorite character?"

"Stuart."

"Mine, too!"

Leo looked at me, as if to say, *Can you believe the coincidence?*

"He makes me laugh," Clara said. "That's my favorite thing."

"I like that," Leo said. "I also like taking notes. I'm probably going to be a marine biologist or a spy."

"Those are both great professions."

Leo nodded and stared at Clara, a child's stare, unblinking. She held it, smiling. She reached into her jacket pocket, pulled out a small box in wrapping paper with balloons on it, and handed it to him.

"Bud said it was your birthday."

His eyes went wide. "Thank you!"

"I had one of these when I was a kid," she said. "And I loved it."

He carefully opened the paper to reveal a Slinky box.

"I love these!" Leo said. He opened it and took it out of the box, played with it, moving it from hand to hand awkwardly.

"Thanks, Clara." He looked down at the ground.

Later, when everyone had gone, taken their goodie bag, and headed home after much running and cotton candy, Leo and his parents stood in front of their house and let go of a single pink balloon. Clara and Tim and I watched as the three of them, hands holding the ribbon, whispered something only they could hear, their heads close, and let go, the balloon rising up beyond the treetops, beyond the roofline of the brownstones, the wind pushing it toward Clinton Street, sideways and higher, out toward the water, a tiny dot of pink in the dimming sky, until we couldn't see it anymore.

Leo's parents waved at us. They turned, their arms around Leo, and walked into the house.

Tim drove. Clara sat up front and I sat in back.

"Where are we going?" he asked.

"I'll tell you when we get there," I said. "Just take the Brooklyn Bridge."

He drove up Hicks Street, up onto the BQE, where we merged and moved slowly in the always traffic, the neverending traffic. Then the exit to go up and over the Brooklyn Bridge, the views never failing to thrill me.

"Take the FDR south," I said.

We drove past the old Fulton Fish Market along the East River, the glass-and-steel towers of Wall Street rising to our right. I pointed to an entrance, the southernmost point on the island, and we pulled in to the small parking lot and I saw that he was smiling.

"Nope," he said. "No, no." But he was still smiling.

"Yes," I said.

"No way. Thank you. But no, thank you."

Two helicopters sat waiting and we watched as another came in and banked over the East River and touched down, the wind and noise tremendous.

I had explained to the company, on the phone, that we would need to lift him in. They had a mechanic who had played college football, they said. They were waiting for us. That's the beauty of New York. If you pay enough, anything is possible. I couldn't afford this, but that's what high-interest credit cards are for.

They led us out to the helicopter and an unusually large man named Tony lifted Tim up and into the seat as if hoisting a toddler. Clara and I got in the two seats behind him. We put on comically large headsets with microphones attached so we could speak over the noise.

The pilot's name was Alan and he said he had flown helicopters in the navy for twenty years and now did this part-time, mostly flying news helicopters. He lived on Staten Island, where he raised his two teenage kids alone, the missus (his word) having skedaddled (also his word) with a dude from the Hells Angels. "What the fuck, man," he added with a shrug, as if this helped explain the situation. "What can you do? Hell, I wanted to go after her and shoot the dude, but who is that helping?"

"Totally," Tim said.

He was clean-shaven, his graying hair done in a buzz cut.

"First time up, my brother?" Alan asked Tim.

Tim nodded.

"Don't need no fucking chair up there when you got wings," Alan said, smiling. Tim was smiling too. "Fuck that, right?" Alan added. They bumped fists. I wanted to be Alan's friend.

How many days do you experience something for the first time?

We rose, slowly at first. We rose and turned, facing the East River, Brooklyn Heights. We rose faster and then pushed forward, the bubble glass so close, looking down over all of it, too much to take in. Up the Hudson River, small planes out the window in the distance, above us the flight path to LaGuardia. The cross streets, the perfect grid; the buildings, different heights, straining toward the sky. We sat in the snug space, faces almost touching the glass, looking down, palms tingling. Clara placed her hand over mine.

We banked right over the Bronx, over Yankee Stadium, to the East River. The city small and quiet below. We should be required to take flight from time to time, to see anew, to see how small and fragile we are.

"You done good, Bud," Tim said through the headsets.

We kept flying.

I HAD A LOVELY EVENING

"Do you walk in your dreams?" Clara asked Tim.

We sat in Tim's kitchen, mostly empty cartons of Thai food in front of us, a near-empty bottle of red wine. Music played low, Oscar Peterson's live BBC concert where he was joined by Joe Pass on guitar and later Count Basie. It was one of Tim's favorites.

For the better part of an hour they had been talking like college roommates who hadn't seen each other in a decade. I sat and listened.

"I used to," he said. "All the time, at first. Less so now. I crawl sometimes."

"I can't run in my dreams," Clara said.

"I can't run when I'm awake."

Clara cackled, her head falling forward. Tim laughed and took a sip of wine, began to refill our glasses but found an empty bottle.

"George," Tim said, handing me the empty bottle. "Be a good man."

I stood to fetch another bottle, found the corkscrew, and twisted it open. I refilled their glasses.

Clara looked over at me, eyes wide. "George?"

"It's true," Tim said. "George Nicholas Stanley."

"You look like a George," she said, smiling.

"You do look like a George," Tim added.

Maybe it was the wine and the music, that time of night, still early, that giddy feeling sitting with friends, a good conversation going, that you don't want to end.

"Where's home?" Tim asked.

"Cincinnati."

"Parents still there?"

"Mother is. Father died last fall."

"I'm sorry."

"Yeah."

"Tell me about him."

She started to say something and stopped. I poured more wine.

"He was the best man I ever met. Firefighter. Lieutenant. Loved it but secretly wanted to be a teacher. Read all the time. He took me to Ireland for my sixteenth birthday. Out west, to Galway and Connemara. To Clifden, where his grandfather was from. Have you been?"

Tim shook his head.

"It's incredible. And the people."

"I must go. And now you're off to Bhutan."

"Yes. Teaching English. Change of scenery. The American belief that if you travel far enough physically you can escape yourself."

Tim liked that. "I know the feeling."

Clara sipped her drink.

"How are you feeling these days?" Tim asked.

She smiled and looked at him. "Better." She nodded. "I'm guessing you might know something about . . . depression."

"All there is," he said, still smiling.

"Hard to describe to the uninitiated."

He nodded.

She paused again, wincing, moving her hand, as if trying to coax the words out.

"You wanted the pain to end," Tim said quietly.

She nodded.

"Can I . . ." she began but faltered.

"What?" Tim asked.

"Nothing," she said, smiling.

"No small talk among friends. Ask."

"I just wondered . . . I mean as someone who . . . with the people I was with and what you went through . . ."

"The answer is yes," Tim said gently. "I thought about suicide."

"I hope it's okay . . ."

Tim shrugged. "Of course. I did more than think about it, actually."

Tim's expression didn't change. He nodded and pulled the sleeve of his sweater back, turned his wrist over, and showed her the thick keloid scar running crossways along the inside of his wrist. He'd told me once he'd gotten it in a boating accident.

"I lied," he said and shrugged, looking at me. "I tried twice. Turns out I wasn't good at it."

"Why didn't you ever tell me?" I asked.

"It's hard to describe what it was like," he continued. "Just a constant twenty on a scale of one to ten. Nerve pain. Anytime I moved. All I did was try to find periods during the day when there was no pain. Moments. I'd doze off. Until the next throb, the next electric jolt. And then there was the reality of it.

The unending nightmare of it. I'd sit there all day and just . . . weep. I was thirty-one years old and I felt like my life was over. And that . . . psychic pain and sadness turned to rage. Just . . . this rage. The world had screwed me and I played an endless loop of *if only*, of *I want my life back*, of *this isn't happening, this can't be happening, this isn't fair*."

He stared at his wineglass and sighed.

"To fully describe what it feels like to be imprisoned in a seated position . . . when you look at me and imagine it . . . it's way worse."

He sipped his wine.

"So, being the clever man I am, I started drinking a lot," he said, pulling a face, looking at his wineglass. "Which, as someone still new to the world of paralysis, was not a good idea. I paid the inelegant consequences. But . . . I didn't care. I mean, I really didn't. I was done. I overdosed on pills once. That was ugly. They had to pump my stomach. But I learned from it. So the next time I used a scalpel, which I had stolen. That's the way to go if you're serious. Were it not for a remarkable trauma surgeon who wasn't supposed to be working that night, you're sitting at a kitchen table in Brooklyn by yourselves."

Clara reached her hand across and touched Tim's hand. He looked up at her. She lifted her glass.

"To failed suicides," she said.

Tim swallowed with difficulty. We touched glasses.

It's strange what you remember. How he brought his wineglass to his lips, sipped, how the wine dribbled down the side of his mouth and onto his shirt. How I thought he was being funny, doing it on purpose. How, in the instant I realized something was wrong, how there was a shift in energy, like a sudden cold front, like a current of danger, of fear. If there were video of it all, it would last two or three seconds. But in my memory, in the near frame-by-frame replay, it's so slow, the feelings so palpable. The glass falls and rolls down his shirt and onto the floor, shattering, the sound an explosion. His eyes went wide and his head flew back, the force of it pulling his torso with him, his chair—the wheels not set in their lock position—going backward. Clara screamed. I don't remember getting there, leaving my seat, of that I have no memory. But somehow I did, my left hand out, catching his head as it slammed to the floor, the wine on his shirt like blood.

He was breathing and I was screaming his name and Clara was on the phone to 911. The paramedics arrived minutes later, Clara meeting them at the door. We watched them in a stunned awe, neither of us knowing what to do. They moved with remarkable speed and calm, placing him on a gurney, but talking to me at the same time, asking questions that I tried to answer while also trying to understand what was happening, as they asked again, his name please, age, my name and number, *bring his prescriptions to the hospital for the ER doctor, no you cannot ride with us, Methodist, we're taking him to Methodist, yes, he's alive.* And they were gone, the siren surely waking the block, faces looking out the windows.

I sat in the large, overlit waiting room of Methodist Hospital in Park Slope. A Hasidic Jewish man and a woman I took to be his wife sat across from me. She stared at her phone and he slept. In the corner, a woman spoke Russian on her phone in a whisper.

It was late now, near midnight, the energy of a hospital during the day faded. The gift shop and cafeteria were closed. The beeping of monitors and low-level chatter at the nurses' station. Clara said she'd stay, but I urged her to go home. She had packing and shopping to do for the trip.

I sat and waited. A world at night, unseen if you are lucky, of waiting and hoping.

I watched a man in his twenties walk in holding a bloody bandage on the side of his head. I watched a woman in her fifties wheel in an older man who she said was having trouble breathing. I watched a man in his thirties help another man hobble in, his ankle swollen. I watched the Hasidic man wake, walk to the vending machine, and get a hot chocolate and a pack of Lorna Doones. He and his wife silently nibbled on them. I leafed through a two-year-old *People* magazine.

Before Clara had left, she looked at me, held the look.

"Your breathing is off," she said.

"What?"

"Little bursts."

"I'm just tired," I said.

"No," she said, shaking her head. "The body holds trauma."

She gently placed her hand on my stomach.

"You feel it here first, don't you?"

She was close now, a few inches from my face.

"I don't . . . I'm not sure what you mean."

"Yes. You do."

She moved her hands a little higher up, along my ribs. "Then here. Your breathing. Little bursts. Fight. Flight."

She reached for my hands, turned them over, ran her fingertips over my palms. "Then here. Tingly. Sweaty. Little jolts of electricity."

She then gently held the sides of my head. "Then here. The thoughts. *Fear. Run. Escape.* And then here." She put her hand over my heart.

"You have a wound," she said. "If it was a cut, you'd have put Neosporin on it, a Band-Aid. But you did nothing and so it festers. You and me and a billion others. We walk around with these deep wounds that alter how we think and what we say, the relationships we have, who we trust, the decisions we make. That keep us from really living."

She touched my cheek. This thing she did. I closed my eyes.

"We hold the past in our body," she said. "It never forgets. But it can learn to let it go."

She held my face in her hands and then kissed my cheek.

It was after 2 a.m. when a nurse who introduced herself as Tara came out and said I could see Tim. She walked me to his room, adjusted his IV, and made a note on her iPad.

"What are you still doing here?" he said. "Go home."

I stood by the bed. He looked pale.

"What happened?" I asked.

"Do you know what deep vein thrombosis is?"

"An English punk band?"

"Close. A blood clot. People in chairs are at very high risk of getting them. This isn't news for me. But I hadn't been feeling well. Shortness of breath. Tired a lot. That was part of the reason for Los Angeles. Specialist at Cedars-Sinai."

"Why didn't you tell me?"

He shrugged.

"So it's manageable."

"In most people, yes. But . . ." He looked at me, his expression changed.

I felt my stomach drop. "What?"

"They said I'll never be able to try out for the Ice Capades."

I heard Tara snort.

"You suck," I said. "You suck so much."

He smiled, pleased with himself.

"It happened before," Tim said. "About ten years ago."

"Oh."

"I felt it. I got lightheaded. Overtired. It's fine. As long as any clotting doesn't break away and make a beeline to my heart. I'm fine. To the extent that a sixty-year-old man half of whose body is dead is fine. Go home. What time is it, anyway?"

"Almost two thirty," I said. I looked at him. "How long do you have to stay?"

"Doctor said a day or two. Observation. Will know more tomorrow. How's Clara?"

"She waited. I told her to go home. She said to tell you that except for you almost dying she had a lovely evening."

"She's nice."

"She is."

Tim stared. "We like her, I think."

"We might. But she's leaving soon for a year."

"So what's a year?"

"A long time."

Tim turned to look at Tara. "Tara. Would you wait for a guy for a year?"

"Absolutely not."

"See? Tara would wait."

"Your friend is quite a character," Tara said to me.

"I was cruel to an internist," Tim said. "Tara, tell him."

Tara grinned. "I'm not saying a thing."

"What did you do?" I asked.

"I told him I had no feeling in my legs. He'd just come in and hadn't looked at the chart. You should have seen the poor man's face when he started testing my legs."

"Made my day," Tara said.

Tim yawned. Tara gave him a pill, which Tim took, accepting the cup of water she held to wash it down.

"We should let him rest now," she said.

"I'll stay over if you want."

"That's only for family, I'm afraid," Tara said.

"He is family," Tim said.

I stood by the side of the bed. He motioned me toward him with his hand. I leaned forward and he kissed me on the forehead.

"Now go. Also, no offense. But I'm tired of funerals," he said.

"Me, too. People talk about how fun they are but I think they're exaggerating."

He closed his eyes, smiling. "You're a moron. That's what I love about you."

SEE YOU LATER

I woke late, around nine, texted Tim. **You good? How'd you sleep?**

Slept well, he replied almost immediately. Saw the doctor. Cleared to go home. Come by at noon? I'd walk but...

I'll be there.

He responded with a disco-dancing man.

I made coffee, shaved, showered, and dressed. I picked up a clean shirt from Tim's apartment and checked the cabinets, made a list on my phone of things I'd pick up for dinner.

Tim kept the car in a neighbor's driveway. It was next to an empty lot that had once, a long time ago, been home to a brownstone, but that had been destroyed in a fire. The family never rebuilt and instead left the plot to the city. A group of volunteer gardeners tended to it. They opened it to the public on weekends.

I made a detour to get him pizza from Fascati in Brooklyn Heights. His favorite. A few slices and a root beer. They made their own. We'd drive up sometimes, talk about the Yankees with Jeff, who owned the place, had worked there his entire adult life with his father and uncle, both long dead now, and who lived on Staten Island but mostly lived and died with every Yankees game.

Fast-moving clouds, the sun sneaking out. Still cool, but the warm weather so close, the trees in bloom, baseball on the radio.

Our lives each day are a series of choices. It's one decision over another. One person over another. One job in a new city over staying at the old job. Whole worlds of what-ifs. What if Jen hadn't had the affair? What if we'd had a baby? What if I had never met Tim? Whole parallel worlds, parallel paths that are there for the taking. It's the chicken over the fish, even though you had no idea the chicken was bad and you ended up with food poisoning, missing work the next day when the gunman came into the office, killing nine, and saving your life. It's the broken washing machine in your apartment building, forcing you to lug your duffel bag of soiled linens five blocks, the strap of the bag breaking, the frustration causing you to burst into tears and a man named Michael stopping to ask if you are okay, Michael with the kind face who offers you Kleenex and who, in two years' time, will be the father of your two beautiful children. Lives are changed by seemingly unconnected, random decisions that change everything. So it is also the detour to get a few slices of pizza and two bottles of root beer so we could eat lunch. Which is why I wasn't in the room when Tim died.

The call with Tim's sister, Louisa, is hazy. She screamed. I remember that. She screamed and said, *No, no, no.* She said it three times. I think I said, *I'm so sorry.* Or *It can't be real.*

I don't remember. She mentioned a flight. I was sitting in the car, with the box of pizza.

You have to identify the body. You have to go into a room in the basement of Methodist Hospital in Park Slope, Brooklyn, near the Barnes & Noble and across the street from the Five Guys and just half a block from the Jersey Mike's Subs, where people went about their day as if nothing had happened. No one stopped or bowed their head. There was no moment of silence. A garbage truck sped by, muffler rattling, leaving in its wake a sickly, putrid smell. A pedestrian gave the finger to an Uber driver who ran a red light. A homeless man in many layers of clothes wearing a baseball cap that said *Life Is Good* looked at me with wild eyes and said, "Jesus ain't Michael Jordan!"

In the hospital, a woman whose name I don't remember greeted me and took me to an office. I had to show my license. I had to sign a form. She put a plastic shopping bag with his clothes on the desk. She talked but I didn't really hear her.

It felt like a movie. The room, the morgue. It felt like a TV show. It wasn't real.

And then I saw him. The same face only different. His coloring gone. He looked peaceful. Maybe it was my imagination, but it almost looked as if he had the slightest smile on his face. Of this memory I cannot be sure. I was tired and confused and couldn't seem to get a handle on my thoughts. There was a buzzy numbness in my head. The room was cold but had a dampness to it, the smell of cleaning products. I wanted to run. I couldn't move.

"I'm sorry, Mr. Stanley. I know this must be very . . . hard. It's just a formality," she said. "We just need you to say, 'Yes, this is Tim Charvat.'"

Where was he, I wondered in a kind of confused shock. Because this wasn't him. This bluish-gray body devoid of life. Where was my friend?

"Yes," I said, my voice sounding thin. "That's Tim Charvat."

THE OBITUARY WRITER

Leo sat on his stoop writing in a notebook, head down, face close to the page. A fire truck wailed in the distance but continued to grow fainter. He looked up when he heard me approach and put the notebook down. He slid over to make space for me and I sat on the stairs next to him, Muffin at our feet.

"Tim is dead, isn't he."

I nodded.

He stared at me. "Are you sad?"

"I am."

"But you know what?"

"What?"

"Like, you knew him and isn't that better than never knowing him even though he's dead now?"

I wanted to reach down and hold him, bony bird of a body, all eyes.

"What do you think about it all?" I asked.

"Well. My grampa died. And we had a gerbil that died. And Lucy my sister. So. I just think *Nope, nope, nope, nope* when I saw their dead bodies because that's not them. I have them in here."

He pointed to his head. "They're all here. I talk to them all the time."

"You do?"

"Course. My sister is always with me. Tim will always be with you."

I had trouble swallowing.

He reached over, without looking, and I felt his little paw of a hand take mine. We sat, looking out at the street, waiting for life to continue, holding hands, holding on.

Clara came over. There was talk of food, of making something, ordering something. We did neither. Instead, we lay on my bed, fully clothed, staring at the ceiling, waiting for sleep to come. I dozed and watched as Clara slept.

In the morning, there was a knock on the door. I opened it to see Esther, her eyes red-rimmed. I wasn't sure what to do. She didn't seem like a person who hugged. She leaned her head against my chest and with her fist pounded my shoulder. I put my arms around her and she sobbed.

In hindsight it was a mistake to go to the office. To lie to Lev the security guard that Tuan needed his inhaler.

I didn't look well. I'd not shaved in a while and I might have been wearing clothes that I had been wearing for a few days. Still, it was my chair.

"Excuse me," I said to the bro. "Get out of my chair."

"Whoa. Bro. Who are you?"

Tuan stood, an alarmed look on his face. "Bud," he said, though I felt he wanted to say more. He had called when he found out, a man who monitored death. We spoke briefly, and then later that evening he dropped off a Thai noodle soup that he said had medicinal properties. He had an Uber waiting and left as quickly as he'd arrived, a brief and awkward hug.

"I'm the obituary writer," I said to the bro. "Like him," I added, motioning toward Tuan.

He stared. "Ohhh. The drunk-obit guy."

I shouldn't have grabbed him by the throat. That was wrong. And I shouldn't have pushed him up against the wall. Nor did I know I was going to do that. It's remarkable what you can do when you don't care what anyone thinks anymore.

"Shut shut shut your fucking mouth," I said, the cadence surprising to me. "I have an obituary to write. Now fuck off."

Apparently my voice was louder than I'd remembered. Because there were people outside of our office now, staring, mouths open, the low murmur of a live event that you almost never fully take in in the moment but remember later. That's when I saw Howard's face. The bro looked at Howard. "Get your boy under control here, dude," he said to Howard. At least I think he said it to him. I was still holding his throat and his speech was gurgled.

Howard didn't say anything for a moment. He looked from the bro to me to Tuan and then back to the bro. And here I thought I was a goner. Surely I was a goner. I was holding the bro by the throat, which isn't nice. Or acceptable by any company policy (nor, apparently, is publishing your own false obituary). Still, the bro was a dick, and if I was going to go out, I was going to go out squeezing the bro's neck like olives at pressing time. But the energy drained from me, as if someone had thrown a switch. The cortisol burst gone. Nothing now. I needed to sit. I didn't feel well. I let go of his neck and he staggered—too dramatically, in my opinion—a few feet and muttered (see if you can guess), "Like . . . bro . . ." *Bro* being a universal word, a cypher, a key to unlock all meaning.

"I'm sorry," I muttered to the bro.

I turned and looked at Howard. A small crowd of my colleagues had formed behind him, looks of concern on their pale faces. It dawned on me that journalists are pale. I wasn't sure why. Maybe all that indoor work. We didn't look like handsome TV people.

I saw Tuan. "Bud," he said, and put his slim hand on my shoulder, my friend.

To Howard I said, "I have to write his obit, Howard."

"I know. I'm so sorry."

Tuan held out typewritten pages, handing them to me. I looked at him, then down at the first sentence.

Tim Charvat, longtime adviser to Sotheby's on twentieth-century art, patron to writers, poets, filmmakers, and dreamers, bon vivant, and man about town, died suddenly at NewYork-Presbyterian Brooklyn Methodist Hospital. He was 59. Mr. Charvat, a one-time Peace Corps volunteer, was a passionate lover of the arts in all forms. He advised the New York City Board of Education and helped design an art curriculum for elementary school students. An accident at age 31 left Mr. Charvat a paraplegic. The accident, and life in a wheelchair, did not slow him down. Indeed, it seemed to drive him to do more for others.

The words began to blur. I turned to Tuan, who shrugged his slim shoulders. "I thought maybe I could help."

I reached for his arm.

I needed to leave, to go home, to sleep. I turned to the bro. "I'm so sorry. I didn't mean . . . I'm sorry." I extended my hand.

"Fuck you, dude. I'm going to sue your ass. Wait till my father hears this."

Howard said, "Get your things." At first I thought he was talking to me. But I saw that he was looking at the bro. "Get your things, leave now. And tell your father to go fuck himself."

Which is when the assembled started applauding.

Louisa flew in from Los Angeles and Esther made soup and Clara got bread from the French place on the corner and we sat at the kitchen table, the sounds of our spoons clinking against the bowls, the tick of the large clock that hung on the kitchen wall.

He wanted sneakers. He'd left instructions for Esther detailing where and how he wanted to be laid out. The funeral home on Clinton Street, the suit, the shirt, the tie. And a new pair of P.F. Flyers, size ten and a half. Esther showed me, asked me if I would get them.

I walked the garment bag over to the Giordano Funeral Home. A man I would come to know as Aldo greeted me. He was the funeral director and would be handling Tim's service. I handed him the bag and asked him for a favor. He looked at me for a time. It was difficult to read his face, his largely flat expression. "It's unlikely," he said to my request, but asked me to write down my phone number anyway.

He called two days later and told me to come by in the late afternoon.

He greeted me at the door and did not seem pleased. I followed him through the old brick town house that had once been a robber baron's mansion, down a staircase and then another, to a brick-walled basement with remarkably clean linoleum floors. We passed a few closed doors with pebbled glass until we arrived at a door at the end of the hallway. He put his hand on the knob, stopped, and looked at me.

"I'm assuming you've never done this before." It was a statement, not a question.

"Done what?"

"Been in the room with a deceased person."

"Wakes."

He nodded. "This is very different. Are you sure?"

I wasn't. I wanted to turn and go but I nodded. He opened the door and we walked in. The floor was white. I remember that. A large and very bright circular light overhead. Two tables, both stainless steel. The one closer to us was empty. On the other one was Tim.

I looked at his face but quickly looked away. I looked, instead, at his suit, at the clean white floor, at the closed cabinets with words stenciled on them that were a blur to me. Something fluid. Something else. Chemical names. In the corner a large sink, the kind you'd find in an old laundry room. The light smell of formaldehyde, sickly sweet.

The room, I realized, was his. Not his in the sense of ownership but his. His office, where he spent his days. I noticed again the organization, the surgical cleanliness, the sharp lighting. Nothing to hide here. I noticed the hum of a fan or air-conditioning. Ventilation, perhaps. It was cold.

"You okay?" he asked.

I nodded, then turned and looked. I stood closer now and looked again at his face, which wasn't his face, was no longer his face. Light and energy gone.

My eyes fell to the dark gray suit jacket, the white shirt, spread collar, silver tie, thick half-Windsor knot, dimple in the center. Someone had taken time to do that, taken care to make it look like that. I looked over at Aldo, who stood still and quiet, his hands behind his back. I wondered briefly if he had been in the military. His bearing. His stock-stillness. This was a man used to standing in a room with someone looking at a dead body.

"What happens?" I asked.

"When?"

"When you bring someone in. When you brought him in?"

"I wonder if we shouldn't focus on the task at hand."

"I'd like to know."

He watched me, as if trying to decide something. "He was placed on the table," Aldo continued.

"But how did he get here?"

"I picked him up. At the mortuary at the hospital."

I don't know why, exactly, but I wanted to know the details. I wanted to know where Tim had been the past few days. "And then? When he got here, I mean."

Aldo looked at me. I noticed, as he blinked, how long his eyelashes were. A prominent nose that looked as if it may have been broken. He had the look of someone who knew his way around a boxing ring.

"The first thing we do is wash the body."

"You did this?"

"Yes."

"Is the water warm?" I asked.

"What?"

"Is the water warm? When you wash the body?"

"Yes."

"Then what?"

Again he waited.

"I'm sorry," I said. "I just . . . need to know."

"We make an incision here . . ." he said, pointing to the base of his neck, just above the clavicle. "We insert"—he turned and pointed to a clear rubber hose, maybe a quarter of an inch in diameter—"we insert a hose and drain the blood from the body."

I continued to listen. Of course I listened. I heard the words—"small incision one inch to the left of the belly button and one inch up." But I also drifted, looked briefly at Tim, then away. I looked at his hand, his ear, his shoeless feet. Where was he? Not this body. But *him*. His essence. That ineffable thing. Is animation, life force, just brain function and electricity? Heartbeat? Is that all it is? Is that all it is that built the Brooklyn Bridge and invented penicillin and wrote "Let It Be" and created Cool Whip?

Aldo had finished. He waited.

"Why do we embalm people?"

"To slow the decaying process."

"When did we start doing it?"

"Civil War. So many dead. The trips home were long. No refrigeration."

More nodding. Not that I understood anything at this point. But the facts were soothing somehow.

"How many . . . How many people have you . . . cared for? Here." I was struggling with syntax for some reason.

"I don't know. Thousands."

"Anyone you knew?"

"Yes. Friends. Neighbors. My brother-in-law. Firefighter at 9/11."

"I'm sorry."

He nodded once. His patience with me seemed limitless. I felt Aldo knew things I didn't.

"Do they all... I'm just... It must be difficult some days... so I'm just wondering if they all... these strangers... if they matter to you? I mean, I could understand if..."

And here I seemed to run out of words, out of steam.

He breathed deeply and I was afraid I had offended him.

"I didn't mean to offend..."

He shook his head. "You didn't."

He paused and examined his hands.

"There are three people in the room when I work. There's me. There's the deceased. And there's God." He shrugged, his enigmatic expression never changing. No sarcasm, no wasted words. Just the thoughts of a man who has seen behind a curtain most of us never will.

"They all matter to me," he added. "How could they not?"

Aldo walked to a cabinet, opened it, and removed the box with the sneakers, the new P.F. Flyers. He placed it on the empty table, opened the box, took a sneaker, and, as if holding a Fabergé egg, loosened the laces, pulled back the cloth tongue, and handed me a pristine Bob Cousy–model reissue P.F. Flyer, size ten and a half.

I turned to Tim's sock-clad foot, gently holding the heel.

"Left," Aldo said.

I looked up, confused. "The other foot," he said. I looked at the sneaker I was holding. Left foot.

I held his foot by the heel and tried to fit the sneaker over it. No luck. Aldo placed a wooden block carved in a semicircle under Tim's heel. "Try this," he said quietly. He took the shoe from me, undid the laces more, pulled the tongue back farther, mimed how he would do it, and handed it back to me.

I fitted the sneaker onto Tim's foot and it went on smoothly this time. I made sure the heel was fully in but pushed too hard and the wooden block fell over. I quickly adjusted it.

"Hey," Aldo said gently. "You're doing great." He mimed placing Tim's foot against his own leg, mimed tying the shoe. I held Tim's heel, propped it against my thigh, and gently tightened the laces, going eyelet by eyelet, a thing a child does a thousand times after school, before a practice, before a game. Sneakers, cleats, skates. That moment leaning over, wiggling your toes in, tightening them up, double knot. He played baseball, soccer, hockey. The freedom of movement. What a thing to be taken from you.

I gently placed his foot back down and moved the wooden block to his other heel. Aldo was waiting with the other sneaker, laces loosened, tongue back. I took it, put it on Tim's foot. Easier this time. Little tug on the laces, pull up the slack, tug, slack. I tied them and removed the block, handing it to Aldo, who replaced it in a cabinet.

Aldo examined my work, gently smoothing Tim's pant leg, adjusting the bows on the laces I'd just made so that they fell evenly, like fallen rabbit's ears. I watched him, this craftsman, this last person who would ever touch Tim, touch the thousands of people who would lay in this room, watched the care with which he did it.

He stood, seemingly pleased with the work, sighed, and quietly said, "Shall we?" extending his arm to guide me to the door.

I nodded but wasn't quite ready to leave. I looked at my friend, at his suit, at where his trousers met his perfect sneakers.

The thought came fast. *Tie them together*, he seemed to say to me. *I dare you.* He would have loved that. Standing, finally, in some distant place, some magical, stardust place where we go, when we go, if we go, Tim finally able to stand, to walk, the joy of it, the sudden desire, in his new sneaks, his handsome suit, ready to burst into a run, and then falling from the knot tying his two sneakers together. "That sonuvabitch," he would have said, smiling.

People lined Clinton Street in Carroll Gardens, waiting on a cool, spring evening, the trees in bloom, crocuses and daffodils seeming to smile in window boxes.

Louisa and I passed friends and neighbors, nods and quiet hellos. I saw Clara in the line and stopped, reached for her hand.

She forced a smile. "Go," she said.

Louisa and I made our way to the entrance, where Aldo stood, waiting for us. He introduced himself to Louisa and led us inside, to the viewing room. She reached for my hand and I walked in with her until she stopped, a few yards from the casket, and let go. Dozens of bouquets of flowers, the smell filling the room. She walked to the casket, stared, then knelt by her brother, her only brother, her last living relative, her head falling forward, shoulders heaving. I looked away and saw Aldo standing at the entrance to the room.

After a time Louisa stood and walked past me, touched my shoulder. I walked over and knelt before the casket. I looked everywhere but at him. At the metal casket itself, the silver handles, the satin lining. And finally at him.

How rude of the dead to die. How selfish. Wherever they are, no pain, in eternal darkness or wondrous afterlife. And here we are, tears streaming down our cheeks, the knotted stomach and clammy palms, a feeling akin to falling, in a dream that won't end.

I wouldn't make the same mistake again, even though I wanted to reach out and touch his hand.

"You can't go yet," I said. "I'm not ready."

I reached out and laid my hand over his.

Louisa asked me to stand with her in the receiving line and I introduced her to friends and neighbors. What struck me most was how much people were laughing. The stories they were telling about him, Louisa in that fragile emotional place of vacillating between laughing and crying. Someone had set up bottles of wine and beer, cheese and crackers. People mingled and drank. It got louder. It was exactly what Tim would have wanted.

I woke in a panic, thinking I'd missed the funeral.

I had stayed up the night before, working on my remarks. Louisa had asked if I might say something. I wrote and rewrote and couldn't get it right. There wasn't enough time, I was too tired, too stressed, *How can I get it down in time?* I had fallen asleep after three, I think. It's all a bit hazy. I showered and dressed, a black suit, and on my way out I opened the door to his apartment.

My phone rang. I looked at the number. Work.

"Hello?"

"Hi, is this Bud Stanley?"

"Speaking."

"Bud, it's Buckley Shames from work."

"Yes. Buckley. Hi."

"I hope I'm not getting you at a bad time."

"Nope. Just on my way to a funeral."

"I get that. That's very funny. Obituary writer humor. So listen. The reason for my call. I wanted to give you the good news that you are no longer dead to the company. You're officially alive."

"Oh. Okay."

"I knew you'd be pleased. We can now prepare the paperwork for your termination. Until then you are still officially suspended from the company. We'll be in touch. Have a great day."

There is a 197-year-old Gothic Revival–style Episcopal church in Brooklyn Heights that Tim would go to on occasion. He had been a consultant on the restoration. Apparently, the original ceiling was painted over. Once they removed that layer, Tim said, this extraordinary painting was revealed. Brilliant yellow-gold stars on a beautiful blue background. A magical night sky. A view to the heavens.

I looked for Clara in the crowd but didn't see her.

Louisa and I made our way into the church.

Louisa spoke. I listened but also drifted. I'm embarrassed to admit it. I wanted to listen but I couldn't seem to focus. I also knew I had to get up after her and speak.

I am not a natural or comfortable speaker. I am too nervous, too aware of my voice, my tendency to say "umm." The walk from the pew to the altar to the lectern seemed to take a long time. I was aware of my breathing, my dry mouth, of trying to clear my throat. I nodded as I passed the minister, who was seated on the altar. She was a woman of perhaps fifty, with beautiful white teeth and dark brown skin.

"Thank you," I whispered to her, although I don't know why.

I stepped to the lectern, placed the pages before me, and adjusted the microphone. I rarely wear a suit and was aware of the collar of my shirt, tight on my neck, my necktie. I cleared my throat again and then turned to the minister and mouthed, "Water?"

Again the lovely smile as she pointed and I saw, on a shelf in the lectern, a bottle of water, a gift from the gods.

"Sorry. I'm just going to do this first," I said into the microphone, too close.

People chuckled. I opened the bottle and drank deeply, then replaced it on the shelf.

I looked out at the nearly full church and picked out faces I knew. Howard. Tuan. Martin. Diminutive Julia Felder. Esther. John and Caroline from the deli. Leo's parents. Benni. Leo. Little Leo. He offered a small wave and I waved back.

Speak, Bud. For Christ's sake. And then I saw Clara and she smiled. Just a small grin that seemed to save me.

"We are here today," I said, "to honor the life of my dear friend, Chaim Lipschitz."

I waited. I looked out over the faces. I'd made a mistake. And then they started laughing.

"I am so sorry," I added. "I've brought the wrong eulogy."

Good man, Bud, I could almost hear Tim say. *Do not let them feel sad.*

"My name is Bud Stanley," I continued, "and I was, like all of you, lucky enough to be a friend of Tim's. I'm not sure why I'm up here. I have little to add to what Louisa said so beautifully. No one knew him better."

Here I looked up, locked eyes with Louisa.

"I'm not exactly sure how to begin to describe Tim Charvat. So I'll start with the time he went skydiving. A man without the use of his legs let himself be pushed out of a plane. I know this because I went, too. One of us screamed. I won't say who but it wasn't him. Now, granted, an instructor was on each of our backs. But in those seconds before the parachute opens, before it jerks you back up, you think, you *feel*, like you are going to die. And what is thrilling is that you don't. He wanted *that*. That thrilling feeling of being alive."

I cleared my throat and sipped from the bottle of water.

"He loved life. I don't mean that as some . . . cliché. He didn't just go through the days. He made them . . . matter. Unable to walk and yet reaching for life every day. With each salon, each party, each random meeting in the street."

I looked up again, out over the rows of people. I hadn't seen her before, but there, in a middle pew, was Jen. Jen, and next to her, the Englishman. Perhaps I stared too long.

"Tim and I spent the last few weeks going to the wakes and funerals of strangers. We went to the wake of Judy Bennett, aged seventy-seven, and the funeral of a Dr. Samuel Gauss, aged eighty-six. To the wake of Jan Kaminski, seventy-six. Molly Donnelly, forty-three, and Eddie Donnelly, six. To the funeral mass of Ava Gutierrez, forty-one, and Vincenzo Marchetti, sixty-three. Tim would have wanted me to mention their names. Tim was, in his own way, trying to show me something. Teach me something. Here's what I learned. Nothing. I learned nothing. In the movie version of this eulogy, they would change that to some bullshit Steven Spielberg ending about how I learned so much, how the scales fell from my eyes and I saw the value of life. But the world didn't change for me because these people—as lovely as I'm sure they all were—were no longer in it. Death didn't . . . It didn't enter my soul and . . . leave a mark."

A siren in the distance outside. The clouds must have shifted because a thin shaft of light came through one of the stained-glass windows on the right.

"And then Tim died. And death entered my soul. I think the question is, what do I do with that? What do *we* do with that? There's this . . . quote . . . from an ancient Sanskrit text, the Mahabharata. And please don't think I knew any of this. It's all Tim. A character in the book is asked what the greatest wonder in the world is. And he answers . . . He says, *The greatest wonder is that every day, all around us, people die, but we act as if it couldn't happen to us.* And yet . . . living is hard. What's the point? Why are we even here? How can we know all this . . . stuff about how to live, about how there is literally a one-in-four-hundred-trillion chance of ever being born and yet, in the next moment, when some jackass cuts me off on the Belt Parkway and then gives me the finger, I give him the finger and wish I had a shoulder-mounted rocket launcher on the passenger seat. Oh, humans. Or maybe it's just the Irish . . ."

I looked out over the faces, at Tuan, at Leo. At Jen. What came out next wasn't on the page.

"People can break you," I said. "Through pain. But also . . . also . . . through love. The feelings so strong, the loss so great . . ."

I faltered, never the good ad-libber. But I kept going.

"I was broken two years ago. And Tim . . . he showed me grace and dignity and kindness when I had none, wasn't able to see it, kind of gave up. Tim saved my life because he showed me how to live."

I looked at Tuan. He was blinking quickly and gave me just a bit of a smile.

"So what now? After we all leave this church, leave the reception, go home, put in laundry, watch a show on Netflix, go to bed, get up tomorrow. And tomorrow. And tomorrow. This has to mean something. Something lasting. I mean, why do we do this thing, wakes and funerals? A sign of respect, of course, for the dead. A sign of respect for the family. But I wonder if it's also for all of us. Each of us here. Surely it's a reminder. But perhaps also a call to a state of grace, if only for a few moments. A pause to remember how fleeting our own mortality is. I had an office mate."

I was tempted to look at Tuan but couldn't quite do it.

"He's a . . . he's a dear friend," I continued, "who I've never told how much I love. And when I first started my job with him and his annoying office habits, he said to me, he said, 'The good news is that someone died today.' I thought he was joking. He later explained that this thing we do, the writing of these things, the celebration of someone's life, it's a gift, a reminder. What death dares us to do, is celebrate it. To celebrate the gift of life in its fleeting face."

I looked down at my speech, at the last line, and smiled. I took the pages, folded them in half, and put them in my jacket pocket.

"Here we are, as Tim would have said, all of us, on this lovely day, alive. What are we going to do with that?"

Louisa invited everyone back to Tim's. There was coffee and wine and food. I don't know how it got there but it appeared. Neighbors, friends. Sal's on Court Street sent pizzas. Esther organized it, arranged it on a table in the dining room. Julia Feldman walked around and filled people's glasses. I saw Clara sitting with Louisa.

Tuan and Howard found me, each surprising me with a hug.

"Thank you for coming," I said.

Howard nodded.

Tuan said, "Your eulogy was beautiful. Who wrote it?"

"I've missed you, Tuan. Speaking of. Our friend Buckley was kind enough to call me this morning."

"You're joking," Howard said.

I shook my head.

"Buffoon."

"What?" Tuan asked.

"I'm alive again. To the company."

"Let's . . . talk about this another time."

Tuan looked as if he wanted to say something. Instead he went to get food. Louisa was calling me over.

"We'll talk, I guess," I said to Howard.

He nodded.

"Hey," I said. "Honestly. Thanks for coming."

Louisa stayed for a few days. I forget how many exactly. I forget a lot from that time. We walked the Brooklyn waterfront, once home to cargo ship piers and then abandoned for decades, now green paths and playing fields. We walked and watched the big orange Staten Island Ferries pass. We watched the massive container ships waiting for high tide. In the evening we ordered in and talked of him. Or not. Sometimes we watched a movie, a *Law & Order* rerun, something, anything, to try and escape for a time.

Louisa slept in Tim's bed.

There were some paintings of his she wanted. We took them to UPS and they packed them for us, mailed them to her home in Los Angeles. There was a dresser that had been their father's, a wedding gift from their mother. There was an old wool jacket from L.L.Bean that Louisa had given Tim years before. She put it on, too big for her, but she rolled the sleeves back, looked at me, and forced a smile.

"I don't like the East Coast anymore," she said as we waited for an Uber. "I used to love it, felt like it was home. This landscape and weather. No more. It's too cold, too dirty. Too many dead relatives."

In March, on Tim's birthday, she would come back and we would go to the family's plot in Connecticut and have a small service.

Her car pulled up and I put her suitcase in the trunk.

She hugged me. "You'll come visit, yes? You'll keep in touch?"

"Of course."

She took a letter from her bag and handed it to me. It had my name on it in Tim's handwriting. She hugged me again and got into the car. I stood there and watched her drive away.

No one tells you about how, in the days and weeks after, when others have moved on, perhaps rarely thinking of the event, the passing, you sit there and think, *How am I supposed to live?*

To my great embarrassment, I believed in Santa until I was twelve, despite the fact that every other kid I knew said it was their parents, that it was all made up. It crushed me to hear them talk like that. I lied when they pushed me to admit it, to say it—*Say it, Stanley! There's no Santa!*

I'm not sure if I actually believed in Santa or wanted to believe so desperately that I convinced myself. It is a bad habit I've dragged into adulthood. (See: marriage, Jen.) There was, for the past many days, a belief in my made-up-stories mind that maybe, maybe, this wasn't real, that this addled, buzzy state of too little sleep and too much coffee, too much sadness, was somehow not reality.

I walked into Tim's living room and waited to hear his voice. Deep quiet has a sound that's almost painful. Not even a ticking clock in the room, just a vast empty quiet. I sat in the chair by the fireplace that I always sat in when we talked. The note was dated a year ago.

If you're reading this, I win. I went first. Wait. Is that a win? I forget the rules. I write this knowing that a person with my condition isn't likely to live a long life. Too many complications. So one prepares, writes notes to dear friends knowing they will be read after I am gone. Fun! Here's what I want to say to you. You saved me. You did. Your childlike wonder masked in sarcasm and absurd jokes. Your asinine comments that somehow make me laugh. I have a tendency toward self-pity. I try not to show it. But alone, late at night, I like to have little pity parties. You wouldn't let me. You were there. The best friend a half-man could have. It never dawned on me, your old-school ridiculous name. Bud. How perfect that that's your name. I don't know if I would have made it without you. Alone in the house. That I want you to have. It's all in my will. The lawyers will take care of the paperwork. Find a good tenant though, please. Someone a bit lost. Someone with a kind heart. Someone who can't afford our lovely neighborhood. Don't charge them much. Invite them down. Play records. Keep the salon alive. Start a new one. The lost souls are out there. And they're always looking for free booze. Thank you for moving in. Thank you for being my friend. One last request. Please, please, please be happy. Try. You're going to die, you know. Trust me on that one. Much love, Tim.

THE HEARING

Before I left the house, Clara had said, "What's the worst they can do? You died already. Everything else at this point is gravy."

She kissed me goodbye, and as she did she put her hand on my cheek. What a thing to have in your life.

Tuan met me in the lobby and escorted me in as his guest up to the twenty-ninth floor.

"Okay," he said when we got to the conference room. "Come by when it's over."

I nodded. Tuan was wearing what appeared to be culottes with espadrilles and a bright yellow sweater with Daffy Duck's face on it.

He turned to go.

"Tuan," I said.

He stopped and turned back.

"I just want you to know," I started, pausing, wanting to find the right words, "that even if I was gay, I wouldn't date you."

The hint of a smile on that beautiful face. "Bland white boy. Please." He turned and walked away.

Megan, Beth, Buckley, Howard, and a woman I hadn't met before who was introduced as corporate counsel. Martine someone. She wore an expensive-looking suit and held a demeanor that suggested she did not want to be here.

Megan started. "Thank you for coming in today, Bud. As promised, we have conducted a full investigation into the illicit publishing of your own obituary earlier this month. We are legally obligated to make a copy of that report available to you."

Megan slid a copy of the slim report to me and passed around other copies to the assembled.

"The sum and substance of the report contains the following: Flagrant violation of company policy by using password-protected company website. Flagrant violation of company policy by improper use of company website. Flagrant violation of company code of ethics by knowingly publishing falsehoods on the company website, including but not limited to claiming you were a member of the Jamaican Bobsled Team, ninth in line to the British throne, and inventor of toothpaste."

She cleared her throat and scanned the document in front of her.

"You will see, attached, a document dated May 22, 2014, bearing your signature that acknowledges your understanding of these rules. Is that your signature?"

I found the page she was referring to.

"Yes," I said.

"It has therefore been determined by this committee that you be terminated from United World Press as of this day."

It's one thing to imagine the impact. It's quite another to hear the words, to feel the shame and fear, the loss. I could hear my heartbeat in my eardrums, feel the heat rise in my face.

Beth, God bless her, said, "For what it's worth, this was not an easy decision, nor a unanimous one."

Both Megan and the lawyer looked over at Beth.

"Unnecessary information," the lawyer said to Beth.

Megan continued. "Is there anything you'd like to say?"

Perhaps it was the shame. It wasn't them I was angry with. It was myself. Might as well let it rip.

"Well," I said, after some time, "let me first off thank you for making me come in here and appear before you to tell me what we all knew was going to happen instead of emailing me or calling me. Always pleasant to come to Midtown to sit in front of you all to be made to feel like a felon instead of an idiot who made a mistake."

"Mr. Stanley." It was the lawyer. "You broke nine codes of employee conduct. We could sue you. Frankly, if it was my call, that's what I'd recommend."

She said all this while looking down at a paper in front of her. I wasn't worth the effort to look up. I was so tired of feeling bad. And I didn't care for her tone.

"Be my guest," I said. It came out too loud. "Have the judge laugh you out of court. Take my . . . let's see . . . I think it's about two hundred thousand dollars in retirement savings. A bit of money in the bank. *Do it.* Like you're going to hurt me? Go ahead. Do it. I just lost my job and buried my best friend."

"Bud." It was Howard.

I hadn't realized that I was standing. I sat back down.

"And just so you know, unlike me, he was actually dead when we buried him," I added.

I got her to look up at least. Howard snorted.

"Bud. I know this isn't easy—" It was Beth. But the lawyer cut her off.

"Do you have anything else to say, Mr. Stanley?"

Whatever brief moment of fight I had in me flitted away, energy drained, a deep sadness at the reality of it all. Not merely loss of the job, but the loss of Jen, of Tim. Of the foolishness of having thought it would all magically change.

"I'm sorry," I said. "I'm sorry for my stupidity. You gave me a job and a paycheck for many years and I owed you better."

They weren't expecting this, if their expressions suggested anything.

I was done. I had nothing more to say. I stood and took my jacket from the back of the chair. And then began speaking.

"But that's not why I'd fire me if I was on your side of the table. I'd fire me because we do the job wrong. Obituary writing. We sit in a room in this building and we make phone calls and type down data and facts and birthdays and *Oh really, he was in a bowling league, sorry about your loss, bye.* And we print it. And people read it. And think . . . nothing. Because it was cheap and easy. It didn't get to who they were. To do that, you have to go to the wake, the funeral. You have to watch and listen and see the grief and try to feel the pain. You have to get to know who they were and what they meant. Each life. We do it wrong."

I looked at Howard, who held my gaze.

"I bet if you looked out that window right now," I added, "you'd see a guy down there waiting for the light to change, the world hustling by him. He's just a guy, both ordinary and extraordinary. And what he doesn't know is that in about an hour he's going to drop dead of a heart attack. You know why?

Because it happens. Who was he? Does he have family? Kids? Friends? Was he in the military? Did he see combat? Does he help coach his son's flag football team? Does he drive his daughter to swimming practice at six a.m. each morning? Is he thinking about a funny story he wants to tell his wife, who's still his best friend? Does he look at his kids when they're sleeping and feel God? I don't know. But an obituary, a good one, from a news company worth its salt, should owe him that. These were whole lives. They mattered. Don't we owe him that?"

I slipped my jacket on.

"Anyway. I'm sorry. As you are now no doubt acutely aware, I am an idiot. But I don't care anymore. I made a mistake. I didn't kill anyone but myself. And now, apparently, I'm alive again. I'll tell you what I'm going to do with that. I am going to start by stealing a Coke from the kitchen as well as several notebooks and pens for my eight-year-old friend Leo."

GROSS NATIONAL HAPPINESS

I picked Clara up the next afternoon. I said I would drive her to the airport. When she opened the door, her large suitcase and carry-on bag at the ready in the small foyer, she took my hand and led me into the bedroom without saying a word.

Do not ask a man to write about sex, to explain sex. It will be boring and expected. It will lack nuance. It will make you wince with embarrassment. Of the many things men are taught, either directly or culturally—how to fix a flat tire, say, or hang shelves, siphon gasoline, track a buck, build a fire in the woods, parachute into enemy territory (not one of which I know how to do)—we are never taught to understand the largely indescribable feeling that is sex when it is far closer to love.

Sex—if my experience with Clara is any clue—is largely about eye contact. Flesh helps. The look of it, the curve of it, roundness. Breast, hip, inner forearm. But also breath, irregular and hurried breath, partially open mouth, the newness of this experience that you've had many times, renewed, made fresh, made alive, the urgency that begs for slowness, the seeing someone so closely, from a place you have never seen them before, just a few inches from a freckle, an eye whose blue, you now realize, contains dabs of emerald green. Now a head thrown back and the shape of a jawline, a long neck, introducing yourself to someone, her fingertips touching your face, barely touching your face, realizing, as it's happening, how strange that your lips aren't touching, simply breathing, as if suddenly in a place, a landscape you have never set foot in. The slow jazzlike rhythm of it, unplanned movements somehow seamless, intuitive, bodies moving in a kind of slow dance, as if they had met long ago, a feeling so exquisite, *Don't end, don't move,* and yet the movement itself a kind of sublime pleasure. This feeling of wanting to laugh, to cry, to say things that in this moment you know you feel without a doubt. This act has nothing to do with sex. You know that now. Because even in the early days, the heady days, with Jen, the sensation was not this. This is something different. This was what you had been looking for. This feeling of being fully alive, connected, emotionally, with someone else.

We stood near the long line at security, as far as I could go without a boarding pass.

"I'm platinum," she said.

"Sorry?"

"I flew so much for the company. I'm platinum." She pointed to an area with no line, where the first- and business-class passengers walked through, without a wait, special people.

"That's cool."

"No, it's not. It's cheating. My father would have killed me."

She looked around, everywhere but at me. There was an announcement for a flight to Cape Town. There was an announcement for a flight to Dubai. There was a final boarding call for a flight to Tokyo.

She looked at me. "Good timing, huh?"

"Swell," I said, forcing a smile.

"Say something else. I mean, I could die. On the plane. Planes crash."

"There's Delta's new tagline."

"If this were the last time you were ever going to see me, what would you say?"

"Is it the last time I'm going to see you?"

"Sorry. We did it at that place. An exercise. The idea of time. That this is it, this is all we have."

"I'm sorry I wasn't listening."

She grinned.

"I like your face," I said.

"Would you come to my funeral?"

"It would depend on what else I had going on. Also maybe don't die."

"Says the obituary writer. If this were a movie, it would be foreshadowing."

I wasn't sure what to say.

"The sex was boring," I said.

"I know, right?" She reached up and gently touched my face.

"A year," I said, not realizing I was going to say it out loud.

"They go by faster now. Think of all the stories I'll have."

She leaned in and hugged me, my face in her hair. She pulled back and kissed my cheek.

"Okay," she said. She took hold of her suitcase but didn't move.

"I love you," I said. It was out too fast. It was a thought in my head and it slipped out. "That's what I'd say. If this was the last time."

She stared at me.

I waited.

She turned to leave, then stopped. "I know. Me too."

She walked through security and didn't look back.

It was the summer that I ran.

I had nowhere to go and I couldn't stay in the house all day, so I walked. I walked from my apartment to Red Hook. I walked to Ditmas Park. I walked through Crown Heights and Brownsville and East New York. I walked until I found a bench and bought a bottle of water and then I walked home.

But it wasn't enough. I wasn't tired enough. So I started running, if you can call what I did running. I am not a natural athlete, but I ran. I ran early in the morning before the heat. I ran in the late afternoon welcoming the thick humid air of a New York summer. I ran in old Rod Laver tennis shoes and dark socks until my feet blistered and I bought proper running shoes. I ran in torrential summer afternoon downpours that had me smiling like a lunatic. I ran to Coney Island and then swam in the ocean, taking the subway back home. I ran late at night when I couldn't sleep, the city quieter, the energy dissipated, the sound of the breeze on the leaves in the trees. I ran welcoming the pain, the searing in my lungs, the lactic acid buildup in my thighs, the ache in my knees. I ran hoping to escape the noise in my head, missing my friend. But it ran right along with me.

I looked after his apartment. I would collect the mail, most of it junk, some of it utility bills, magazine subscriptions. I watered the plants. I kept the drapes closed against the heat of the day. I kept lemonade and iced tea in the otherwise empty refrigerator. Sometimes I would sit in his living room and read. The old house, thick masonry, the high ceilings, kept the worst of the heat of a New York summer out.

I would sometimes turn on a fan and pull down a book from his collection. I read *Anna Karenina* over July and August. I read *Moby-Dick*. These books I was supposed to have read in college. I read *Ulysses*. Fine, that last one is a lie. I tried. I didn't make it far. I doubt Mrs. Joyce even read it.

At night, alone in my own apartment—I couldn't go down to his place at night yet, though I'm not sure why exactly—I drank a cold bottle of beer or two and listened to the Yankees game on the radio, uninterested in the score, soothed by the voices. No rush, baseball. The pause after a foul ball. Snippets of information. Batting average, on-base percentage. "Loves fly-fishing in the offseason."

At night sometimes I would call his phone. I would wait for the answering machine message, listen to his voice. After a while I stopped calling. The bastard didn't answer.

I kept running.

During the last week of summer, the energy of Cobble Hill a kind of suburban quiet, families at their summer homes out east, on vacation up on Cape Cod, fewer people on the streets, the asphalt playgrounds empty, Tuan invited me to Fire Island, that thin thread of land off the southern coast of Long Island, a place on a map that looks as if it became unglued from the mainland. There are no cars allowed. People walk and bike along the miles-long stretches of well-worn boardwalk, past scrub pine and garbage-seeking deer.

Tuan had rented a house with a group of friends he had known from his restaurant and bar days years before. There was Ian who was a book editor and Lucas who was a publicist, Patrick who was a strategist at an ad agency and Ryan who was a producer on the *Today* show. He invited me for a night. I stayed for three. He gave me a small room in the attic, under the eaves, a window fan pulling in cool ocean breezes at night, the sound of wind through the pine boughs.

I slept late, drank iced coffee, walked the beach. I swam in the ocean, the cold and salty Atlantic, and lay on a thick towel in the sun, half listening to Tuan and his friends talk of love and sex and what to make for dinner. In the late afternoon I returned to my attic room to read and nap.

In the evenings, after an outdoor shower, impromptu dinner parties seemed to materialize magically. Friends of friends came over, brought food and wine. They had names I don't remember and interesting jobs. Later, I followed as they walked to the beach and built a bonfire, watched these men who had been bullied as children, taunted as teenagers, had to hide their true selves, but who were, now, here, tanned and laughing, fully themselves, inviting me, daring me, to join them. *Everything is waiting for you,* they seemed to say, in the moonlight, in the firelight, in the joy and beauty of being alive.

"What do you think of Lucas?" Tuan asked as we walked along the water's edge one afternoon, the sun on our shoulders. I wore baggy swim trunks, and Tuan, like his friends, wore what appeared to be a bit of fabric left on a cutting-room floor. His thin body was nut brown, the tips of his spiky hair dyed purple, his fingernails with tiny peace symbols on them.

"Which one is Lucas?"

"The really handsome one with the great body."

"They're all handsome with great bodies."

"With the mustache."

Lucas was at least ten years younger than Tuan. He was the kind of man Tuan had often dated in the past, men who were unkind to him, who dumped him quickly.

"He's not good enough for you," I said.

Tuan slowed his pace and looked at me. Then he turned and looked down at the sand. "I know," he said, his voice quieter. "But I'm lonely."

"I know. But make sure they deserve you."

He looked as if he wanted to say something but didn't.

"If this were a buddy movie," I said, "I would put my arm around your shoulders."

"Please don't touch me."

We walked, the waves rolling gently over our feet.

"I'm sorry," I said after a time.

"For what?"

"Being an idiot. Giving you more work. Making you work with the bro."

He seemed to think about this.

"There's so much about you I don't like," he said, looking at the sand. "Where do I even start?"

"I know," I said, smiling.

We walked on for a bit before turning and slowly walking back.

LIFE AFTER DEATH

I moved into Tim's apartment after Labor Day. September has always been, for me, the beginning of the new year. Back to school. Back to life.

I rented out my apartment, putting an ad up online showing photos, listing the address, but not putting the rent amount, simply saying that the rent would be "under market value." I had something like 214 emails in two days.

I set aside a Saturday to interview people. One man offered to pay a year's rent up front. A woman who looked barely thirty said she'd pay $4,000 a month. I said I would be in touch. A woman named Mariel stood out, though. She was thirty-one, originally from Honduras, and worked at the Marriott in downtown Brooklyn cleaning rooms. She was studying to get her GED and hoped to go to college one day. She had a six-year-old son named William. I asked her how much she could afford to pay each month, and she said $1,000. I gave it to her for $300. I told her about Tim.

We're having our first salon soon. Mariel has promised to come.

Professor Avner Chartoff was eighty-two and one of the leading experts of the archeological dig site at King Herod the Great's winter palace in Jericho. He had taught at Yeshiva University. There was a page on the university's website with his complete bio. There was a Wikipedia page on him with links at the bottom to articles. It could not have been an easier obit to write. I sat there, reading about him, typing in notes, but that's all it was. Notes. I read about his wife, Greta, who survived him and who lived in Scarsdale, a leafy suburb north of Manhattan. So I called her and asked if we could meet. He was my first new post-obit when I got back.

Howard had called and asked me to meet him at Gallagher's. I assumed he was taking pity on me. But he had an idea, he said. A new section on the extraordinary lives of ordinary people who'd died. *Life Stories.* Not just obituaries but a longer form, more fully told tales. It flew in the face of everything the company had been doing of late. Reducing staff, chopping stories, aiming for bombastic headlines. Click, ad, click.

"What do you think?" he asked.

"Sounds amazing."

"You want to work on it?"

"I'm kind of busy fending off offers from Target and Walgreens." I stared at him. "Is this a bad joke?"

He shook his head. "Your little . . . speech. The eulogy. This is your idea. They like it upstairs. Think it could be something. Maybe more than words. Videos. Reminders of people's lives."

"I think Tuan would be great for this too. The two of us, I mean."

So it was, a few weeks later, that I signed many documents in the presence of Beth, Buckley, and two stone-faced company lawyers attesting to the fact that I would never again knowingly post blah blah blah. I signed in the hope that my days of writing my own obituary were over.

And so on a cool fall morning, I took the Metro-North train from Grand Central to Scarsdale, a half hour from the city, and walked down Garth Road to a Tudor-style apartment building. Mrs. Chartoff had coffee and cake and I listened as she talked about her husband for two hours, talking and crying and talking and laughing. She showed me photos in old albums, the pictures covered with plastic, trips they had taken, vacations in Israel, photos from the dig site. Greta. Her name was Greta and she had taken care to do her hair and had on a long skirt and a yellow sweater, a small gold Star of David around her neck. Her face was deeply lined and her blue-green eyes appeared especially large behind her thick glasses.

"Would you like coffee?" she asked.

"No, thank you."

"Oh." She looked away, as if disappointed. "I still make eight cups."

"What's that?"

"I make eight cups. The night before. I've always made eight cups. In the Mr. Coffee. The night before. I always have too much now."

She forced a smile. "The things you do. These . . . After fifty-seven years . . . He brought me a glass of ice water, each night, before bed, and put it on my nightstand. In case I got thirsty in the night." She stared at me, but I don't think she was seeing me.

She turned and looked out the window.

"You know, I would actually love a cup of coffee," I said.

She turned back and smiled.

She talked and I listened. I asked a few questions, but there really wasn't any need. All I had to do was listen carefully as she told the stories of their life. She told me that when her husband was on the site, it was common to find pieces of ancient walls. And on the walls were painted frescoes. When her husband would pick up a piece of wall, touch his finger to it, pigment from the fresco would rub off.

"Pigment made by another hand two thousand years ago. He would tell me about that," she said. "It stayed with him, that connection to the past. Can you imagine that?" she asked, wide-eyed, alive in the memory of it all.

It was Leo's mother who stopped me one afternoon.

"Bud," she said, blinking a lot. "I wondered if I might ask a favor."

"Of course," I said.

"Leo has a school thing. A kind of show-and-tell. It's usually a parent but . . . he'd like to ask you. If you don't mind."

Which is how I found myself, in late October, on a small wooden chair in Ms. Son's classroom, decorated for Halloween, at PS 29, waiting my turn. The other adults, mostly parents or grandparents, spoke about their jobs. Claims adjuster, investment banker, pediatric nurse. Each child introduced them. Then it was Leo's turn.

He had insisted on wearing a sports coat and tie and asked me to do the same, as he felt this was what serious people did during presentations. As always, he held his notebook.

"Mmm . . . good morning. My name is Leo Hoyt and I am in third grade at PS 29 school in Brooklyn. I chose for my show-and-tell my friend Bud who is also my neighbor from five houses away but the houses are connected, so if you think about it except for the bricks it's kind of the same house."

I looked over at Leo's mother and father, watched them watch him. Leo looked up at his classmates and hesitated for a moment, suddenly shy, and then looked over at his teacher, who smiled and nodded.

"Do you know what an obituary writer is? Well, neither did I. It is a person who writes about dead people. But isn't that sad? you might ask me. No, it isn't, because to do a good job you have to write about their life and the good things because that's what life is. When someone writes your obituary, you will like it because you will have laughed a lot during your life and you had friends and a dog and went to birthday parties with balloons and to the beach and so many things that at night, each night, when you go to bed, you will think, *Wasn't that a great day.*"

Leo's mother wiped at her eyes and her husband put his arm around her shoulders. I wondered what I could possibly add to that that would make any difference.

I see a red cardinal from time to time, out the back window, on the old ash tree, occasionally hopping onto the back deck. They are hard not to notice. Their color, their particular beauty. I did a search online and came across an interesting story. Apparently red cardinals can be spiritual messengers.

The word *cardinal* comes from the Latin word *cardo*, meaning *hinge* or *axis*. Like a door's hinge, the cardinal is a kind of doorway between Earth and the spirit world, the story said. There are, depending upon how late you are willing to stay up and how much you want to read and how much you miss your friend, many myths around the cardinal having to do with renewal and good health. They are, say some, a visit from the other side.

I don't understand death. The biology of it, yes, but not what remains for the living. Pain and memory and an empty place. I think to fully get it, you have to feel it so profoundly that it upsets your sense of the world. It has to make you a little crazy. But it also has to make you love this miracle of existence to the point of bursting. If it doesn't, well, then you don't get it yet.

Life prevails. How strange and wondrous. In the midst of death, life prevails, calls to us, begs us, says, *Come, please, don't you dare waste this precious gift.*

It's just after 7 a.m. on a cold December morning. The sky brightens later now. I sit and wait for it. The coffee is on. I can smell it. Tim's apartment—it will always be Tim's apartment to me—ticks and creaks in the early-morning quiet. The vague smell of old fires, of polished wood and clean floors. The man who delivers *The New York Times* just tossed it up on the landing, hitting the door. I open the refrigerator and see that I need milk and eggs. I'll go later.

There is an obituary to write. I want to do it in a way that reminds anyone who reads it that that person's life mattered, that we won't forget. It is so easy to forget.

Tim said we are all obituary writers because we get to write our life every day. Write it. Please. It's your life.

Also, it will certainly make my job easier.

AUTHOR'S NOTE

This book was inspired by something my brother, Tom, said the last time I saw him. He died in June 2019 at age sixty-five.

Tom was a firefighter, like our father and both grandfathers. He was also a rescue team manager on the Massachusetts FEMA Urban Search and Rescue Team who worked at the World Trade Center during 9/11. He had walked into burning buildings. He had saved lives. He was the man.

He had been diagnosed with pancreatic cancer and my four other brothers and I had been visiting fairly regularly. His condition worsened, and Tom's wife, Kathy, called to say we should visit as soon as possible.

I arrived before my other brothers. Tom was sitting in a reclining chair, a blanket over his thinning frame, but still himself, still in there somewhere, still sharp, quiet, darkly funny.

We talked, and after a time I heard a car pull into the driveway and I looked out the window.

"The others are here," I said to Tom.

With a Buster Keaton stone-face, Tom dropped an arm over the chair, let his head fall to one side, and, trying to suppress a grin, said, "Tell them they're too late."

ACKNOWLEDGMENTS

People I would like to thank, in no particular order.

Adam Bernstein, longtime obituary writer at *The Washington Post*, kindly responded to an out-of-the-blue email from me and graciously answered my many questions. He daily keeps the art of obituary writing alive, taking care to honor the lives of the dead. Adam said he looks forward to writing about me one day soon.

Chris Bucci, my agent at Aevitas, and fellow corduroy jacket wearer. Along with David Kuhn and Kayla Grogan. And Michelle Weiner at CAA. How lovely to find people who believe in your work.

Zibby Owens, publishing pioneer, who took a chance on a male author.

My editor, Kathleen Harris, whose nimble hands made this book far better.

The team at Zibby Publishing, Anne Messitte, Sherri Puzey, Katie Teas, Graça Tito, Sarah Fradkin, Jordan Blumetti, Gabby Capasso, and Chelsea Grogan.

Trusted early readers: Debbie Kasher, Rick Knief, Tom Drymalski, Jennifer & Michael Goldfinger, Judy Watkins, Beowulf Sheehan, and Mike Kenney.

Susan Morrison and Emma Allen at *The New Yorker* for continuing to publish my Shouts & Murmurs pieces and making me obscenely rich in the process. That second part is a lie.

Special thanks to my dear friend, mentor, and guide, Lynn Hendee.

Tim Watkins for inspiring me with his grace, wit, and courage.

My wife, Lissa, reader, editor, wise critic, supporter.

My children Lulu and Hewitt. As I say to them every night before they go to sleep, "I am so lucky to be your dad."

ABOUT THE AUTHOR

John Kenney is the bestselling author of two novels and four books of poetry, including *Talk to Me*, *Love Poems for Married People*, *Love Poems for People with Children*, and *Love Poems for Anxious People*. His first novel, *Truth in Advertising*, won the Thurber Prize for American Humor. He is a longtime contributor to *The New Yorker* magazine's Shouts & Murmurs column. He lives in Larchmont, New York, with his wife, Lissa, a therapist, and two children, whose names currently escape him.